Other books by Stephanie Rowe:

UNBECOMING BEHAVIOR
SHOP 'TIL YULE DROP (Anthology)

IF THE SHOE FITS

STEPHANIE ROWE

MAKING IT®

January 2007

Published by

Dorchester Publishing Co., Inc.
200 Madison Avenue
New York, NY 10016

ISBN 0-505-52700-6

The name "Making It" and its logo are trademarks of Dorchester Publishing Co., Inc.

Printed in the United States of America.

Visit us on the web at www.dorchesterpub.com.

This book is dedicated to all the wonderful folks in Nike product creation who were my teammates for the eight years I worked in footwear product testing. I've never met so many dedicated, hardworking folks who were so inspired by their work. I miss you guys! Special thanks to those who inspired me to raise the bar and who gave me the opportunities to succeed and challenge myself in a field that never ceases to innovate: Ellen Devlin, Steve Roth, Robert Conradt, Deb Zaveson, Brian McCloskey, Jeff Pisciotta, Howard Banich and the rest of the tennis group, and of course, the entire Category Product Testing team (you guys ROCK!)...the list is endless. And to those of you whose friendship made each day brighter: you know who you are.

Thank you.

ACKNOWLEDGMENTS

Thanks to my wonderful friend, Guinevere Jones (product-testing goddess extraordinaire), for coming up with the fabulous title to this book, and for being my buddy.

As always, thanks to my inspirational agent, Michelle Grajkowski, for keeping me going when I thought this book would never get written.

And thanks to my editor, Kate Seaver, for helping me brainstorm this book and believing in my ability to pull it off.

A special thank-you to the art department at Dorchester for creating such an amazing cover for this book.

And of course, Josh, whose unflagging belief in me still blows me away.

ONE

It was the first time I'd noticed the mold on the walls of my office.

It was the first time the odor of dead rat emanating from the HVAC vents had bugged me.

It was the first time I'd contemplated that the mysterious stain on the carpet might actually be from a nefarious act involving death and dismemberment instead of a more innocuous incident.

Being faced with the failure of my dream sort of made it hard to ignore the fact that our offices were located in the underbelly of Boston's corporate world. Well, not really the underbelly. More like the slums of the underbelly's poorest cousin.

It was two in the morning on a Wednesday night, and the coffee machine was broken. Again.

Hi, my name is Paris Jackson and apparently I suck at sales.

Either that or every footwear company in America is shortsighted, cheap, risk-averse and generally stupid. After four years of research by my two esteemed scientists, with my additional contribution as a biomechanical and technical expert, we'd perfected the ultimate cushioning system for running shoes. Truly, it was brilliant. Brilliant!

So why had every single footwear company turned down our technology? Too expensive. Wouldn't work. Didn't like the color. Afraid of the future. Stuck in the past. Stupid idiots. Blah, blah, blah.

Not that the "why" really mattered. The fact was that we were out of places to sell Sfoam to, and we were out of options. Life sucked.

But as the leader of PWJ, Inc., it was my job to rally the troops after delivering the bad news. So what if we were broke, directionless, sleep-deprived and forced to use antibiotic soap after walking through the halls of our building to reach our offices? No need for depression and angst! I raised my can of cheap beer. "Here's to perseverance. We're not through yet."

Will Foster, one half of our megatalented research team and also the man who'd been playing twinkle toes with me occasionally over the past six months, left his beer unopened on the table. He shot me a skeptical look. "How are we not through?"

My raised can of beer lowered a couple inches. "I'll think of something."

Jodi Harpswell, the other half of our scientific unit, was lying on one of the picnic table benches currently serving as conference room chairs. Yeah, so it wasn't the most sophisticated seating option in the world. It matched the garage-sale picnic table, so at least our décor blended, right? Jodi had her sweatshirt over her face and her feet up on the table, not an unusual position when she was trying to work out a problem with one of her experiments. "This sucks."

My beer dropped to the table with a dispirited thud. "Why are you guys being so down? So what if we can't sell our technology? It's just a little blip." More like a monstrously huge blip that had totally knocked me for a loop. This last rejection had come from the company that had been our safety. Sure, it was a small company, but it was innovative and risk-taking. I'd been certain they'd at least offer us a little money for our technology. But no, they'd actually laughed and walked out of the conference room while I was in the middle of my presentation.

And it was a really nice conference room.

Jodi sat up, dumping her sweatshirt on the carpet. She'd have to wash it before she put it back on. We'd gotten the carpet at a garage sale, and even multiple rounds with the steam cleaner hadn't quite cleared up the strange odor emanating from it. Sometimes when we were too fried to think at four in the morning, we would have contests about what nasty thing caused that smell.

Frankly, the carpet scared me.

"Listen, Paris, I can't keep doing two jobs. And neither can Will. And neither can you. We're out of time and we're out of money. We can't afford to rent this space anymore. We can't afford any more materials for research. Plus I can't even fork up the dough to buy enough coffee to keep me awake during the day when I'm at the job that actually pays the bills." Jodi flopped back on the bench, her head cracking against the wood with a thud. "Ow."

Will drummed his fingers on the picnic table. "I know you're really counting on making PWJ fly, but . . . well . . . I was counting on the money from this sale. I'm sorry, Paris, but I'm running out of options. You know I'd never bail if I could help it, but . . ." His voice faded, no doubt smothered by the look of horror on my face.

Will bailing on me? If he bailed, well, it would be like having my feet cut off. He was always there, no matter what. I counted on him, and he had never let me down. "What do you need the money for?" Oops. My voice was a little squeaky there.

Calm down, Paris.

This was the first time I'd heard Will talk about the money. He'd always been in it for the fun and the challenge of researching. As a guy who lived in jeans and T-shirts, money didn't matter to him as long as he could afford to eat and didn't have to sleep on the sidewalk. In fact, immediate financial gratification had never been a motivating factor for any of us, which was good, considering our joint venture had been a major financial drain for the past four years.

Will frowned, as if he hadn't intended to say it out loud. "Nothing."

"Nothing? What does *nothing* mean?" Since when did he hold out on me?

He shook his head. "It's not a big deal."

"Not a big deal?" This company was my life, and Will was a critical piece of the biz. It was a very big deal. "But—"

"Hey, lovebirds, I hate to interrupt your discussion of Will's plans, but we have a decision to make." Jodi sat up again. "I love you guys, and I love this company, and I love doing the research, but frankly I don't see how this is going to work. I'm tired of this whole scene." She hesitated. "I vote to disband."

My gut plummeted, and I looked at Will.

He touched my arm in apology. "If there's any way to salvage it, I'm in. But otherwise, I need to get going on other projects as well."

Well, shit. Without my scientists, I had no company.

Which meant I had no dreams.

Nothing.

Everything I'd been working for during the last four years. Gone. To them, this was merely a business. To me, it was my world. It was my everything.

My gut started to churn and my head began to pound. I couldn't let my dream go. Couldn't give up. I had to find a way to make our company viable. Had to. No choice. Couldn't let Seth down.

I so needed to come up with a brilliant rallying speech. Or better yet, a plan.

But before I thought of anything inspirational, the front door rattled and we all sat up.

"Think we're being robbed?" Jodi asked hopefully. "Insurance payout could save us."

"I haven't paid insurance in six months," I said.

"Oh. Bummer."

We all stared at the door as someone tried to get in. In this area of town, there wasn't a whole lot of good that came from someone trying to get in your door at two in the morning.

Then someone pounded on the door. "I saw the lights on! Open this door!"

We all relaxed, then I got up to open the door. "Hi, Lindsey."

The fourth member of our group of friends from college strode into the conference room aka lobby aka office aka kitchen of PWJ. Her red hair was flying out at all angles; she was wearing jeans, cowboy boots and a tight, black T-shirt. And she was limping—quite badly, actually. Not that she seemed to care. Her cheeks were flushed a bright red and her eyes were glowing. "Did you guys change the locks or something? My key doesn't work." She sounded way too happy for the wee hours of a Thursday morning.

Jodi took one look at Lindsey and rolled her eyes. "You were risking death again, weren't you?"

"Not at all. Just having some fun."

Yeah, right. Lindsey had always been adventurous, but for the past four years she'd been flirting with serious bodily harm, ever since our dear friend Seth had been killed. Risking injury or death was the only thing that put that look of sheer joy on her face nowadays.

Lindsey peered at the broken coffee machine, then picked up Will's unopened beer and sat down at the picnic table. "You guys look like hell. What's going on?" She wobbled slightly, and I caught the faint scent of alcohol. No wonder she'd had trouble with the key.

I shut the door and straddled the bench next to her. "Why are you limping?" As her friends, Jodi and I had appointed ourselves "Protectors of Lindsey" to save her from herself.

"I went to that new country-western bar and rode the mechanical bull. I told them to put it on high." She pursed her lips. "I tried ten times and I think I stayed on for a total of one second." She rubbed her knee and grimaced. "Thought I broke my kneecap on that last one."

"Did it occur to you to have them put it on a lower level?" I asked.

"What fun is that? It's only fun if you could get hurt. Adds an element of the unknown."

"Yeah, like a broken neck," Jodi grumbled.

Lindsey shot her a look as she cracked open the beer. "Lighten up, Jodi. It's my neck."

"And you're my friend, so I have a right to be concerned if you're being stupid."

"Stupid? I'm stupid? Just because you're a brilliant scientist, you think the rest of us are peons?"

"Hey," I said. "Intentionally getting thrown off a mechanical bull repeatedly isn't exactly the path toward enlightenment."

Lindsey slammed her beer down on the table. "I come by here to chat with my friends and you guys are all over me."

Will grabbed her arm as she tried to stagger to her feet. "Hey, Linds, you know it's because they care."

Lindsey sighed. "But they're so annoying."

He grinned. "But you love them."

She rolled her eyes and sat back down. "Fine." She shot a pointed look at us. "Back off with the harassment."

I glanced at Will, and he gave me a single shake of his head. He was probably right. Broaching the subject while Lindsey was drunk and still on the high of nearly paralyzing herself wasn't the right timing.

We all eyed each other for a moment, and I realized Lindsey was looking worried. Upset.

My bad. So I hugged her. She sighed and hugged me back; then Jodi jumped on top of us and knocked us off the bench onto the floor, where we descended into laughter and hugs while Will looked on as though he would never understand women.

So I grabbed his elbow and Jodi latched onto his waist and we pulled him down with us. "Hey!" he protested as he landed with a grunt.

"Hey, what? Most men would give their family jewels to roll around on the floor with three gorgeous women," I said.

"Well, show me the three gorgeous women, and I'll give you the family jewels."

I bopped him on the head. "Watch your language, Buster, or we'll cut you out of the biz."

He laughed and gave me a hard kiss that had Jodi and Lindsey groaning. "You have no biz, sweetie. It's all gone into the tank, remember?"

Lindsey rolled to her knees and set her hands on her hips. "Cut the kissy-face for a minute. What do you mean, the business has gone in the tank? As your legal consultant who would be responsible for filing all the bankruptcy forms, I demand to know what has happened while I was out breaking wild mustangs on the prairie."

Jodi propped herself up on her elbows. "Paris let us all down."

I threw her sweatshirt at her. "Liar. I did not. You did, because your product apparently sucks."

Will put his hands over our mouths. "Will you two quit with the mudslinging for one minute?" If he weren't so cute, I totally would not let him get away with that, just so you know. He turned to Lindsey. "The last company turned down Sfoam. There aren't any more places to sell it."

Lindsey put on the contemplative lawyer expression that she did so well, then ruined it with a bitter beer face after taking a sip of our company beverage. When Lindsey wasn't trying to get herself killed or hanging out at PWJ in the wee hours of the morning, she was a successful lawyer. Wore nice suits, ate at expensive restaurants and drank wine that was a lot better than the beer she was attempting to swallow. She was our legal consultant, which didn't require her putting any money into PWJ.

Translation: she was the only one of the four of us who was solvent. "You can't tell me you've approached every single company that makes running shoes."

Will lifted his hand from my mouth. "You can answer the question."

"Gee, thanks for your permission, Your Highness." I climbed to my feet and sat down on the picnic bench. "And yes, Lindsey, I've approached every single company that might possibly be interested. There's nowhere else that makes running shoes."

She finished a long swig of beer. "So, what's your solution, El Cap-i-tan?"

"I'm still thinking." See? Lindsey had faith in me. She didn't think our company was a lost cause. So there. I wasn't delusional after all.

"Could you use Sfoam in something other than running shoes?" Lindsey asked, and both Jodi and Will snorted.

"Come on, Linds. Paris is the ultimate running snob. You know she'd never consider anything else," Jodi said.

"And you're a reverse running snob," I shot back. "You think exercise in any form is unnatural and bad for your health."

"It is! Your body is so messed up from running that by the time you're fifty, I'm going to be pushing your wheelchair around because you'll have such bad arthritis."

"Your body will be made of jelly by then because you never use it for anything other than sitting."

Will groaned and climbed to his feet. "Will you two cut it out for five minutes?"

I slung my arm around Jodi's shoulder, who immediately returned the favor. "The verbal bantering keeps us intellectually stimulated."

"Well, it's annoying as hell to the rest of us," Will grumbled. "And it's not getting us any closer to a solution." He sighed and turned to me. "Why don't we think about what other uses Sfoam has? You might care only about running, but Jodi and I are personally invested in the technology itself. We'd like to see it put into a real product."

Typical scientists. Only in it for the research. They had no concept of what a true mission was. They didn't understand what PWJ was all about. I could never give up on it. Never. "It has to be running shoes. You know it does."

Jodi elbowed Will. "You're sleeping with her. Can't you change her mind? Withhold sex or something?"

"Jodi!" As if the occasional romp with Will gave him special influence over me. We hooked up on occasion. That was it. Nothing more. There were no undying declarations of love or whispers of forever. He was getting over a breakup with She-bitch-from-hell, and I was just barely ready to start dating again after being shredded by my ex-husband. So we had a no-pressure, no-strings relationship that included occasional overnight stays and a non-negotiable agreement to keep it light. And we'd promised that it would never, ever cross over into work. Which most definitely included him using sex to change my mind.

Will quirked an eyebrow at me, and I blew him a kiss. Agreement reinforced. No matter what Jodi said, we would never cross that line. Orgasms had no strings attached.

Lindsey set her beer down. "Okay, so you can't sell Sfoam to any running companies. Paris holds the veto on applying it to any other technologies. Seems like you're a little bit screwed. Unless . . ."

We all looked at her. "Unless what?" I asked.

"Ever think about manufacturing the shoes yourselves?"

Excitement flared inside me, then faded just as quickly. "We don't have the resources," I said. "We need money, manufacturing facilities . . ."

"What if I could provide the manufacturing facilities?" Lindsey asked, her eyes beginning to get that glow that only risking death generated. "And you could get a loan from a bank or something."

I sat up straighter. "Are you serious?"

She grinned at me. "Deadly."

"Hang on." Will looked a little worried. "Are we talking about opening our own footwear company? Because that's a very different deal than what I signed on for."

Ideas began to flow. "Actually, we could manufacture some shoes, show that the technology works, and then have a bargaining chip to take back to the companies. We'll hand them proof that it works, and then they'll have to take us seriously." That had been part of the problem. We made the foam and it passed the tests in the lab, but we hadn't been able to put it in shoes because we had no resources for manufacturing shoes . . . until now! I felt like bouncing in my seat. Instead I practically skipped over to the whiteboard nailed up over the worst of the peeling paint. I grabbed a red marker and started jotting down ideas. "We could recruit a tester base of our target consumers and get them to testify to how well it works for them."

After being a runner my whole life and on the cusp of the Olympic trials before my accident, I had so many ideas about how to make great running shoes. How cool would it be to actually put Sfoam into the shoes our-

11

selves? I turned to my partners. "What do you say? I think it's a great idea."

"What kind of manufacturing facilities are you talking about, Lindsey?" Jodi was sitting up now, and she looked much more awake. She gestured at the labful of obsolete equipment we'd gotten when one of the local universities had built a new science building and tossed all their outdated equipment. "There's no way we can build shoes with that."

"One of my clients has a specialty business where he builds custom orthopedic shoes for about a thousand bucks a pair. I'm sure he'd be happy to take in some extra income letting you guys work in his lab after hours," Lindsey said. "Since your state-of-the-art running shoes aren't exactly competition for him, I doubt he'll mind."

Oh, baby. My mind was rolling now. "Let's go see the lab, at least." Suddenly, my deflated dream was gaining new life. I might be able to put Sfoam in running shoes myself! I could practically taste the culmination of everything I'd worked for.

A slow grin spread over Jodi's face. "I'd love to see Sfoam through. I mean, I've spent four years developing the technology. I'd hate to see it fail without a real chance."

I danced across the room and high-fived her. "Rock on, girlfriend! We're totally going to make this fly."

We both looked at Will, who was frowning. "What about money? I'd been banking on the fact that we were at the point where money would start flowing from PWJ to us, not the other way around."

My elation faded. Crud. He was right. Manufacturing cost money, and money was not exactly falling from the sky right now.

"I can't put any more in," he said. "I have to get out of debt."

Jodi frowned. "I'm pretty tight right now too."

I pursed my lips. "I'll do it."

Will looked at me, his face surprised. He knew exactly what I was talking about. "But you wanted to keep them separate."

"Keep what? What are you talking about?" Jodi asked.

"It's time." My gut thudded. Me, nervous? You bet. I'd kept my day job separate from PWJ for the past four years. Telling your boss you have another job that you like more than the one he's paying you for isn't exactly good for your career. But sometimes you have to be willing to risk for your dreams. "I'll get a loan from my bank."

"Give us a minute," Will said to Lindsey and Jodi as he stood up, grabbed my hand and pulled me into the lab, shutting the door behind us. "Paris. You don't have to do this. Asking your bank to float a loan to PWJ could get you into trouble, with all those rules about not financing personal investments through the bank."

I heard the floor outside creak, and I knew Jodi and Lindsey were listening. Privacy? What privacy? "I'm going to do it."

Will shook his head. "Listen, we've all given up a lot for PWJ in the last five years. I think Sfoam is amazing, and I love the fact that I was part of the team that created it, but maybe it's time to call it a day. Is your career really worth risking for this?"

I met his gaze. "Yes."

"You might end up unemployed."

"I know."

"And PWJ might fail anyway."

I nodded.

"You could wind up homeless."

I pressed my lips together. I knew the risks, but I couldn't walk away.

After a moment, he sighed and tucked my hair behind my ears, then kissed my forehead. He knew why this dream was so important to me. He didn't need to ask. "If you want to go forward with this, then I'm in."

The sincerity in his tone would have made a lesser woman turn into a blathering idiot. I hooked my hands behind his neck and kissed him. "Thank you."

He hesitated. "If things go badly, well, you can always move in with me."

I stared at him as his offer filled the air that had suddenly become oppressive. We never talked about things like that. I couldn't handle it, and I knew he wasn't interested in getting serious either. We simply didn't have that kind of relationship. For him to offer to let me move in . . . I didn't know what that meant. All I knew was that I felt a fist beginning to close over my chest, making it difficult to breathe. "Um . . ."

He sighed again, this time even more heavily. "Don't freak out, Paris. I didn't mean it like that. I just meant I have your back, as your friend."

"Oh." I let the air out of my lungs in a whoosh and suddenly felt stupid. "Right."

"Even if I wanted to get serious, I'd never ask you to move in for real."

I lifted a brow, trying to keep the conversation light while I regained my composure. "Why not? I'm not good enough in bed?"

He didn't laugh at my joke. "Because asking you to get serious would be the fastest way to lose you. If I wanted you in that way."

"Which you don't." Just double-checking to make sure the rules hadn't changed. I needed Will in my life as my friend, as my lover and as my business partner. I'd never be able to handle it if that got screwed up because one of us started hankering for white picket fences.

He trailed his fingers through my hair, fluffing it the way he liked to do. "Can you imagine the two of us in a serious relationship? We'd both break records for sprinting in the other direction."

I nodded. "I know."

He gave me a light kiss on the lips. "So, if you find yourself broke and homeless and eating grass for dinner, give me a call. I'll let you sleep on my couch, except when we want sex, and then we'll share the bed."

I grinned and felt the last bit of tension ease out of my body. We were cool. "Sounds like a plan." I cleared my throat. "Thanks for your support on all this. I . . ." I what? What did I want to say? "I couldn't do it without you." Crap. Did that make me sound wimpy? Or needy? Or as if I was trying to break the rules I'd just reinforced? "I mean, you know, because you're a scientist and I'm not and . . ."

He just smiled and kissed me. Not a little kiss. It was an I'm-going-to-distract-the-hell-out-of-you-by-making-you-so-hot-you-can't-even-think-anymore kind of kiss. The kind of kiss that has you ready to drop to the linoleum floor and start ripping off clothes even though you know your friends are listening at the other side of the door. I had my hands inside his shirt and my right leg around his thigh when I heard a light rap on the door.

"Um, guys? What did you decide?" It was Lindsey's voice.

Will released my mouth and grinned. "Tell her quickly and then I need to ravage your body."

I shoved him aside, but I was laughing. As usual, Will

had known how to reach inside me and yank me out of my foray into melodrama and serious topics that I wanted no part of. He'd been doing that for the past four years, and I'd never have survived without him. "I love you, Will." Not Love, just love. But he knew that.

"Yeah, you tell that to all the boys who want to get into your pants." He put his hand on the doorknob and started to turn it. "But if you do move into my place, I'll let you pay your share of the rent with your body."

"For nightly sex with you, it would almost be worth it to give up my freedom."

"'Almost' being the operative word," he said. "Probably best if you try to avoid getting canned. Who knows if we'd be able to survive so much proximity."

"I'll do my best." And not just to avoid moving in with him, though I'd do a lot to avoid that. I simply wasn't ready to fail. Not at my job and not at PWJ. The failure of my marriage was enough failure for me, thanks so much.

Lindsey knocked again. "Jodi and I also vote that you avoid getting yourself fired. It would be idiotic to lose your job over PWJ."

Will squeezed my arm. "Follow your dream. I'll catch you if you fall," he whispered.

Every girl needs a guy like Will to be her rock. No way was I going to risk losing him by moving in with him. Especially when I was half-certain I was going to fall flat on my face and need him to pick me up off my sorry behind before I got run over by a street sweeper. "Thanks."

He nodded just as Lindsey pushed the door open. Jodi was right behind her. They both planted their hands on their hips and gave me their "don't be a fool" glares. "Well?" Lindsey demanded. "What did you decide?"

I met their gaze with my steeliest look. A look I hoped didn't reveal the fact that I was scared to death at the thought of what I was proposing, even knowing Will would be there with his superglue to bail me out if the worst happened. I didn't want to be saved from myself. I wanted to make this work! "Anything worth having is worth taking a chance for." Those words sure sounded a lot better when it wasn't my job and my income at stake. Who came up with that kind of stupid saying anyway?

"Not this kind of risk for this kind of reward," Lindsey said. "Don't be a fool."

I shoved past them and walked over to the picnic table. "I'm not asking any of you to jeopardize your jobs. You guys should be happy I'm willing to put my neck out there for PWJ."

"Actually, I'll just feel guilty if you get fired," Jodi said.

"And I'll probably have to support you," Lindsey said. "Seeing as how I'm the only one of us with money."

"I'm not asking you to give me money or permission!" I slammed my palms down on the table. "I have to do everything I can to make this fly. Risking my job is nothing. Why can't you guys understand? I already tried to get a loan from other banks, and it won't happen. It's either my bank or we shut down. How can I possibly give up without doing everything possible to make it work? How?" Will understood. Why couldn't they be like him? I mean, it really wasn't that complicated, not for anyone who'd been a part of my life for the past four years.

Will touched my arm. "Okay, Paris, calm down—"

I pulled away. "Don't placate me. I'm going to get us a loan through my bank, and I expect everyone to do whatever they need to to make PWJ succeed."

Jodi's eyes flickered with anger. "You can't put pressure

on us just because you're willing to take stupid gambles. I'll keep doing what I'm doing, but I'm not endangering my own interests for PWJ."

"That's all I ask." I looked at Lindsey. "You'll hook us up with that shoe guy you know?"

"Even if I have to sleep with him, I'll get it done."

"Okay, then." I took a deep breath and surveyed the wary faces. "So that's it. We're moving forward." I grabbed my beer and shoved it skyward. "Here's to PWJ."

Will lifted a beer can immediately. "To PWJ. And Paris, who inspires us with her passion and her willingness to take risks for what she believes in."

And I could tell he meant it. This business never would have made it without his support and his belief in me. Someday I needed to find a way to pay him back.

Lindsey sighed and raised a beer. "Fine. It's not my money."

Jodi groaned. "You know I would love for this to happen. I really would."

"Then toast us," I said. "Because it's going to."

She shook her head, but she picked up a can and lifted it. "To PWJ and manufacturing our own shoes." A glimmer of excitement glittered in her eyes. "And to Paris, for refusing to give up even if it makes me want to strangle her sometimes."

I grinned. I could see the tentative hope on each of their faces. They might not have wanted to admit it, but they were just as excited as I was at the prospect of seeing our company succeed.

Then I thought about what I'd just done.

I'd committed to doing something unethical at work to make PWJ fly.

My gut contracted into a knot. Was Will right? Was it worth it?

I thought of the boy I used to love.

I thought about how I'd cried at his funeral.

I thought about the Olympic trials I'd watched from my hospital bed.

And I knew it was worth it.

Somehow I had to make PWJ work.

Two

Business tip for the day: If your future employment at the day job is already in peril, don't let your boss find you passed out at your desk, drooling all over a set of loan documents.

I was dreaming that I was in an important meeting at the bank. I'd fallen asleep at the conference table, and I couldn't wake up. Co-workers were pelting me with paperclips and rubber bands, and I was trying desperately to rouse myself, but I couldn't make myself open my eyes, couldn't find the strength to lift my head.

"Paris?" An insistent knocking started bugging me. "Paris. Wake up."

I sat up quickly, blinking at the sight of my very hot boss standing in my doorway, the corners of his mouth curving in poorly hidden amusement. Damn. I'd been dreaming that I'd been dreaming. In actuality, I had been sleeping at my desk and I'd been totally busted.

Crap.

I wiped the drool off my cheek and tried to think of a really good explanation. "I have narcolepsy."

Thad Wilkins was maybe a couple years older than I was, and he took his bank career very seriously, as evidenced by the fact that he was considerably higher than I was on the career hierarchy at NorthEast Savings Bank. Like Will the hottie scientist, Thad didn't fit his role. He might have been a banker, but there was a controlled sexuality about him that reminded me of a predatory cat. All muscle, sinew and stealth, as though he could sneak up behind me and eliminate my defenses before I had time to take a breath.

Since the day he'd taken over as my boss six months before and introduced himself to me over coffee, there'd been an undercurrent of sexual tension between us. Maybe that was why we'd never gone to coffee since. He was my boss, I was his underling, I was already engaging in the occasional midnight massage with Will, and I still had ex-hubby baggage. Yet I was attracted to Thad, and I was pretty sure he felt the same way about me.

Scary stuff that had no room in my life, thanks so much.

But that didn't mean I was able to keep myself from leaning back in my chair and letting his presence wash over me when he leaned on my doorframe in that casual catlike way. Too bad the drool incident probably meant that he wasn't entertaining the same thoughts about me.

There's nothing sexy about a girl with saliva hanging off her face, you know?

"Got a minute, Paris?"

"Sure." My heart started beating a little faster, as it always did when I was in close proximity to him. "Anything for you, Boss." I used his title as a little reminder to both of us. I'd never had a boss I was attracted to before. Especially not when I was already involved with someone else, though technically I was free to date anyone I wanted, as was Will. My attraction to Thad was more than a little unsettling. But it made for some nice day-dreams during boring staff meetings.

I hopped up and cleared a stack of files off my client chair, catching a whiff of his scent as I moved past him. Thad smelled like soap. Clean, fresh, well-scrubbed. No cologne or other frills. He was a straightforward, honest guy, and it was enough for me.

Crap. What was I thinking?

Sleep deprivation or not, it was time to get a grip.

I felt my cheeks heat up and retreated back behind my laminate desk. Had he found the loan documents yet? I'd left the loan application for PWJ on his desk. I'd tried to approve it myself, I really had, but in the end, I couldn't do something that unethical. So I figured I'd let him take a look, and if he didn't have any problems with the trans-action, I'd 'fess up and try to get him to make an excep-tion. I might even be willing to sell my body for it. A great sacrifice, yes, but for the good of the company, I might be able to bring myself to do it. "What's up?"

He tugged at his bow tie. (How many guys nowadays wear bow ties? I think Thad was the only one. A guy had to be pretty sure about himself to wear a bow tie. And trust me, it worked for him.) "I had a meeting with my boss this morning."

"Sylvie Myers?" At his nod, I grimaced. Since Thad had never once reported to me about a meeting between him and Sylvie, I immediately decided that it might be time to get nervous. "About what?"

Then I had a bad thought. He'd noticed my name on the loan documents and he was going to fire me before I had a chance to come clean? Shit, shit, shit.

"The meeting was about you."

"Ah." Great. This was going to be special. "And?" I didn't think it was about Thad asking permission to court me without getting fired for sexual harassment. Was I about to get busted on the loan application? I should confide about the loan documents before he called me on it. Act like I was going to tell him all along, which I'd been planning to.

But what if it wasn't about the loan? What if it was something else? Should I 'fess up about the loan, when he might not even realize my name was on it? I mean, was it really my fault if he wasn't detail-oriented enough to read the fine print? But did I really want to risk my job if he had seen it?

"There's some concern about your performance."

"My performance?" My gut sank. It didn't just sink. It plummeted like an elevator whose cables had been cut and smashed into my toes. This sounded way bigger than one loan application. "Are you firing me? Just tell me now. Otherwise I'll obsess about it and I won't hear anything else you say." That's me. I was all about being direct. I hate people who can't lay it out the way it is. But damn, being fired? At two in the morning when I'd pledged to risk my job for PWJ, I hadn't thought he'd actually fire me. I couldn't afford to lose my job. Really, I couldn't. But could I afford to let PWJ die? Impossible choices . . .

"No, no. I'm not firing you." He shook his head firmly. Phew. Some of the pressure in my gut eased.

"But there are some issues."

Pressure back. "But I'm not being fired?"

"No." He gave me a half-smile. "Not today, at least."

Well, I still had a job. That was good. I couldn't afford to be unemployed. I forced myself to take a deep breath. "So what's wrong?"

He set a small pile of documents on my desk. "You've had typos in six different sets of loan documents in the last two weeks, all of them important."

Ow. Not good. "Really?" I took a quick glance. Yep, those were my loans. Yep, an extra zero on the loan amount probably wasn't a good thing. Apparently even the expensive Starbucks caffeine wasn't enough to make up for four hours of sleep a night. I aimed for six, but it hadn't been happening lately. Certainly not last night, when I'd stayed up way too late working on a new business plan for PWJ. And I wasn't drinking Starbucks anymore either. It was cheap convenience store coffee nowadays. Totally not the same thing.

"You come in late. You take long lunches. You leave early," he said. "And I'm guessing you're not visiting clients when you're out of the office, are you?"

"Um . . . I stay until six." Couldn't deny my tardy arrivals. Or that I hadn't been off visiting potential clients.

My arrival time had gotten later and later recently. I'd get up early to work on PWJ stuff, but I'd forget to stop so I could go to the job that actually paid the bills. Okay, so maybe my priorities were a little confused. Follow your dreams or be able to afford food? Not always an easy choice. Damn it! I'd been working so hard at both jobs! I'd thought I was doing it okay. I was so tired all the time, and for what? So I could fail at one and get fired from the other? In case you hadn't guessed, I really needed my day job. Food. Shelter. Such annoying needs that seriously limited my freedom to be fiscally irresponsible.

No. Unacceptable. I wasn't going to get fired.

Thad peered at me over the rim of his glasses. "Your salary is seventy percent commission. You should be selling during the business day and doing paperwork after hours. You know that."

I pressed my lips together. I did know that. And I was also aware that my paychecks hadn't been as big lately as they used to be.

"Plus you look like hell."

Yeah, that one I already knew. It figured the first comment my hot boss would make about my appearance was that I looked like hell. He couldn't have noticed a new blouse that showed off my boobs? Maybe he didn't feel the same sexual tension I did. Maybe I had completely misinterpreted everything.

Great. So not only was my job in jeopardy, but my fantasy lover wasn't even returning the fantasy. Every girl needs a fantasy lover to make herself feel better when real life is in the shitter. No such luck for me, apparently.

"What's going on, Paris?" He leaned forward, and the sympathetic expression on his face actually seemed genuine. As though he really cared.

Like any good boss would.

He wasn't trying to catch a glimpse down the front of my blouse at all. He never had. Maybe I needed a new fantasy lover. If he'd stop coming into my office all the time and reminding me of how sexy he was, it would be a lot easier.

"Paris? What's going on? When I first joined this department, all I heard were rave reviews about you. But I haven't seen it. Either I'm a bad boss, or something's up with you."

Oh, nice one, Thad. Guilt me into revealing all. "It's not you."

"Then what?"

How do you tell your boss that your professional aspirations lie elsewhere? Wasn't that the fast track toward a farewell party?

A tendon in Thad's neck twitched, the only sight that he was anything less than completely patient. Maybe having one of his star employees blow it wasn't a good thing for his career either. So I was bringing him down too? Could this day get any worse?

"Paris, if you don't tell me, I have nothing to take to Sylvie to convince her to give you a chance to fix things." To his credit, he didn't look like he was enjoying this discussion. Even his bow tie looked droopy.

I tapped my fingers on my desk while I tried to think of the best way to deal with this situation. Not an easy task when your brain is too tired to form a coherent thought. The caffeine needed reinforcing every twenty minutes, give or take. How to get a boss to support extracurricular job interests . . . hmm . . . "Do you have any dreams, Thad?"

He looked startled and his cheeks flamed red. "What kind of dreams?"

Holy cow. What kind of dreams did he think I was asking about? A trill of something raced through me, but I managed to contain it. For now. "If you were independently wealthy, what would you be doing all day?"

His faced relaxed. "Oh. Job dreams. I'd be working here. I love my job."

It was my turn to be surprised. "Seriously? It's a bank."

"And I love it." He tilted his head. "You don't?"

I sat up and leaned forward, twisting my fingers. "Well, did you look at the loan file I put on your desk this morning?"

"For the shoe technology? Yes, why?"

"What did you think?"

He narrowed his eyes. "Is there something you'd like to tell me about that company?"

"Um . . ." *Should I confess? What if he didn't notice my name listed as one of the owners? What if I could get away with it? For PWJ, it would be worth it, wouldn't it?* "It's a nontraditional company, but it has great potential. I think it would be a good investment for the bank."

He nodded, his face neutral. I couldn't tell if he knew. "Anything else?"

"No."

He looked at me.

I looked at him.

Then I broke. "Okay, fine, I'm one of the owners of the company. I know it's not allowed, but it's a great company and it has a promising future and I know it's a good investment for the bank. I couldn't get a loan from anywhere else, so I had to submit it here. I was going to tell you but I wanted your opinion on it first—before you knew it was from me. You'd never look at it otherwise and—"

I stopped when he held up his hand.

"It's against policy."

I sat up and leaned forward. "But it's my dream, Thad. I've been working on this company since I graduated from college. I know it'll work. We just need some money and—"

"Shut up."

I blinked. "What?"

27

"If you ask me to finance a loan for your company, I'll have to fire you."

"You'd really fire me for that?" Apparently, I wasn't the hero I'd made myself out to be last night. Risking my job didn't really count if I hadn't actually believed there would be repercussions.

I was so disappointed in myself. Where was my passion?

"I'd have to. If I didn't, I'd be fired as soon as someone found out." He leaned forward, his gaze intense. "I was happy to look at your loan application and give you advice on putting it together so you could submit it to other banks. Isn't that why you left it on my desk?"

"Um . . . yes?"

He nodded. "Next time you fill out a fake one, you shouldn't do it on company letterhead, or someone might think you were actually submitting it against company policy."

Damn. I wasn't going to get the loan. I slumped in my chair. "Got it."

He lowered his voice. "If anyone, and I mean anyone, thought you were trying to pass off a loan you had a personal interest in, you'd be done. I couldn't save you, and I'm not even sure I can save you now, given your job performance as of late."

I pressed my lips together. Did this suck or what? Not only was my loan application being rejected, but I could lose my only source of income. No dream and no money.

I suspected Thad was too straightlaced to consider trading sex for a good review. Not that I'd really have considered it, but seeing as how he was already my fantasy lover, was it such a big leap to turn it into the real thing?

But even a good review wouldn't help the fact that I'd let down PWJ. If only I'd managed to be enough of a liar that I kept my name off the loan documents entirely. By putting my name on there and leaving it on Thad's desk, it was as if I wanted to get stopped. Damn it! Why was I so ethical? No, I wasn't ethical. I was a wimp. I blinked hard as the full ramifications of my actions hit me. I'd failed PWJ, and I might lose my job anyway.

"Paris? Do you have a response?"

A light knock sounded at the door. A respite! Any distraction was welcome. Gave me time to try to figure out how to save the situation before I had to commit to anything stupid. I smiled brilliantly at the admin who supported the loan department. "Dani! Hi! Come on in!"

Thad shot me a skeptical glance. Busted. He totally knew I was trying to avoid the situation.

Dani gave Thad an apologetic smile. "Sorry, Thad. I didn't realize you were in here." She looked at me. "Someone named Greg McFee is here to see you. Shall I have him come back later, or will you be available soon?"

Greg?

Greg?

Greg?

My ex-husband was named Greg. I hadn't heard from him in five years, since he took off in the middle of the night. He couldn't be back. It couldn't be that Greg McFee.

Could it?

Black spots started dancing around in my office and the room began to spin, slowly at first, but picking up speed.

"Paris?"

I tried to focus on Dani, but she was wavering in and out of focus. "Are you sure he said his name was Greg McFee?"

"Yes. Why?"

"What does he look like?" My heart was racing so hard my ribs were starting to hurt.

She glanced at Thad. "Um, short, light brown hair. Pretty tall. Kinda thin."

Could be anyone. Didn't have to be Greg. Lots of guys had light brown hair and didn't eat enough. Greg. Common name. Right? Or a joke? A really bad one. I swallowed hard. "Did he . . . um . . . have any scars? Like on his forehead?"

Her cheeks turned pink, as if she was embarrassed to be caught gawking at clients. "Yes."

Oh, shit.

"Paris? You don't look so good."

That was Thad's voice, but it was somewhere in the distance, echoing in the vast emptiness of my brain.

"Is she going to pass out?" Dani was talking now.

"I don't know."

I felt firm hands on my shoulders. "Take a deep breath. Fight it off."

Right. Fight. It. Off.

I could do this.

I scrunched my eyes shut and willed myself to get control. I focused on Thad's grip on my shoulders. On his hand rubbing my back.

Oh, wait. That would mean he had three hands, seeing as how two of them were holding me up. Must be Dani who was rubbing my back.

Bummer.

I took a deep breath, and the buzzing in my ears faded.

"I think she's going to be okay." Thad again, only this time his voice was right next to my ear.

I opened my eyes and found him standing directly in

front of me, his face so close I could have planted one on him with minimal effort. I could actually feel his breath on my face.

He smiled. "You going to pass out?"

You going to kiss me? Hah. Nothing like having your ex-husband show up unexpectedly at your office to make you want to be caught in a compromising position with another man. "I'm fine."

He lifted a skeptical eyebrow at the word "fine," but didn't argue. He did, however, help me sit up, his hands holding me securely. What a good boss. He was well on his way to redeeming himself as my fantasy lover too, coming to my rescue like that.

Dani was standing next to my desk, looking worried. "Should I call an ambulance?"

How sweet was that? I patted her wrist. "No, I'm all right. Skipped breakfast."

She didn't look as though she believed me. What was with all these suspicious people? Just because I'd nearly died of an anxiety attack wasn't any reason to be concerned.

"So, what do you want me to tell Mr. McFee?" she asked.

"Tell him I died last week and he missed the funeral." I sat up more erectly and Thad let go of me. Sob.

"Seriously?"

Before I had a chance to say yes, I was absolutely serious, Thad interrupted. "She'll be available in five minutes."

"Okay." Dani darted out of the room before I could stop her.

So I glared at Thad. "What's up with overruling my death claim?"

"It's a client. I don't care if you're feeling sick. You still have to meet with him."

I felt like sticking my tongue out at him. "He's not a client. It's my ex-husband."

Gawk. He definitely gawked at me. "You're divorced?"

"Yep. Haven't seen the bastard since he left, either." I eyed my window. "Do those open?" I could probably fit through it. I wasn't as skinny as I had been when I was training for the Olympic trials, but it was a very big window. And it was only three floors up. I could survive a fall from that height, couldn't I?

Thad cursed under his breath. "Listen, I'm sorry I interfered. You never talk about your personal life. I had no idea you . . ."

"Had a personal life? Now you do. I'm the CEO of a financially strapped company that makes foam, and I have an ex-husband. Anything else you want to know?"

"Got a boyfriend?"

"What?" I gaped at Thad, and he looked completely shocked at his question.

Awkward silence, anyone?

I should have said yes, I really should have. Or at least sort of.

But I didn't.

I didn't say no either, though.

After a long silence, Thad cleared his throat. "So, um, about your job here. I assume you don't want to get fired?"

"Good assumption." Why had he asked me if I had a boyfriend? Why? Why did I care? Thad was only a fantasy lover. Not the real thing. Not. Not. Not. For heaven's sake, he was my boss! I couldn't go around sleeping with my boss. Way too complicated.

"So let's meet next week. Monday morning? Put together a strategy for improving your job performance and we'll go over it. I'm meeting with Sylvie in the afternoon, so I need to have something to take to her." He stood up. "So, um, yeah. See ya."

And then he was gone.

His soapy scent hadn't even faded from my office when a lean brown-haired man with a scar on his forehead appeared in my doorway, escorted by Dani.

If I hadn't been sitting down, my legs would have given out. My heart felt as if it might anyway.

Why?

Because the Greg McFee standing in front of me was definitely the one I'd been naked with on my honeymoon.

The one who'd been an arrogant prick to me too many times.

The man who had walked out on me, leaving me a note instructing me never to speak to him again.

The scum who had his attorney mail me divorce papers so he wouldn't have to see me.

The bastard I'd loved once, who had eviscerated me a month after he'd pledged his eternal love and fidelity.

It had taken me almost five years to get over him.

And he was here to see me.

THREE

Should I rise and shake his hand and act like it's all business? No, maybe it would be better to remain seated, like he's not worth standing up for. Or I could pretend to hug him and then slam my knee into his crotch. Perhaps an open assault with the letter opener in his throat would be best. Or maybe I ought to pretend I don't recognize him? Greg? Greg who? I'm sorry; I don't know anyone by that name.

Pride got the best of me, and I settled for the professional response. Stand up. Shake his hand. No assault to the family jewels. So hard to resist. "Hello, Greg. Nice to see you." Did that sound neutral enough? Or could he sense the sarcasm dripping from every word?

His fingers closed around mine, and I felt a weird sensation rush through me. I wasn't sure what sensation it was, but it was definitely not neutral. Dammit! How could I not be totally over him? The scum-sucking pig testicle deserved nothing from me.

On the plus side, he looked a little worried. Sort of shocked, actually, as if he couldn't believe he was in my

34

office. I'd never seen him flustered like this before. He'd always been the arrogant, obnoxious, life-of-the-party kind of guy, with a drink in one hand and a girl's butt in the other (except during the four weeks we'd been married and two weeks we'd been dating, of course. Then it had been my butt his hand was wrapped around). And now he looked like some meek little ferret who was afraid of getting stepped on.

He was scared of me? Cool. After all these years, the power was in my corner, and I was down with that.

That was me, all control and dominance. Then I caught a whiff of his aftershave and all delusions of grandeur vanished. It was the same delicious scent that used to make my knees quiver. All of a sudden, I could feel him pressed up against me in bed, telling me about his day while he played with my hair.

I'd always loved it when he played with my hair.

I bit my lower lip and tried not to think about the past. Yeah, so easy to do.

He shut the door, and the sound of it closing made me jump. Right. I was in my office. At work. Not in bed with him, scantily clad and hoping to soon become completely naked.

"Paris. You look great."

"I know." No way was I thanking him for anything, even a compliment. I spun away from him and settled in my throne of domination behind my desk. I let my breath ease out between my lips. Okay, so being in the same room with him was a little hard. It had been almost five years. How could he still affect me like this? "Are you here for a loan?"

"No."

Figured. I hadn't thought he was, but a girl could always hope. What if he was here to ask me to try our relationship again? What if he'd had some cathartic rebirth? Too damn bad. There was no room for ex-husbands, even if they did still make me think about being naked.

He'd left me. How could I have even one longing thought about him? Probably a residual bond from that "I pledge myself to you forever" thing. Well, time to get over that.

He remained standing, and I noticed that he was wearing a very expensive suit. Probably Italian. Definitely custom-made. And his loafers were a gorgeous leather that made my mouth water. I knew shoes. I noticed nice leathers, and he had 'em.

So, in the five years since we'd been hitched, Greg had gotten rich. I'd gotten poor. Obviously I should have gone for alimony. When you're one month into your senior year of college, you don't think about things like that.

"I'd like to take you to dinner tonight."

My eyes bugged out in that really unattractive way I had. I could feel it, but I couldn't stop it. "Why?"

"We need to talk."

"About what?"

He frowned. "We were married, Paris."

"Well, yeah, I know that. But you took off and left me a note never to bother you again." That hadn't been my best moment, finding that note. "I kinda figured obligatory dinner dates weren't my problem anymore." I drummed a pen on my desk and looked at my watch as obviously as I could. "What do you want? Why are you here?"

"We need to talk."

Yes, he'd already said that. "Sorry, Greg, but—" Wait a sec. I wasn't sorry. "Scratch that. I'm not sorry. You're an ass, you treated me like shit, and my time is too valuable to be wasted on an evening with you." Yay for Paris! Be strong, girlfriend! Oh, sure, a part of me wanted to fall at his feet, grab his ankles and beg him to tell me what went wrong with our marriage. If he'd shown up a year or two after leaving me, I might have done it.

But not anymore. I wasn't the same woman he left, and I wasn't falling for him again. I gave him an evil half-smile, hoping he'd realize I was picturing him with a butcher knife sticking out of his chest.

"Tomorrow night?" he asked.

"I have a life now. It doesn't include you." I couldn't believe Greg was standing here in my office, demanding that I make time for dinner with him. My tongue felt as though it was sticking to the roof of my mouth. I wondered if it sounded as though I was lisping. If he asked, I'd claim a recent trip to the dentist and a mouthful of novocaine.

He lifted a brow that was perfectly shaped. Did he pay someone to do that for him? I didn't recall him having fashionable brows before. In fact, when I'd married him, he had long hair that was shaggy and unkempt. He'd worn cutoffs and flip-flops to our wedding. To him, dressing up meant grabbing a T-shirt off the floor. Who was this well-dressed guy standing in my office looking all weepy and apologetic?

I didn't even know him.

"What about lunch today?"

"I would rather clean dog shit off my shoe than eat lunch with you." Where were these great comebacks coming from? I was so witty. They must have been accumulating over the last five years. Who knew I had it in me?

He sat down and folded an elegant leg across his knee. "Lunch tomorrow?"

Um, hello? Did all those years of partying fry his brain, or was he simply ignoring me? The old Greg would have been all up in my grill at my attitude, but this new, wimpy Greg was still gazing at me with a hopeful look on his face. I shifted, ordering myself not to feel sorry for him. I didn't know what his plan was, but I wasn't falling for it. "Don't you get it? I'm not going out with you."

"I'm not leaving until you agree. I need to talk to you."

I glared at him. "You can't control my life anymore."

"Oh, come on, Paris. We have a lot of stuff to talk about."

"No." I stood up, walked to the door and opened it. "Leave."

He didn't move.

So I peered out the door. "Dani."

My admin looked up at me. "Yes?"

"Can you please call security to escort Mr. McFee out of the building?"

"Really?" Her eyes widened even as she hit the red button on her phone.

"Yes." I caught a whiff of Greg's aftershave, and he was suddenly standing next to me. "Or are you leaving on your own?"

"I'm leaving, but I'm not giving up." He shoved a business card into my hand. "My cell phone number is on there. Call me."

"Stalking is illegal in Massachusetts. My mom's a lawyer, and she loves to protect women from men. And she's not exactly a big fan of yours anymore." Who was?

He looked a little desperate. "But I really need to talk to you."

I shook my head, even as a part of me was screaming to grab his hand, drag him back in my office and beg for his love again. The more my subconscious wanted to forgive him for the five years of hell I'd endured after he left, the more I had to get him out of there. "We stopped having anything to say to each other when that greasy divorce attorney showed up asking for my signature. Go back to whatever manure pile you've been living in." I caught a glimpse of a rent-a-cop hustling down the hall toward me. Excellent. I pointed toward Greg. "That's your man."

The guard took Greg's arm and tugged him out of my office.

"Paris . . ." He shot one last plea at me over his shoulder, but the instant my gut curled up and ordered me to run after him, I charged into my office, slammed the door and leaned against it. My knees were shaking, my hands were trembling, pain was screaming through my temples and my mouth was so dry I could barely swallow.

Greg was back. After almost five years of silence, he was back, and I could tell he wasn't going to go away. Today the victory was mine, but what about tomorrow? Or the next day?

I needed reinforcements.

Shoving myself off the door, I doddered on shaking legs to my desk. Pulled out my cell phone and speed-dialed the troops.

Lindsey was waiting for me at Octopus 8, an outdoor bar on Boston Harbor where all the business execs gathered after work on Fridays. Since it was only four o'clock on Thursday, it was pretty much just us.

She'd already ordered, and my glass of wine was sitting across from her. That meant she was footing the bill. If I was buying, I had water. Hard to get drunk off water, but it was even harder to stay alive eating your carpet.

I slid in opposite her and gulped down half the glass of wine.

Lindsey lifted her brows. "A little stressed?"

"Where's Jodi?"

"In the bathroom. She had to fake death and dismemberment to get off, but she made it. She said to tell you if this crisis wasn't adequately life-threatening, she was going to hire a professional hit man to take you out." Jodi worked in the lab at a local hospital doing blood analysis. Nothing like the creative research she got to do for PWJ. That was why she put up with PWJ even though she wasn't an athlete and didn't give a hoot about running shoes. For Jodi, the big attraction was the research. Unlike Will, who loved the challenge of proving his technology was the best. He was about the end result. Jodi was about the process.

I was about making the dream a reality.

Oh, screw the dream. I had bigger issues right now. "What about Will? Is he here yet?" I needed Will. Oh, who was I kidding? I needed all of them.

"Coming soon. Why? What's going on?" Lindsey was all proper in her black suit and modest pumps. A perfect lawyer. She was still limping from the encounter with the ornery mechanical bull, though. Not good.

At that moment, Jodi walked up to the table, a frozen daiquiri in her hand. "This better be good. I had to use one of my best excuses to get out of work, and I try to save all my sick time for PWJ issues." She was wearing her typical work outfit: white cotton pants, white sneakers and a white T-shirt. Since she had to wear a lab coat all day, she didn't worry about looking good. Not that Jodi was ever overly concerned about her appearance. Clothes were more about function than fashion for her. "So what's your crisis?"

"Greg."

Her brows skyrocketed. "McFee?"

I took another swig of my wine and drained the glass. How could it be gone already? Less than an hour since Greg forced his way back into my life, and he was turning me into a lush. "He came to my office today."

"No kidding? What did he want?" Jodi sat down and ran a finger through the condensation on the outside of her glass.

"He wouldn't say anything, other than that we had to go out and talk."

"Huh." Lindsey took a sip of her wine. "How'd he look?"

"Rich. He wouldn't leave until I promised to go to dinner with him." I considered licking the last drops of wine out of my glass and decided that was too uncouth even for me.

"So are you going?" Jodi sounded hopeful.

Hopeful? What was up with that? "You want me to go out with him? I thought you agreed that being skinned alive and turned into a pair of boots was too good for him." We'd had many Greg-vilification parties after he left. Going out to dinner with him had never been submitted as an option.

She shook her head. "Not at all. I was just curious. Are you going?"

"I called security on him." I was still proud of that move.

"Impressive." Lindsey lifted her drink in a silent toast. "Did they handcuff him?"

"No, but I'm thinking of filing for a temporary restraining order to keep him away from me. Could I get one?"

Lindsey grinned. "Not yet, but give me a little more to work with and I could make it happen." She sighed. "How cool would that be to get a TRO for him? If you do, can I serve him?"

"Be my guest." As if I wanted to get face-to-face with him again. Thanks so much, but I'll decline.

"So how'd you leave it?" Jodi asked.

My smile faded. "I think he'll be back. He made it pretty clear."

Jodi frowned. "He refused to say what he wanted?"

"Uh-huh." I nodded at the waitress and gestured for another glass of wine. When PWJ sold for millions, I'd buy Lindsey drinks for a year to pay her back.

"You said he's rich?" Lindsey asked.

"Yep." How unfair was that? Maybe he'd get kidnapped and tortured for a ransom. That might even things out a bit between us.

"Maybe he wants to start paying you alimony," Lindsey said. "Might be worth it to go."

"I think you should hear him out," Jodi said. "You never know. Maybe he wants to apologize."

I stared at them. "Are you serious? He broke my heart!"

"Five years ago. You're over him now," Lindsey said. "I mean, if you weren't, you'd still be mooning over his photo instead of riding the hobby horse with Will."

"If I'm over him, then why did I want to grab him, drag him into my office and beg him to take me back?"

"Oh." Lindsey frowned. "Really? That's not good."

"So you still care about him?" Jodi said. "All the more reason to go out with him and see what he wants."

"Drag who into your office?" Will walked up to the table. He was wearing his day job uniform, which was the same as his PWJ outfit: jeans, T-shirt and whatever footwear was closest to hand when he got dressed. He was the only man I knew who could look so incredibly sexy in castoffs. Whatever male pheromones Will had, they did it for me. Big time. Heavy-duty sexual attraction was a good thing in a lover, don't you think? Will worked in a lab at a local university performing experiments for a chemistry professor. They were researching some medical drug I could never remember the name of.

"Who'd you want to jump?" he asked.

"No one." Suddenly I felt weird discussing Greg with Will. Will knew I'd been married, and he had even met Greg a couple times before Greg had taken off, but Greg was much more a part of my past with Lindsey and Jodi than with Will. Will was my friend first and my lover second, so I should have been able to talk to him about Greg but . . . I don't know. It felt weird.

Will lifted a skeptical brow at me. "No one, huh?" He looked at Jodi. "Who is she talking about?"

"Greg."

His brows went even higher. "Paris's ex-husband?"

"Yep. He came to her office today and wants to go out and 'talk.'" Jodi ignored my foot kicking her foot.

"Huh." Will sat down next to me. "What did he want?"

His easy, nonjealous tone relaxed me. He was acting like the friend he was, not a jealous lover. I needed him, and he was there for me. Everything was going to be all right.

I gave him the quick summary of the encounter. Yeah,

I was sleeping with Will, but our sexual relationship wasn't developed enough for him to have any sense of ownership about me or any jealousy toward past loves. My no-commitment relationship with Will was working perfectly.

I'd been ditched by my dad when I was four.

My college boyfriend had died on me.

My husband had bailed on me.

Any wonder why I wasn't about to get all picket fence and patchwork quilt with anyone? Will's attitude and mine were peacefully compatible, as evidenced by the fact that he wasn't remotely threatened by the reappearance of my ex-husband, at least not in terms of whether it would affect his nightlife.

When I finished, Jodi spoke up first. "Go out with him. I want to know what he's after."

Lindsey nodded. "I agree. Try to get some money out of him. Want me to come along and threaten him into paying alimony? You could put the money toward PWJ."

Will held up his hand. "I don't think she should go."

Thank heavens for that! I didn't want to go either! I shot him a grateful smile, and he squeezed my shoulder. As usual, he was there for me.

Lindsey frowned at Will. "Why shouldn't she go? You think she can't handle it?"

Will kept his hand on my shoulder. "Honestly I'm not sure she can."

I didn't like the sound of that. I sat up straighter. "What does that mean?"

He sighed. "Don't be offended."

"I'm not offended." Okay, so I was. "Why don't you think I'm capable of handling a dinner with him?"

"Look at you. You've downed two glasses of wine,

you're pale, and you freaked out so badly you called all of us out of work at four in the afternoon for consultation."

"This is nothing. You should have seen her the first few weeks after he left," Lindsey said. "She wouldn't even get out of bed."

Will gave her a dry look. "I moved into your house right after Greg took off, remember? You needed someone to pick up his share of the rent."

"Of course I remember," Lindsey said.

"Then you recall that I was present while Paris was still incapacitated? You're acting like this whole nightmare with Greg is a secret the three of you have that I don't. I was there. I was part of the discussions on how to get her to shower."

I decided to stop the conversation before it descended into a discussion of how much of a mess I'd been when Greg had left me. "Listen, that was almost five years ago. I'm totally over him now, and I can handle dinner with him."

Will shook his head. "I think it's a bad idea. Don't go."

Jodi snorted. "You're just being a jealous lover."

Will's eyes flashed, but I was the one who spoke first.

"That's crap and you know it, Jodi. Our relationship isn't like that. I could go sleep with Greg if I wanted to and Will wouldn't care, or he could get back together with She-bitch-from-hell and I wouldn't mind."

"Well, then, you guys are messed up," Lindsey said. "You should care if Will goes back to She-bitch, because it would be wrong, and he should care if you start shtupping Greg, because Greg's a bastard and he'll break your heart again."

Will leaned forward, his jaw tense. "Paris meant that our concern for each other is as friends. Not jealous lovers." He glared at Jodi. "I don't think Paris should go out with Greg because he almost destroyed her. It took all of us almost four years to get her functioning again. It's really only been the past year that she even looked at another guy."

Had I really been that bad? I'd been functioning for far more than the past year, hadn't I? And I'd looked at guys. Sure, Will had been the first (and only) one I'd slept with, and yeah, maybe that was because he was safe and undemanding and was dealing with his own brutal breakup, but that didn't mean Greg had crushed me.

I was uncrushable, damn it, and I was going to prove it! "I'm going!"

Will shook his head. "You have too much going on with PWJ and your job right now to risk falling apart again. If Greg really wants to talk to you, have him send you an email or something." He studied me. "Are you really so certain he can't affect you anymore?"

I swallowed hard. I wasn't sure at all, and Will saw it in my eyes. He grabbed my wrist. "Listen to me. You're a different woman than you were five years ago. You're smart and motivated and on the verge of breaking through with your own successful business. Yet one meeting with Greg has already sent you spiraling backwards. Walk away." Urgency gave life to his words, and I stared at him. He really was worried about me. I smiled and slipped my hand under his.

It felt good to have him care—unlike Greg who'd used me, abandoned me, and now was back for his own agenda.

"Go out with Greg," Jodi said.

"You deserve the chance to find out what really happened," Lindsey added. "Go out with him. Ask all the questions you wanted to ask five years ago. Get some money from him. Then kick him in the nuts and walk out."

I snickered. "I like that last suggestion."

"Or maybe you shouldn't dwell on the past," Jodi said. "I mean, who cares what happened five years ago? Go to dinner with him to see what he wants, but use it as an opportunity to move forward. Maybe you guys could rebuild your relationship again."

"Get a restraining order and let the bastard ruin someone else's life," Will said.

I wanted to kick Greg in the nuts.

But a morbid curiosity also wanted to find out what he had to say and to ask a few questions about what happened five years ago.

But most importantly, I had to prove I was strong enough to face Greg again without falling apart. I'd done it today, and I wanted to show myself it wasn't a fluke. It made me feel good that Will was worried about me, but it also made me feel weak.

I wasn't weak anymore. I wasn't the woman who let Greg McFee devastate her. Greg no longer had the power to hurt me, and I wanted to prove it. I needed to prove it. To Will. And to myself.

I pushed my glass of wine away and picked up a glass of water. "I'm going to go out with him."

Will groaned. "Paris—"

I leveled a look at him. "I'm going, and I'll be fine."

Famous last words? Not on my watch.

Four

The next Sunday night at seven-thirty, I stood naked in my bedroom with my hair done and makeup on and stared at the clothes I'd laid out on my bed.

Jeans, sneakers and a T-shirt to prove to Greg that I wasn't trying to impress him?

Slinky black dress to show him he'd let a good one get away?

I thought about his expensive suit and manicured eyebrows.

The dress won.

Sheer black nylons. A simple diamond pendant my mom gave me when I graduated from college. A strapless push-up bra to augment the generous endowment I'd been blessed with.

And my flats.

I frowned at my reflection.

Lindsey would be all over me for wearing flats with this outfit, but what other options did I have? Oh, sure, I had the pair of heels that she'd bought for me when she saw me trying to wear flats to my office Christmas party the year before, but it had taken me almost two months to heal my sprained ankle after that incident.

High heels weren't my best friend.

I'd have worn my running shoes if I could, but even I knew that wouldn't fly.

Oh, who was I kidding? I wasn't a sophisticated diva who could pull off some slinky black dress, even to try to impress my ex-husband. Crud. I stared at my jeans and felt depressed. Jeans just didn't seem to be sufficient, and I wasn't about to wear one of my bank outfits.

I kicked off the shoes and then jumped when my buzzer rang. He was early! Omigod. My heart started racing and I ran across the floor in my stockinged feet. I punched the button. "Hello?"

"It's us," Lindsey said. "We thought you might need moral support."

"You're the best!" I buzzed her in, opened the door and collapsed on the couch. Thanks heavens for Lindsey. She could give me the final check on my outfit and make sure I oozed sex and everything that Greg wasn't allowed to touch anymore.

When I heard the elevator door open, I jumped up and bolted into the hall, and then stopped. Lindsey was there. And she'd brought Jodi. And Will.

Shit. Will had been pissed off since I'd told him I was going to go out with Greg. He hadn't even come over for our usual Friday night whipped cream game.

But he was here now, and I could tell he was itching for a chance to say, "Told ya so."

"This was more important than work," Jodi said. "I came down with a migraine and bailed. Serves them right for assigning me to the night shift on a Sunday." She kissed my cheek. "You look hot." She walked past me into my condo, but Lindsey paused to give me a disapproving stare. "Don't even tell me you were thinking of wearing flats with that."

"Um . . . yeah . . ." Did I make the call on Lindsey and the flats or what?

She rolled her eyes. "You are so hopeless. Get inside so I can finish fixing you up." She disappeared into the condo, shouting at Jodi to grab her a soda, leaving me standing in the hall with Will.

"Hi."

His gaze skimmed my bosom. "I've never seen that dress before."

I suddenly became uncomfortably aware of the cleavage poking out above the diving neckline. "Yeah, I don't have many occasions to wear it."

His eyes narrowed slightly. "We go plenty of places you could wear it."

There was so not going to be a way for me to win this discussion. Current lover catches you showing major boobage for ex-husband when you've never done the same for said lover. I mean, yeah, we had no commitment, but I didn't want to exactly throw it in his face. "Um . . ."

"You said you were over him."

"I am."

"Then change your clothes."

Crap. I didn't want to. I didn't want Greg, but a girl has to have some pride, you know? Why couldn't Will understand that? "Will . . ."

The elevator door opened and we both jerked around. It was Greg. Wearing an even nicer suit than he'd had on before. And he was carrying a dozen roses. Scratch that. It looked more like two dozen. He gave me a big smile. "You look gorgeous."

Cringe.

Will stepped in front of me. "Hi, Greg. Remember me?"

Greg eased to a stop, his brows furrowing, his gaze flicking between us. "Um . . . do I?"

"Will Foster. I went to Morrison College with you guys."

Greg's frown didn't lessen. "Oh, well, hello then."

"I picked up your share of the rent senior year when you bailed on the girls." Ooo. Totally loaded sentence there. A dig on Greg for walking out on me and the rest of us, plus staking a claim on the women and house Greg had left behind. Will had moved into our house and our lives five years before, and he was still involved, while Greg was not. This was Will's turf now, and he was making sure Greg knew it.

Something ticced in Greg's cheek, but he kept his expression smooth. "Nice to meet you."

"Paris is with me now. Just thought you should know."

Okay, then. Now I knew why Will had come. To brand me as his woman in some caveman fashion. He was going to get quite the earful when Greg left. I wasn't his. Not by any definition of the word.

Yeah, I knew he was trying to protect me, but it still rankled. I did not do commitment to men anymore. Period.

But I'd let it go for now. If he wanted to make Greg feel like a loser, then I certainly wasn't going to jump in and interfere. My fight with Will would be for private audiences only.

Greg nodded, then handed me the roses. "For you."

Talk about awkward. I had no choice but to accept the flowers. Did Greg mean to insult Will by giving me the roses? If he thought Will and I were a couple, it was a totally uncool move. Of course, he probably felt stupid, standing there with the roses. What else was he going to do with them? Should I give Greg the benefit of the doubt or not?

A shriek erupted from inside my condo, and Lindsey and Jodi came flying out the door. "Greg!"

Will and I stepped back as Lindsey and Jodi flung themselves at Greg, the three of them engaging in a big bear hug. They all started yakking at each other, big grins on their faces, as each woman took an arm and escorted Greg into the apartment, leaving Will and me standing in the hall.

Will touched my arm. "Still want to do this?"

I swallowed. "I'm not sure."

"We could leave. Go have sex at my place."

I narrowed my eyes. "Say it a little louder, why don't you?"

"What's wrong? Did you decide you want him back? Don't want to be naked with me when he's around?"

"Oh, shut up, Will. Don't be an ass. You know this is hard for me."

"Then why do it?"

"Because I have to prove to myself that I can."

He studied me for a moment, then his face softened. "You're right. You do."

"I do?"

He nodded. "You never got the chance to show him the amazing woman he walked out on. He needs to see it."

Amazing? "Keep telling me that."

He grinned. "Just be careful with the dress. He's going to think you want to sleep with him."

I lifted my brow. "Isn't that the point?"

Will stepped in front of me, catching me by my upper arms. "Do you think I wouldn't care if you slept with Greg?"

I nodded.

"You're wrong."

Oh, crap. "I thought we already had this discussion."

He ignored me. "I joke about the sex all the time, and I love sex with you. It's great. But that's not what this is about."

"It isn't?" I had no idea what he was talking about, and I really couldn't concentrate on it, not when I could hear Lindsey and Jodi chatting with Greg. What were they discussing? Was I obsessing about my ex-husband? Damn it. I was. I refocused my attention on Will. "What's your point?"

"I would care if you slept with Greg, because he doesn't deserve you, and even though you pretend you're so tough, it would mean something to you." He gave me a small shrug. "I just don't want you to get hurt. It sucks."

My throat suddenly got a little tight and my eyes stung. "You're right. It does suck."

"I love Lindsey and Jodi, but they have other agendas when it comes to Greg. I don't. I think he's a prick and I just want to prevent him from screwing you again."

I grinned. "Literally?"

He laughed softly. "Yeah, I guess. Just watch yourself."

"So you think I shouldn't go?" *Maybe I shouldn't.* I hated Greg, but there was no doubt I wasn't immune to him.

"Go. And kick his ass." His fingers slipped around my elbow and cupped gently. "Let's go get it done."

"Okay." Kick his ass. I could do that. Keep up the attitude I'd given him when he stopped by my office. I sighed, and Will echoed it, though I could barely hear him over the chatter coming from my apartment as Lindsey and Jodi babbled cheerfully to Greg.

Where was the loyalty? Sure, Greg had been friends with Jodi and Lindsey as well, but hello? He'd broken my heart and maintained radio silence for almost five years. Didn't that count for anything?

Apparently not.

At least Will was there for me. Sometimes he knew better than I did whether I needed sympathy or a shove. I took a deep breath and stared at the open door to my condo. I didn't want to go in. I really and truly didn't.

Then Will took my hand and squeezed it. It wasn't sexual. It was a show of friendship and loyalty.

Public displays of affection weren't my gig, but today I needed it. So I held on tightly and followed him into the apartment.

The three musketeers were bonding on the couch, Lindsey and Jodi babbling with excitement. I hadn't seen that much life on Jodi's face in ages. I moved closer to Will so my shoulder was against his arm, and then I cleared my throat.

No one noticed.

I glanced at Will, surprised to find him watching the exchange with a yearning look on his face. We'd all been his women for the last five years, and just like that, Greg had snatched them away.

I leaned against Will more firmly, so that we were pressed against each other. So that he knew I wasn't going to abandon him for Greg, even though I knew he'd never admit he was worried about it. He shot me a soft smile and I grinned back. "Forget it, Will. Let's go. We don't need this."

He looked at me. "Seriously?"

"Yes. I'll just grab my shoes."

He gave me his lecherous look, wiggling his eyebrows and leering at my breasts. "Don't change the dress. I like it, as long as you're wearing it for me."

I laughed. Sometimes being ogled is exactly what a girl needs. "Can I wear sneakers?"

"You can wear anything."

I knew it was because he was going to rip it off the instant we walked into his apartment, but it was still sweet. "Thanks."

He pressed his lips to the palm of my hand. "Anything for you, my love."

I realized suddenly that the room was totally silent, and I felt my cheeks heat up as someone cleared their throat.

Will's face tightened, and we both turned toward the couch. All three of them were looking at us, but Greg's face was totally inscrutable.

Lindsey was the one who spoke. "I talked to my client. The one who does orthopedic shoes. He's happy to rent time in his lab to you."

I blinked. Now was the time to discuss shoes? "Great."

"Did you get the loan?" Jodi asked.

I didn't want to have this conversation with Greg there. "Let's talk about it later, okay?"

Jodi sighed and flopped against the couch. "You didn't, did you? I knew it. A waste.".

Greg looked at all of us. "You guys need money? I have money. What do you need?"

Will muttered something uncomplimentary under his breath, Jodi perked up and Lindsey looked thoughtful.

"Forget it, Greg." No way were we going there. "I'll get my shoes and we'll go." I caught a surprised look from Will at my change of plans and touched his hand. "I'm sorry, but I think I should go with Greg after all," I said quietly, for his ears only. "I'll meet up with you afterwards, okay?"

He shrugged and leaned against the wall. "Whatever."

Damn it. Now I felt bad.

"We need a few hundred grand," Lindsey said to Greg. "That would set us up really well."

Total betrayal. There was no other way to describe Lindsey's words. Time to end that discussion. "I'm going to go put on my flats," I announced. "I'll be right back."

"Flats? You can't wear flats!" Lindsey fell into my trap and raced after me, forgetting about her little financial proposal to Greg. Jodi joined her and they dragged me to the bedroom and shut the door.

Lindsey dove into my closet and emerged with the break-my-ankle heels. "You have to wear these."

You know what? I wanted to wear them. I wanted to be Greg's equal, with his beautiful suit, two dozen roses and his ability to toss money at floundering businesses without even bothering to find out anything about them.

Why was he willing to do that? I was going to find out.

"Don't screw this up, Paris."

I looked up at Jodi. "Screw what up?"

"The money. This is our chance. Greg has the money to fund whatever we need. If you let your baggage from the past screw it up, then we all lose."

I set my hands on my hips as Lindsey put the shoes on my feet. "There's no way we're letting Greg get involved with PWJ. How could you even suggest it? He's an ass, he's unreliable, we have no idea where he's been for the last five years, and . . . and . . . he's Greg!"

"You don't have to have sex with him or marry him," Jodi said. "But if he wants to rejoin the fold and give us a bunch of dough, maybe we should let him."

I folded my arms across my chest. It had a nice effect on the cleavage. "No."

"Let it go, Jodi," Lindsey said. "She's too stressed to think about that." Lindsey stepped back and inspected me. "Looking pretty good, I have to admit. Nothing like that sweet college girl he married."

"That's the point." I took an experimental step in the shoes, and my ankle wobbled. "I should really wear my ankle brace with these shoes."

"Yeah, that'll complete the look nicely." Lindsey smacked me on the butt. "Have no mercy, girlfriend."

I cocked my head. "You seemed pretty chummy with him a few minutes ago. And now you want me to 'have no mercy'?"

"I was trying to lull him into a sense of complacency so you could destroy him before he realized what was happening. Go, go. Be mean. Show him what he can't have anymore. Make him regret what he gave up. And talk about how good your orgasms are with Will."

And with that great advice, I headed out to dinner with my ex-husband.

I didn't wait for dessert.

I didn't even wait for our appetizers to arrive.

We sat. We ordered. I asked the million-dollar question. "So, Greg, why did you need to talk to me so badly?"

He met my gaze. "My therapist told me to."

I blinked. "What?" Greg was so not the type to have a therapist.

"It's time for me to heal."

"Heal what?" This was absolutely not what I'd expected. Greg was the strong, silent type, which was part of why I'd fallen for him. All the mystery. Girls loved that. I certainly had. I mean, he hadn't been silent when he was running around at a party, hitting on all the girls, but he'd been silent when it came to his emotions. Greg had always been a rock. After Seth died, he'd never shed a tear, never talked about his feelings. Instead, he'd sat and listened to me bawl night after night. As Seth's best friend, Greg had been the one I'd chosen to share my grief with.

One thing led to another, and two months after Seth's death, Greg and I had gotten married. August fifteenth. We had a great honeymoon, headed back to school for our senior year, surprising Lindsey and Jodi with our unexpected union. Then a week after we arrived at the house the gang was sharing, he'd disappeared.

And that was the last I'd seen of him.

"My wife left me," he said.

"Your . . . wife?" The word stuck in my throat. Clearly he didn't mean me. He'd done the leaving in our relationship. Finding out your ex-husband already married someone else? Ouch.

"Yes. After we got divorced, I remarried." He shook his head. "Didn't work at all. She left."

Well, shit. I'd spent the first three years after Greg left pining for him, and he'd gone off and married someone else. Him, rich and remarried. Me, broke and alone. You see a problem with how this story unfolded? Not that I'd let him know it bothered me. I was going to play it cool. "Well, they say third time's a charm. Maybe you'll get it right next time."

He ignored me. "After she took off, I got depressed and tried to kill myself with a safety razor."

I stared at him. "You tried to commit suicide?" Goosebumps popped up on my arms. The Greg I'd known would never have let himself get that depressed. "I don't know what to say. I mean, that sucks." I hated him, but I didn't want him to suffer like that.

Or maybe I did. I mean, it was only fair, right?

But how could I want that kind of pain to be inflicted on him? I'd loved him once.

But it had been another woman he'd loved that much, not me.

But I'd felt that kind of pain and it was horrible. Even though he'd ripped my heart out and shredded it, I didn't really want him to suffer.

Or did I?

Damn it! I didn't even know how to react!

"I went into counseling about six months ago," Greg continued. "Turns out I have issues. Apparently, attempted suicide with a safety razor is more of a cry for help than an actual death wish."

Well, damn it. How was I supposed to be flippant and obnoxious when he was telling me about how he almost killed himself? "I'm sorry to hear that, Greg."

"The thing is, I wanted my wife back, so I basically picked a method that I knew wouldn't kill me. My therapist says I basically faked a suicide attempt to force her to come back."

Ah, there it was. The Greg I knew so well, making sure

I understood it was for his other wife that he'd been driven to such extremes. He didn't even care that he'd left me behind as he'd breezed onto a new life. This conversation was all about him and his needs. He thought he could just breeze back into my life without the smallest consideration for my feelings. No apology for the past; he just launched into his own sad story and expected my sympathy. He was still a bastard. So I picked up my wine and gave him a demure smile. "So it's difficult to kill yourself with a safety razor? Is that what you're saying?"

He blinked. "I'm trying to share here."

"And I'm trying to learn. See, I didn't try to kill myself after you left, so I'm not all that familiar with the methodologies. I actually opened my own business and I'm on the way toward changing an entire industry. I didn't have time to feel sorry for myself and engage in metaphorical cries for help." I stopped when I realized he was staring at me. "What's your problem?" Me, hostile? You bet. A girl has to have some pride, you know? There was no chance in hell I was about to let him know what he'd put me through after he left, not with him flaunting money and subsequent wives.

"You're so different now," he said.

I nodded. "Yep."

"Before . . . you were soft. Needy. Dependent."

Shudder. Obviously I used to be an embarrassment to liberated women everywhere. Not anymore. "Greg, I'm not here for you to dissect my personality. I'm here because you wanted to talk. Talk." Our drinks arrived, and I took a long swallow of my sparkling water.

No wine for me. I wanted a clear head to deal with Greg.

He regarded me with a speculative look that made me squirm. "I came here because my therapist felt I was still conflicted about our past. I have feelings of guilt from the accident and the divorce. If I divest myself of these emotional burdens, then I will heal and be able to get my wife to take me back." He grimaced and smacked his head. "Ex. Ex-wife. I keep forgetting."

I didn't want him back. I really didn't. But the thought of him overhauling his entire personality into a touchy-feely softie just so he could win back his second wife didn't exactly do wonders for my ego.

He took a deep breath. "I'm sorry."

I waited. It was a start in the right direction.

He picked up his wine and took a sip. "So tell me about your company. What do you need the money for?"

Um . . . hello? "That's it?"

"What's it?"

"That's why I had to go to dinner with you? So you could say two words?"

"They're very important words." He stretched and looked pleased. "I feel a lot better now. It's been weighing on me for a long time."

I drummed my fingers on the table. As if he was going to get off that easily. "What exactly are you sorry about, Greg?"

His self-satisfied look faded. "What do you mean?"

"What are you apologizing for?"

He pulled his perfect brows together in a frown.

I waited. I wasn't going to let him off easy.

After a long moment, he said, "I'm sorry about my role in Seth's death, and I'm sorry I left you the way I did." He shifted in his chair. "And I forgot to get your acceptance of my apology."

I didn't know what to say. It was the first time I'd ever heard anything like that out of Greg's mouth. Not that I bought it. Note that he said he was sorry about how he left me, not *that* he left me. Big difference.

Besides it was only to get his wife back. He'd already faked a suicide attempt to win her over. A fabricated apology to his first wife was a hell of a lot less effort to pull off.

"My therapist says I need your forgiveness in order to move on." He noticed me studying him, and his cheeks flamed red. "It's kind of embarrassing, though. Having a therapist and all. So don't tell anyone, okay?"

I laughed. This was the Greg I knew, trying to pretend he was a tough guy. I'd always thought there was more under there than he shared. And now he was here, sharing secrets with me and apologizing. . . .

No.

Not enough.

I sat up straighter and cleared my throat. "You're really back in town to do therapy work? That's it?"

"I'm not very good at saying this stuff. My therapist says I've repressed my natural need to share my emotions because I've been trapped by societal expectations of male behavior." He laid his hands out on the table, palms up. "I hereby offer my innermost secrets to you. Ask whatever you want to know."

Oh, wow. How much did I want to find out what he really thought? Get inside his head for the first time ever? Find out if he was the man I thought I'd married, a quality soul beneath that harsh exterior? What if he'd really redeemed himself?

Or what if he was still a manipulating bastard who was

trying to destroy me again? He'd married me once to assuage his own guilt (that was my theory, anyway), then bailed without a second thought. And now he was back, using me to try to get his wife back. "There's nothing I want to know," I said. It even sounded as though I was telling the truth. I hadn't realized I was such a good liar.

He nodded and took his hands off the table. "I did very well in my second marriage," he said. "I used my wife's money to start my own business, and now I'm set for life. Apparently I'm very good at the venture capitalist business."

I wondered how long I had to sit here and listen to his good fortune. Why was he telling me? Had I somehow given the impression that I cared?

"So I'd like to give you the two hundred thousand you need for your business. Is that enough? That's what Lindsey suggested."

"What?" My jaw dropped and my heart rate soared. Two hundred grand? For PWJ? Saliva pooled. Then I mentally smacked myself. I couldn't take a handout from Greg. I wasn't that pitiful. "Why would you give us that kind of money? You don't even know what we're doing."

He looked a little taken aback at my challenging tone. "You were a mess after Seth's death, and I can't imagine my leaving was easy to deal with. I had never realized how awful you must have felt until my wife left me last fall. It's a horrible experience, and I can't believe I did that to you. I can't change the past, but if I can make up for it by helping you now, the money is yours."

"Actually, Greg, you're wrong. You didn't hurt me. I was glad to have you leave. Note the lack of safety razor scars on my wrists." I held out the body parts in question, even as excitement pulsed through my body at the thought of all that money being infused into the PWJ coffers. *Think of what it would mean for us.* But I couldn't. I had too much pride to let him pay off his guilt with a check, and I certainly wasn't going to owe Greg anything. "No, thanks."

"Don't be a fool, Paris. Take the money."

"I don't need it." But, damn, I wanted it.

But there was no way I was going to accept it. Ever.

I hadn't spent five years healing to let Greg back into my life.

But I hadn't spent four years on PWJ to let it die when the money was right there.

Greg leaned forward and fixed his baby blues on me. "Paris. I'm back, and I'm not leaving until my therapist says I can. You need my money. I need to do some work on myself. It's the perfect setup. I give you money. You forgive me. I help you launch your company into a highly profitable state. My ex-wife realizes I'm not such a bad guy, and we all go away happy."

I shook my head. "I don't want you in my life." Especially not on those terms.

"Then you need to work on yourself as well."

"What?" Like I needed a live-in therapist. No thanks.

He nodded as though he was some wise sage. "If you don't want me around, then it's an indication that you're still holding some level of antipathy toward me. It's not healthy. You need to embrace me, and together we can work over our issues and move on."

Embrace him? Hah. I'd sooner embrace a deranged were-wolf with rabies and a deep-seated aggression against women. "Forget it, Greg. There's no chance."

He arched an eyebrow, and I saw a glint of the old

Greg in his eyes. Plotting, manipulative, so certain of what he wanted. For so long, he had fooled me with his friendship and his smooth exterior. But it was all part of his master plan to service his own needs. When his needs conflicted with the mores of decent human behavior, guess what won out? On the outside, he was awesome. On the inside, he was ready to sell out his friends for his own well-being. Or for his wife. At the moment, he might be playing the role of the victim, but I didn't buy it for a minute. Not anymore. But at least this time I knew he was using me to get what he wanted, so I could protect myself.

"Are you willing to give up on your business?" he asked. "Without my money, it's over, according to Lindsey and Jodi."

Such a low blow. Typical ex-husband. Totally knows where to hit. "I'll find the money."

He set a business card on the table, along with a hundred-dollar bill; I assumed for the dinner check. "In case you tossed the other card I gave you, here it is again. My cell phone number is on there. Call me when you're ready to take my money, and when you're ready to heal." Then he stood up. "Have a nice evening."

"I won't call you." There was one other option. I hadn't wanted to do it, but it was time. "Trust me, I don't need you."

"You'll call." He looked so sure of himself that I wanted to kick him in the shins. I should have nailed the family jewels in my office when I'd the chance.

And then he left. Our food arrived moments later. My stomach was too upset to eat, so I had them package both dinners to go and kept the change. You know you're pathetic when your biggest revenge on your ex-husband is to claim his food, keep his change and refuse to take money from him. Watch out. I was such a badass.

Hah.

FIVE

I stopped at my mom's condo on the way home. I figured a little unconditional love would help me reclaim my equilibrium. Sure, it was getting late, but my mom often burned the midnight oil working till all hours, even on a Friday night. Like mother, like daughter. I inherited my workaholic gene, in case you were wondering.

And yeah, I was going to ask her for a really big loan.

When I let myself in, my mom was sitting at her marble kitchen table with a glass of expensive white wine, Godiva chocolates and fresh strawberries. Papers were spread all over the table. A very common sight for my mom.

She was out of her business suit, opting instead for a pair of linen slacks with a silk tank top, her hair still in a bun.

"Hi, Mom."

She looked up quickly, and her eyes widened in startled shock. Then her features contorted into the expression a kid might wear if he were caught with his hand in a bag of cookies being saved for dessert. Total guilt. Pink cheeks and everything. "Paris! What are you doing here?"

She lunged for the papers, trying to gather them up before I could get close enough to see them.

"Interrupting something, apparently." I sprinted toward the table as she tried to sweep all the papers into a pile. "Whatcha got, Mom?"

"Nothing." She swept, I dove, and we smacked heads.

"Crap!" I reeled, my hand pressed to my forehead while my mom collapsed in her chair, doing much the same thing I was, except her swears were much more ladylike than mine. She still blames my foul mouth on the four years we lived with my dad before he left.

Whenever I point out to her that she's been the only influence in my life since I was four years old and she'd had plenty of opportunity to fix it, she develops selective deafness and leaves the room.

My head still throbbing, I fished a piece of paper off the floor. "What are you working on?"

"Can't you respect my privacy?"

"No more than you did when I was a teenager. Remember those weekly searches of my room to ensure I wasn't a drug addict? Sometimes a gross violation of personal space is for your own good." I scanned the paper, and then frowned. "'Dear Babolicious, I like smart women with attitude. I'm also a lawyer. I'd like to engage in some courtroom battles with you. Email me at sosueme555@contingencyfee.com.'"

I glanced at my mom, and she appeared to be trying to melt into her kitchen chair. It was so rare to see her embarrassed that I couldn't resist the temptation to torment her just a little. I picked up another paper. "Dear Babolicious, bring some handcuffs and you can try to break me out of jail any time you want. Sandm69@statepenitentiary.gov." I set the paper down. "Are you Babolicious?"

"Maybe." She grabbed the paper and turned it over. "So what?"

"You put an ad in the personals?"

At her nod, I collapsed into the nearest chair. I couldn't believe it. My mom, who had nearly disowned me in an effort to dissuade me from marrying Greg. A women's rights activist who was against marriage because it stripped women of their identity and rights. A successful lawyer who hadn't had a boyfriend since my dad had walked out. My mom, whose only needs in life were work and her own fabulous daughter. A personal ad? "Tell me it's a research project."

She sighed, got another glass and poured me some wine. "Have some chocolate."

Harassing her could wait a moment. I shoved three-thousand calories into my mouth. "So?"

She swirled the wine in her glass. "I turn fifty soon."

"In four years." My mom was twenty when she had me. Apparently I went to law school with her, dirty diapers and all. Having a kid wasn't about to slow her down. Personally, I think earning her law degree was her way of trying to silence all the people who claimed she was a loser for getting knocked up by a no-good scumbag. "And so what if you're nearing the half-century mark? You look thirty-five."

"I went to a funeral last month."

"Oh." Bummer. "Someone I know?"

"No. I got my directions messed up and ended up at a funeral by mistake. So I decided to go in." She sighed. "It was really a lovely funeral. Apparently, Harold Oaks was quite a nice man before he started stealing Social Security checks from mailboxes."

And this had what relationship to a personal ad?

"You're too rich to have to worry about stealing Social Security checks. Is that what you're worried about?"

"Of course not. The point was that Harold was dead."

"Was he young?"

"Ninety-three."

I took another chocolate. "Sorry, but you've totally lost me. What does this have to do with men in prison wanting to have bondage sex with you?"

"I want to be like Harold, of course."

"You mean, you don't want to be like Harold."

She rolled her eyes. "No, I want to be like him."

"Because he didn't die until he was ninety-three? Call me skeptical, but going on dates with guys in prison might not do much for increasing your life expectancy."

"Even though Harold was a thief and apparently enjoyed berating children until they cried and trained his Chihuahua to attack the mailman, his wife was still there, crying her eyes out."

"Probably because it took that long for him to die."

She glared at me. "No. Because she loved him. Despite the fact that he was pretty much a lowlife, she loved him. Unconditional love." She got this dreamy look on her face. "And even though his kids were drinking champagne and wondering how much they'd inherited, there was this whole feeling of love in the air. Love for Harold Oaks."

"I'll cry at your funeral, I promise. I'm sure I could bribe Lindsey, Jodi and Will to cry too, if you like. Or we could toast your death with champagne. Whichever you prefer."

She sighed and ran her fingers over the papers strewn in front of her. "When I die, I want a man to be crushed.

I want a man to love me so much he can't live without me. If he killed himself after I died, that would be best. That's the kind of true love I want."

I blinked. "Since when?"

"Since Harold's funeral. The man was amoral, cranky and generally unpleasant, yet his wife was devastated by the loss. I had no idea that kind of love really existed. Now that I know it does, I want to see what it's like before I end up in a can of ashes on your mantle."

I frowned. "You want me to keep your ashes on my mantle? Isn't that a little morbid?"

She gave me a haughty look. "Quit making a joke of it. I'm completely serious." She sank her teeth into another chocolate. "I raised my daughter. I have a great career. Now I want love."

"You want to get married?"

"Yes." There was no doubt in her voice.

"All because Harold Oaks was a schmuck before he died?" I didn't even know how to respond. I had been my mom's reason for living for the past twenty-five years. And now I wasn't enough? She needed a man?

After trying to brainwash me into thinking that no woman needed a man, she was now yearning for love and marriage? I didn't get it. I really didn't get it. I mean, I was finally at the point where I realized I was better off single, so how could she be changing the rules on me? It wasn't easy to find a female role model who believed that women should have all the sex they wanted but never commit to one man.

"Something like that." She patted my hand. "Don't worry. I'll still love you and I'll protect my inheritance for you. I just want to see what true love is like."

"But don't you want to be independent?"

"Of course. But I also want love." She picked up a stack of emails and set them in front of me. "As long as you're here, you might as well help me screen. I'm looking for a man who's smart, emotionally stable, financially independent and has a sense of humor."

I started laughing. "That's what every woman wants."

"Yeah, well, I'm going to get it."

My mom got everything she'd ever wanted. Why would this be different? I didn't want a dad. I didn't want to have to fight for time with the one stabilizing force in my life. With any luck, this was a phase. I mean, how long could the Harold Oaks influence last? My mom was too entrenched in her world to change.

This was definitely a temporary condition, and that thought made me feel much better. I could handle a deranged mom for the short term. "Sure, I'll help you find a man. I assume anyone who's in prison is out?"

"Depends on what they're in for. Insider trading might be okay. Serial killers probably not." She shot me a curious look. "What was it like to get married? To have someone declare their eternal love to you?"

"A lot better than getting the divorce papers a month later."

She smacked my arm lightly. "You don't have to be so negative. Why not look on the bright side of things? A man loved you enough to commit his life to you. That kind of love never goes away. I'll bet he still loves you and he's getting the nerve to come back and find his true love again." She brightened. "What about Will? Has he mentioned marriage? He sure seems to love you."

"Will and I aren't about love."

"Why not?"

I stared at her. "Who are you and what have you done with my mother?"

"Hey, I don't want you to end up with no one at your funeral either. I went to one last week and—"

I held up my hand. "Hold on a sec. Don't tell me you went to another stranger's funeral?"

"I saw this obituary and it was so short and had this cold tone about it. So I went to the service. Do you realize there were only two people there, and the other one was his garbage man who told me the deceased used to give him two-thousand-dollar tips every Christmas? Here was a man who was so generous that he gave a trash collector huge tips, and no one else cared enough to come to his funeral." She gave a dramatic shiver. "That was the day I put my ad in the personals. I refuse to end up like Ike Isenhauf."

"Ike Isenhauf? That was his name?"

"Yes. Did I tell you he was fifty-one? Heart attack. I'm almost fifty. That could have been me."

"It's not going to be you. You have tons of friends."

She leaned forward. "It's not the same thing. Wait until you get to be my age and alone. You'll see." She pulled out a section of the newspaper. "There's another funeral on Saturday. For a woman named Rebecca Munson. It looks like another low-attendance one. I'm going to go and give her some respect. Want to come?"

I blinked. "You're going to start going to strangers' funerals on a regular basis?"

"It's my new resolution. I can't let these poor people be buried with no one caring."

"Or you could. Just a thought."

"Don't be callous, Paris. If you come, you'll understand what I mean." She shook her head. "I can't believe it took me this long to realize what was important in life. The value of your life can be summed up in who attends your funeral and how upset they are. Keep that in mind, and you'll be happy."

Or locked up in a padded cell with a straitjacket and no sharp objects. "As someone who is a lot closer to the dating scene than you are, can I make a suggestion?"

"Of course."

"If you really start going on dates, don't take them to funerals. At least not on the first date. They might not understand."

"I may not have a lot of practice dating, but I'm not a total social zero."

"Right. Sorry." I decided today wasn't the day to tell my mom that Greg was back in town and Will's public displays of affection were making me itch. I was too afraid of the advice she might give me. The mom I knew would have told me to tell them all to shove off and to jump in the sack with Thad instead. But this new mom might suggest something less appealing, like grabbing one of them and hustling off to the altar.

Been there. Done that. Not trying again.

I was totally thrown by my mom's new attitude. What do you do when the foundation you've counted on your whole life changes?

But what scared me the most was that all her talk of marriage and love was stirring up feelings long buried, feelings I didn't know how to deal with and didn't want to. It made me wonder whether maybe, just maybe, I was missing out by banning marriage from my life.

And that scared the daylights out of me.

Time to change the subject. "So, Mom . . ."

She didn't even look up. "No."

"But you don't even know what I'm going to ask."

"You're going to ask me for money for PWJ." She paused to read one of the letters, then tossed it in the trash, muttering something about perverts.

I blinked. "How did you know that?"

"I've been waiting for you to ask for the last four years." She threw another letter in the trash. "I'm impressed you waited this long to ask, but I would have been even more impressed if you hadn't asked at all."

How can you be twenty-six and still vulnerable to the parental one-liner that makes you feel like a total failure in everything you've ever accomplished? I sagged, but continued my quest. "Well, we decided to manufacture some prototypes ourselves and develop proof that they work. Then we'll go back to the companies with a revised proposal."

She nodded. "Sounds like a good plan. What do you think HWP means?"

"Height-weight proportionate."

That got her attention. "How do you know?"

"Lindsey put an ad in the personals once. She wanted to see how many people would respond to an ad looking for a vampire to date."

"How many did she get?"

"Over a thousand."

"Really?"

"She put a picture of herself in a bikini in the ad."

"Ah. Did she meet any real vampires?"

"Jodi and I burned all the letters before she could set up any dates." We'd figured that letting Lindsey go off with someone who claimed to suck blood simply wasn't a good idea, given her self-destructive state of mind. "So . . ."

"No."

Argh! "Why not?"

"Because the only way to be proud of yourself is to make the business a success on your own, taking no handouts. Getting money from your mom qualifies as a handout." She looked up and patted my hand. "You'll figure out a way, and you'll be so much more proud of yourself than if you took money from me."

"It's a loan. I'll pay it back. You'll be a bank." I couldn't believe she was pulling the ol' "doing it for your own good" shtick on me. She'd used it when I was in the hospital with a broken pelvis, she'd used it when I was attending the funeral of my boyfriend, and she'd used it when Greg had walked out, all three times when I was so miserable and depressed I wanted to give up on everything and move back home. She'd locked the door in my face (metaphorically speaking) and told me the tough love was for my own good. The only time I got real support from her was when I was flying high and didn't need it.

When I needed the love, I got a kick in the ass. And you know what? I still didn't like it. What was wrong with a little pat on the back and a few encouraging boosts? My mom's boosts consisted of a smack upside the head and a lecture not to feel bad for myself because I was the one in control of my destiny and I was damned lucky. "Please?"

"No." She held out a picture. "Does this look like it's been altered? I've never seen someone with a triple chin and washboard abs."

"It's fake." See, the problem with having a mom who raised a baby solo while putting herself through college and law school without taking a dime from anyone, was that it set the bar a little high for her offspring. "Can't you at least think about it?"

"You'd never forgive me if I let you take the short cut."

Oh, but I think I would.

She handed me a stack of letters. "If you find a man you want, feel free to take the letter. True love, ending in suicide because your husband can't live without you when you die. It's the path to life fulfillment."

I thought of Greg and his episode with the safety razor. Did that mean he'd found true love with wife number two? He was no better than snake entrails.

Maybe I should take that money from him. It would serve him right to have to empty his bank account on my behalf. But I had a feeling the money wouldn't be string-free.

Argh. Why weren't there any other options? What was more important to me, PWJ or my personal vendetta against my ex-husband?

When I looked at it that way, there seemed to be only one mature response. The question was, how mature was I?

When I got home, Will was watching television and had cleaned out half my fridge. His feet were up on my coffee table, his shoes in the closet, the roses from Greg in a vase in the kitchen.

I hadn't put the roses there. Had Will? It felt weird to have him taking care of roses from my ex-husband. As a friend, totally normal. As a lover, not so much. "Hi."

He looked up quickly. "I didn't hear you come home."

For a moment, there was an awkward pause. Though Will and I had known each other for five years and seen each other naked more than a few times, we were still in that newlywed phase where we always got up to welcome the other one home.

But this time, Will took a second or two before standing up, and my gut did some weird thing.

I didn't want what Will and I had to change.

He walked over, gave me a quick kiss and a light hug, then released me.

I needed a real hug, from my friend Will, and he had to have known it. But instead he treated me like a miffed lover.

Things were changing.

"So how'd it go?" He walked into the kitchen and opened the fridge, staring at the contents as if he didn't care about the answer.

"He's here because his therapist told him he needs to revisit his past and get closure."

Will eyed me over the top of the fridge. "Seriously?"

"That's what he said." I handed him the take-out containers from dinner. "Hungry?"

"Sure." He handed me a bottle of water from the fridge, then shut the door. "What else?"

Was there something ironic about your lover eating the leftovers of your ex-husband? Oh, wow. That could totally be taken the wrong way. Except I wasn't a leftover, damn it. "What do you mean, what else?"

"Did you talk about PWJ? About him putting money in?"

"Maybe."

"Lindsey and Jodi talked to me tonight," he said. "They want me to support bringing Greg into the business."

I frowned. "Why is it so important to them?"

He looked at me. "The better question is, why are you hesitating? Yesterday you were willing to risk getting fired to make PWJ fly. Today you turn down money merely because it comes from some guy that you were married to for less than a month. Seems to me that if you really were over him, you'd take the money without a second thought."

"It's not that simple."

"Or are there still sparks flying between you two?" He reached over and ran his hand over my arm, an undertone of tension in his voice. "Afraid you'll want him back in your bed?"

I pulled away, remembering his claim earlier in the evening. "What was up with the 'Paris is with me' comment earlier tonight?"

He gritted his jaw. "I knew that would piss you off."

"So why'd you do it?"

He shrugged. "Felt right at the time."

Something about his tone caught me. "And now?"

"Feels stupid." He sat back down in his chair and clasped his hands behind his head. "I guess I wanted to protect you."

"I don't need protection." Though I had to admit, I was feeling a little lost right now. Which is why I had sworn off marriage again. I didn't want to let myself rely on a guy again. It left me too vulnerable. Sure, Will was a guy, but he was a friend, so it was different. He'd been burned by his true love as well, so he didn't want serious either.

So why were things changing just because Greg had shown up? Shouldn't our friendship be stronger than that?

"I disagree."

"Oh, come on, Will. Just because we're sleeping together doesn't give you the right to rule the rest of my life."

"Maybe, but the fact that we've been best friends for

five years does." He flipped his hands dismissively. "But if you think you're fine, then whatever. Do your thing. Take his money."

"Gee, thanks for your support."

"What do you want from me?" He scowled. "I tried to give you support and you got pissed. I give you space, and you get sarcastic. Pick what you want, Paris."

"Support isn't the same thing as claiming to the world that we're a couple."

"Is it the couple thing that's bothering you, or the fact that I made the comment in front of your ex-husband?" His eyes were glittering. "You want him back?"

"Damn it, Greg, I don't want him back! Can't you quit bugging me?"

His jaw tensed. "You just called me Greg."

"I did?"

"Yeah." He stood up. "I think we should skip the overnight tonight. I'm not in the mood."

"Fine."

"Fine." He paused at the door. "Take the money, Paris. If you can handle Greg, take the money. For the rest of our sakes, don't piss it away."

He slammed the door behind him, leaving me very alone in my condo.

It was my first fight with Will since we'd started dating.

Shit. I really could have used a casual night of loving. Someone holding me till dawn without making any demands on me.

Damn Greg for coming back into my life. He was going to screw everything up, wasn't he?

SIX

At seven-thirty the next morning, I dragged myself to the café in the lobby of our office building for my breakfast meeting with Thad. I hadn't slept well, and I was looking good. Not. When my alarm had gone off this morning, I'd been in the middle of a dream.

Greg and Will were in a mud-wrestling fight, while I sat at the bar and counted a large pile of cash, which was then sucked into the floor in a huge vortex, which then reversed and spit out a wrecked Jeep Cherokee covered in blood. Then Jodi and Lindsey ran into the room, waving bottles of ibuprofen at me, which turned into scraps of newspaper articles about how PWJ was in bankruptcy. Then Lindsey's right arm and left leg fell off, and Jodi had to drag her to the bar, where my mom was making out with a guy in prison overalls and leg shackles. And then a huge chandelier broke and was falling on me, but just before it hit, Thad came riding through the bar on a Harley. He was naked except for a leopard-print thong and a bow tie made of handcuffs, and he yanked me out from under the chandelier and threw me on the back of his bike. But as he was driving out of the bar, I fell off, landing face-down in the mud. When I sat up, everyone was sitting around laughing at me and drinking really expensive champagne from glasses with Greg's company logo on them. They were toasting the takeover of PWJ by Greg's venture capitalist company.

I liked my simple sex fantasies about Thad a lot better. Not that it mattered.

Right now I had to fight for my job, and I hadn't pre-pared a thing for the meeting.

Thad looked as cute as ever in his bow tie, and there was no heavy baggage in his gaze. Just a boss. Just my fan-tasy lover. No strings. No past. So nice.

I set my chin on my hand and gazed at him as he walked to the table with his croissant and coffee, and wondered what it would be like to start over, to date someone who knew nothing about my past. Who was separate from my world. It had some serious appeal.

Thad gave me a smile as he slid across from me. "So, how'd it go with the ex-husband?"

"Huh?" How'd he know about my ex-husband?

"The other day. In your office."

"Oh. That."

He lifted a brow. "That good, huh?"

"Ex-husbands suck. You ever been married?" It was to-tally not part of our relationship to discuss personal stuff, but who else did I have to talk to? Everyone I was close to was tied up in my past, had agendas.

He gave a mock shiver. "Heck no. I'm staying away from that."

"Really? That's awesome."

He regarded me suspiciously. "I thought all women wanted to get married?"

"No way. Tried it. Once was enough." I'd thought a no-strings-attached relationship with Will was the answer. Maybe it wasn't. I didn't like the possessive glint in his eyes. Made me itch. "Got a question for you."

"What's up?" He broke off a piece of his croissant and popped it in his mouth. A croissant. Greg seemed as though he'd be a croissant guy nowadays, even though he used to be a cold-pizza-and-beer-for-breakfast guy.

"My ex wants to give us money for my company. My partners want me to do it, because they're friends with him and we need the money. I think it's weird."

Thad stopped chewing, then swallowed. "Are you kidding? The last thing I'd do is let my ex-anything get their claws into something that's important to me."

I grinned. "That's what I thought too."

"But if you really need the money, you should take it."

I frowned. "But you just said . . ."

"You could make him sign a contract that limits his control over your company. You take his money, and he shuts up and lets you do what you want with it." He grinned. "Then, if your business fails and your ex gets hit with the loss, that's fine. But if it succeeds, then you make sure the contract says he only gets back the money he put in, with moderate interest, so he can't benefit big if you guys hit it off."

I stared at him. "That's not a bad idea."

He shrugged. "I have three sisters who've been wronged by many guys over the years. They're very good at revenge. I pay attention so I can protect myself if some woman decides to take revenge on me."

Thad had sisters? It was weird to think about him as having a life or being a person. He was my boss and my sometimes fantasy lover, and that was it. I wasn't sure what I thought about humanizing him. "You don't seem like the type to piss women off."

He grinned. "Because I'm a banker?"

"Yeah. You're, well, you seem like a nice guy."

"It's my work persona. Really I'm quite the jerk when it comes to women. I don't like to get serious. Most women want commitment after a certain amount of time and don't appreciate my approach." He shrugged and took another bite. "I have an unlisted phone number and sprinkle garlic over all the entrances of my condo. Seems to keep them away."

I laughed. Couldn't help it. This was so not the Thad I knew. Maybe we should have gone to breakfast sooner. Did it feel good to laugh or what? Besides, he'd just described my perfect man: fighting for freedom. Maybe we should move from fantasy lovers to the real thing? "Do you date vampires or something?"

"It wouldn't surprise me if some of them ended up falling into that category. What about you? Any vampires in your life?"

I shrugged. "I'm sort of dating someone." There. I'd told him. See? I didn't have designs on him. "It's not going so well at the moment."

Thad grunted his understanding. "Let me guess. He's not happy about the ex-hubby showing up and wanting in on your business, huh?" •

I nodded. "We're supposed to have a casual relationship, but now that my ex has appeared, he's getting sort of possessive. Putting pressure on me. On us."

"Been there. That's what always happens. One person

wants to get serious and the other doesn't." He gave me a speculative look, a mischievous twinkle in his eyes. "Maybe you're the woman I've been looking for. We should try dating."

"Ha ha. You're such a funny guy." No way was I making the mistake of taking him seriously on that one. But when I swallowed, my mouth was suddenly dry. "What's up with the Mr. Friendly approach this morning? Usually you're all business."

His cheeks got a little pink. "Well, last night I was thinking about you."

He was? What about me? My heart sped up a little and I leaned forward. "And?"

"You used to be a great employee. Now you're not. You have all this personal stuff going on, right? Ex-husband, second business. Difficulties that affect your ability to work. If I'd been a good boss, I would have known about all this and figured out a way to help you succeed." He shook his head and made a noise of disgust. "I realized I didn't know any of my employees personally. How can I be a good boss if I don't know you? So I'm going to breakfast with each of you once a week. You get Thursdays."

Talk about a major ego deflation. I was part of his business plan? It sure threw a damper on my warm and fuzzy feelings toward him. But it was probably for the best. I didn't have room in my life to start eying another guy. Thad was impersonal and that was good. That was what I needed, actually. A friend who wasn't really a friend. Who wouldn't press me for more than I wanted. An acquaintance who didn't know anything about my past life and didn't need to.

Yeah, I needed someone like that in my life.

Plus I liked his idea about letting Greg invest but binding him to a contract. I was going to have to talk to Lindsey about that.

Then I noticed the way Thad's eyes were gleaming. Had his eyes just skimmed my breasts?

Oh, wow. Was his business plan all talk to cover his ass in case I wasn't interested and would have claimed sexual harassment? Or was I delusional? What was really going on here? "Thad . . ."

He cleared his throat. "So, let's get to the point of this meeting. Your job."

Uh-oh. "I'll shape up." Had he realized that I'd been thinking about him as more than a boss? Had he read it on my face and jumped to redirect the conversation? Or was I getting paranoid? Maybe he was simply trying to keep us focused. Yeah, that was it. Too bad.

"Did you write up an action plan?"

"Um, not exactly."

A muscle in his neck tensed. "Paris, I'm on your side, but you have to help me."

"I'll be at work by eight. Won't leave before six, unless it's to visit potential clients. I'll do extra work at home at night. I swear I'll get it together."

He drummed his finger on the table. "That's not enough."

"Why not?"

"Because it's not about hours. It's also about your intellectual and emotional energy. You can't give it all to both jobs. You need to make a choice, Paris. Either commit yourself to PWJ and make it fly, or commit yourself to the bank."

I stared at him. I didn't want to make a choice. I wanted it all. I mean, I wanted to work for PWJ full-time, but that wasn't an option. I couldn't leave either of them.

"You have thirty days. In that time you need to show me your full commitment to the bank, or resign from your job."

"You can't fire me for having another job."

"I'll have to fire you for bad performance. The other job doesn't matter."

Well, damn. Your fantasy lover wasn't supposed to fire you, was he?

"Until then, I want to see your loan documents before you submit them."

"Fine." Ouch. That hurt. I'd been autonomous for four years. It was major ego blow to have to get approval on my loan documents. Here I was, CEO of my own company, and I couldn't even take responsibility for my own loan documents.

It sure made me want to take Greg's money so we could go forward with PWJ. Was being my own boss worth having to do business with my ex?

That was the million-dollar question.

SEVEN

I do my best thinking when I run. I always have.

So we got together and ran after work on the streets of Boston.

Or, rather, I ran.

Lindsey rode her bike without a helmet.

Jodi rode one of those electronic scooters so she didn't have to sweat.

I wore running shoes, black leggings and a sleeveless running shirt.

Lindsey was wearing bike shorts, a sports bra and not much else.

Jodi was wearing glasses, a baseball cap and beige painter's pants that didn't fit her all that well.

No one said anything for the first twenty-five minutes. They knew I wouldn't have anything to say until I'd sweated out my frustrations. Since my hip had been bothering me lately, I was running more slowly than usual, so they upped the time from the usual fifteen minutes.

It gave me time to wonder what Thad would really

look like wearing nothing but a leopard-print thong and a bow tie. I know, I should've been thinking about how to deal with Will, or whether to take Greg's money, or how to save PWJ, but I couldn't deal with any of it anymore.

I wanted to escape, and fantasizing about Thad was my top choice for escapism.

"So, Greg looks good." Lindsey interrupted my fantasy just as I was peeling off Thad's thong with my teeth. Damn. "Did you sleep with him last night?"

"Of course I did. And Will. At the same time."

She rolled her eyes. "Don't knock it. It could be fun."

"And Thad. A three-on-one." Can you imagine? How screwed up would my life be after that? I stepped to the right to jog around a couple walking hand in hand and looking all cozy. Rolled my eyes at Lindsey, who grinned. We understood each other.

"Thad? Your boss? Since when did he become a player?"

"He's my fantasy lover."

Lindsey looked surprised. "You have only one?"

"I'm monogamous in my dreams. Can't do it in real life."

"And why should you? Monogamy is for the birds."

"You guys are idiots. Monogamy is awesome. How can you sit there and disparage having someone who loves you unconditionally?" Jodi interrupted as we slowed down to worm our way across the street against the traffic. Who needs crosswalks? Not pedestrians in Boston, that was for sure. Waved at a cabbie who honked and flipped us off. He should be glad we held him up—gave him a chance to pad his fare.

"You should talk to my mom." Two people in my life preaching love? Yuck.

"Monogamy doesn't necessarily translate to unconditional love," Lindsey said. "Plus, you don't need sex for unconditional love. I love you guys, but I don't want to do you."

I laughed. "Exactly. Why do we need men to break our hearts?" I gave Lindsey a look. "Have you ever met Thad?"

"No. Is he hot?"

"Yeah, kinda."

She arched an eyebrow at me. "And?"

I hopped over a manhole cover and dodged a homeless guy with a coffee cup full of coins. "I don't know."

"You do know."

Yeah, I knew he was my boss and it would be a foolish thing to do.

"Know what?" Jodi asked. Funny how she wasn't having trouble breathing. Wonder if the electric scooter had anything to do with it. "What are you guys talking about?"

"Paris might have a fling with her boss."

"No, I wouldn't," I said quickly. Laying it out there like that didn't sound too good. Well, it sounded good, but it also sounded bad, which is why it was appealing. Was I messed up or what? Maybe I should mug the hot pretzel vendor on my right and get carted off to prison for some quality alone time.

"But what about Greg?"

I looked at Jodi sharply. "What about him? Don't you mean, what about Will?"

Her cheeks flared red. "Well, um, yeah, like for sex. But I was thinking about Greg in terms of PWJ. What about his money?"

Lindsey and I exchanged looks. Something was up with Jodi. "How did we get on the topic of Greg's money?" I asked. "I thought we were talking about sex."

"Sex and money are often linked."

"Yeah, with prostitutes," Lindsey said. "Is there something you're not telling us, girlfriend? Maybe an alternate source of income for our celibate friend?"

Jodi's cheeks got even redder, and she shoved past a group of yuppies standing in line at a streetside café. "Shut up. I'm sorry if I think my financial and professional future is more important than Paris's bedmates. Did Will talk to you? He's on board with taking money from Greg."

She shot over a curb on her scooter and almost took a header. I reached out to grab her, but she righted herself on her own. "I talked to Greg this morning and he said you turned him down. And . . ."

"You called Greg?" Didn't that border on betrayal? "Why'd you do that?"

"Because you wouldn't tell me what happened." She lifted her scooter over the next curb and sailed down the sidewalk, blithely endangering pedestrians of all shapes and sizes. She was usually quite the considerate scooter-rider. Guess Greg was getting to her as much as he was bugging me. "You turned down money that would save PWJ without even consulting me! We're equal partners and I'm not letting you wreck this business because of your own baggage. Will and I voted to accept Greg's money, and you're overruled."

"Will voted against me?" That wasn't a Will kind of thing to do. One thing he valued more than anything was friendship. He'd never turn against me like that. Would he?

"Sure did. Either take the money or get out. Greg's got the business talent. Will and I can work with him if you don't want to be a part of it."

I stopped running, and Lindsey nearly crashed into me with her bike. "You're trying to cut me out of the business?"

She braked her scooter, frowning. "That's not what I'm doing."

"Then what exactly are you doing? What little games are you playing with Greg?"

"Nothing! What's your problem? Can't you see I'm just trying to save the business? You're so caught up in your baggage that PWJ is going to crash and burn, and it's Will and I who are going to pay. Greg has appeared as our savior, and we're taking it. You're in or you're not."

Lindsey cleared her throat as she settled on her bike, one foot up on a nearby trash bin. "Actually, PWJ bylaws require unanimous consent of all three partners for this kind of decision. You can't take Greg's money without Paris's support."

It wasn't until the stress eased from my shoulders that I realized how tense I'd become after hearing Jodi's threat. Phew.

Jodi scowled and started driving her scooter again. I had to sprint to catch up, Lindsey cruising along easily on her bike. "Jodi."

"I wouldn't have actually cut you out." She looked pissed. Wonder why. Maybe because she'd just vowed to kick me out and she'd just found out she couldn't, and now she had to figure out damn fast how to repair the relationship. "I was trying to pressure you into making the right decision for the team."

"Well, that's nice to hear." But I didn't know for sure anymore. Even the mere threat had been unexpected. "But I'll never know for sure, will I?"

She shot me a look. "We promised that we'd keep business separate from our friendship. Don't take it personally."

"Right." Yeah, so easy.

"See, this is why I didn't get involved. The three of you are going to screw up your friendship because of this damn business." Lindsey rode up between us. "Will's the only one who keeps us on an even kilter, and he's already got his nose out of joint about Greg." She looked at me, and the bike wobbled. "Maybe you shouldn't take the money. Kick Greg out, let PWJ die, and put your friends first."

Lindsey had a point. What were we doing to our friendship? I glanced at Jodi's face, but it was still tight. "I want PWJ to fly," I said.

"Really? It doesn't really seem like it. Seems like you're more caught up in some stupid-ass dream and some baggage from your past." Jodi stopped and Lindsey swerved to avoid hitting her. "For God's sake, Paris, Greg's a good guy. He made a mistake, he's back to make amends. He's not going to hurt you again. Forgive him, take his money and let's make this business a success!"

I didn't necessarily agree that Greg was trustworthy, but that didn't matter as long as we had Lindsey the expert lawyer on our side. But Jodi was right about one thing: I was letting my personal issues stand in the way of my dream, and that was wrong. "Lindsey, Thad suggested we have Greg sign a contract that says he has no influence on any business decisions. We take his money, he'll get back some interest on it if we succeed, but if the business goes under, he has no recourse against us. Can you do it?"

"Sure thing. I'll make it ironclad. It'll put his testicles in a vise he'll never be able to get out of."

I grinned. "You're the best legal consultant ever."

She fluffed her hair and puckered her lips. "I know."

Jodi was standing with one foot on her scooter, her eyebrows puckered as she watched me.

I speed-dialed Will's number on my cell phone and he picked up on the fourth ring. He used to pick up before the first ring had stopped. "What's up, Paris?"

"If Lindsey can write a contract that makes Greg powerless in PWJ, should we take his money?"

Silence.

Aha. Jodi had lied about Will's readiness to cut me out of the biz. I wasn't a big fan of her lying to me. It felt good that Will hadn't been so quick to sell me out. Maybe all wasn't lost between us. Yet.

"If we take this money, how long until we're ready to go back to the footwear companies for another round? Can we do it in a month?"

I frowned. "A month? That's pretty fast. Why the time crunch?"

"I need the dough."

"For what?"

"I just do. A month. I'll give this a month and then I'm out. Do whatever it takes to make it happen."

Shit. We really needed Will. "Six weeks?"

He hesitated. "Fine. Six weeks. That's all I'm giving you."

I hung up and looked at Lindsey and Jodi. "He's in."

Jodi nodded. "For only a month, huh? I knew that would be a problem. Can we get it done that fast?"

I frowned. "What do you know about his deadline?"

Jodi immediately started wheeling her scooter across the street toward the park. "Nothing."

I fell in beside her. "Jodi."

"What?"

"What's going on?"

She shook her head. "It's up to him to tell you, not me."

"Since when does he tell you things he doesn't tell me?" I mean, yeah, I knew they spent a lot of time together in the lab, but I hadn't given it any thought. Until now.

"I don't know what he tells you and what he doesn't."

I shot a glance at Lindsey, who shrugged. What was going on with Jodi and Will?

"So since Will agrees, and Lindsey can write up the contract, are we in business?" Jodi hoisted her scooter over the curb, while Lindsey and I hopped up easily.

"Nice try on the change of subject."

Jodi shoved me in the shoulder. "Oh, come on, Paris. Lighten up. This is much more important than any kind of bickering between you and Will."

"Yeah, you are kind of serious," Lindsey said. "Both of you, actually. You both need to lighten up. Want to go to the circus with me next weekend?"

"The circus?" We took a left off the sidewalk and headed into Boston Common. The softball fields were packed and the paths were full of runners, walkers, bikers and commuters heading home. Despite the leash law, there were even some dogs running free, chasing down Frisbees.

"I'm thinking of going to clown school and joining the circus. I have a meeting with the clown director after the show. If PWJ fails, you guys can join me. Think of what fun we'd have on the road."

I ducked as a wayward Frisbee whizzed by my head. "You're really thinking of quitting your job as a lawyer to become a clown?" I didn't buy it. Lindsey loved to have money to support her lavish lifestyle. No way could she survive on cheap beer and last season's clothing.

"Well, I'd prefer trapeze artist, but I don't have the skills."

I wondered if Greg's therapist had time to fit Lindsey in for a few sessions.

Jodi cleared her throat. "Before we get off on the subject of Lindsey's alternative careers, can we focus on PWJ for a sec?"

"Fine." I wondered, should I take Greg's money? If we could keep him from interfering, but still get his money . . . oh, wow. We could manufacture the shoes. We'd be back in the game. We would still have complete control of the company, with the added benefit of emptying Greg's bank account.

My heart started beating faster.

Her eyes widened, and hope lifted her features. "Fine, what? Fine, we can talk about PWJ or fine, you'll agree to take Greg's money and we can go forward?" Jodi's scooter ran off the path and started bumping over the grass, but she didn't seem to notice.

I felt a grin coming over my face. Maybe it was insanity to take money from my ex; maybe it was a brilliant business decision. Seeing as how PWJ was dead in the water without it and seeing as how I'd been sacrificing everything for it for the last four years, it seemed pretty stupid not to take one last chance. "Yes?"

"Is that a question or a statement?" Jodi stepped off the scooter, her hands clenched by her sides. "Paris?"

"Both." I grinned. The chance that we could make

PWJ fly . . . It was too much. I was so excited! "As long as Lindsey can handcuff him, I'll do it."

Jodi whooped, and Lindsey grinned. "Handcuffing men is one of my favorite things to do. Consider it done."

The three of us stared at each other as the reality of the situation dawned. We were going to make shoes. We were going to make shoes with Sfoam. We were going to do it.

Yahoo!

Lindsey screamed. I screamed. Jodi screamed. Then we grabbed each other and started dancing around in a circle, hopping and jumping and screaming. Our celebration descended into a Dallas Cowboy cheerleaders spoof we'd perfected at a college toga party our senior year that ended up with us in a pile on the ground, laughing hysterically.

Very fitting for drunken kids in sheets.

Not as appropriate for sober twenty-somethings in the middle of the Boston Common at six-thirty on a Monday evening.

Who cared? We were going into business!

Eight

"Excuse me. Are you girls all right?"

Girls! He'd called us girls! I beamed up at the sinewy runner staring down at us with a look of concern on his face. "We're brilliant. Want to test some shoes for us?"

He frowned in obvious confusion.

What? Was there something random about being asked to test shoes by a woman sprawled on the ground?

"Seriously." I extricated myself from my friends' extremities and climbed to my feet. "We're developing the ultimate running shoe and we need runners to test for us. Interested?"

Jodi slapped a PWJ business card in his hand. How convenient that the electric scooter enabled her to carry her purse and her stash of business cards. "I'm one of the scientists, and I'm a genius."

He looked back and forth between us. "You guys are serious?"

Lindsey stuck her manicured hand between us. "Lindsey Miller, outside counsel. I'll be sending you a testing agreement. Confidentiality oath. Waiver of liability. You know, if you step in an open manhole and break your femur, you can't blame the shoes and sue us. But it's a great opportunity to be on the inside of an innovative new product that'll change the running world forever."

"I'm the designer and marketing person," I said. "I qualified for the Olympic trials in 2000 in the ten-thousand meter. I'm the running expert in the group."

"No compensation, though," Lindsey said. "Strictly voluntary due to the fact that the company hasn't sold any shoes yet. But you'd get free shoes and you'd get to help shape the future of global running."

We all gave him blinding smiles, and after a moment he grinned back. "Cool. I'm in. How do I get involved?"

Score! We had our first tester! "Email us at the address on the business card and that'll get things going," I said. "And we're looking for men and women, so if you have any running buddies, pass the word."

Jodi dropped a stack of business cards in his hand. "Here you go. Pass 'em out to any runners you know."

"But only serious runners," I said. "No joggers."

Jodi rolled her eyes. "She's such a running snob. Thinks nonrunners have nothing to offer this world."

"Not true! I just think that the shoes should be tested by real runners."

"She does let you do all the invention stuff," Lindsey pointed out. "Even though you're not a runner."

"That's because I'm brilliant and she knows it."

Tester numero uno cleared his throat. "Um . . . I guess I'll be going."

Whoops. Totally forgot about tester number one. I

gave him a brilliant smile and pumped his hand. "Welcome on board. Have a great day and don't forget to email us."

"I won't." He tucked the business cards into his sock—ew! sweaty business cards!—gave us a wave and took off.

We stared after him.

"Nice form," I said.

"Nice ass," Lindsey said.

"Hope he's smart enough to be able to communicate his feedback effectively," Jodi said.

"Incoming." Lindsey pointed toward another hottie sprinting toward us in an easy gait. Easily a fifty-mile-a-week runner.

"Perfect," I sighed. All these serious runners were so wonderful. I was in heaven. "Who wants him?"

"I do." Lindsey grabbed a business card and stepped onto the sidewalk and waited for him to approach. He was running past her when she stuck her foot out and tripped him. He went flying and crashed to the pavement. She fell to the ground next to him, both of them grunting. Lindsey rolled to a sitting position. "I can't believe you just ran into me! Don't you look where you're going?"

He cursed and jumped to his feet. "Geez. I'm so sorry. Really. Are you okay?" He helped her up, still apologizing, while Lindsey fussed and fumed and generally played the role of the upset, beautiful maiden in distress.

Impressive. Maybe she should leave her legal career and give Hollywood a try. Nah, probably not enough risk of death.

He left with a stack of business cards, a commitment to testing and a promise to recruit at least ten other people for her.

Lindsey grinned. "Am I good or what?"

"You're crazy, girlfriend."

She tossed a couple of cards at Jodi. "Your turn."

"Mine? I'm not going to tackle anyone."

"Of course not. That's my modus operandi." Lindsey nodded at a couple female runners stretching by a softball game, watching the men run bases. "Go talk to them."

"I can do that." Jodi left her scooter and trotted across the grass toward the women in question.

I opted for flagging down runners.

Lindsey continued to tackle.

An hour later, we had thirty-two new testers, and Lindsey had a bunch of new bruises and two dates for the upcoming weekend. We also had been called stalkers, crazy bitches and one woman had even threatened Lindsey with pepper spray. Bostonians were way too uptight.

Exhausted and worried about having the police escort us off to jail, we finally bought snow cones and flopped down on the grass to revel in our financial future. For about five minutes, until I noticed Lindsey giving me an odd look.

"What?"

"You're rubbing your hip."

I immediately stopped the massage. "Am not."

"You were limping when you were running."

"So what? You're limping too."

"I'm limping because I got kicked in the knee by a mechanical bull. You're limping because your hip is bothering you again."

"Go to the doctor," Jodi said.

"I'm fine. Besides I don't have time to go the doctor. Too much to do. Plus you're the one we're worried about."

Lindsey looked surprised. "Me? Why?"

"Because you're going to get yourself killed one of these days," Jodi said.

Lindsey snorted. "Give me a break. I can take care of myself." She looked at Jodi. "You, on the other hand, are heading in a bad direction."

Jodi frowned. "What are you talking about?"

"Does the phrase 'lonely old spinster who has too many cats' mean anything to you?"

Eye roll from Jodi. "Give me a break. I have two jobs. No time for dating."

"When was the last time you had sex?" Lindsey subtle? Not when it came to naked romping.

Jodi's face instantly flamed bright red. "What?"

"Sex. Riding the hobby horse. Intercourse. Doing it. You remember?" She stretched out on her belly, propped her chin up on her hands and let her feet flop up over her butt. "It's always Paris and me talking about sex. You just listen. So now I want to know."

There was an interesting shade of burgundy on Jodi's cheeks now. "College."

"College? That was four years ago! With who?"

The color drained from her face with one blink, until she was so pale she looked half-dead. "No one."

Lindsey shot me a look, and I shrugged. Whoever it had been wasn't someone Jodi wanted to discuss. What had happened? Obviously that was a question for when she'd tossed back a few. "Fine," I said. "It doesn't matter. What matters is that you sequester yourself in the lab and never go out. You've talked to more people today than in the last three years combined."

She frowned. "How did this conversation get turned on to me? I thought it was Lindsey we were worried about. Isn't her death wish more important than the last time I had sex? And your hip is kind of an issue too."

"I don't have a death wish. And yes, Paris's hip is a concern."

"My hip is fine. You're the problem."

"Jodi's the problem."

Jodi was laughing now. "You both are the problem."

"We're all the problem," Lindsey announced.

I started to laugh. "We are, aren't we?"

Jodi folded her arms across her chest. "Speak for yourselves. I'm fine."

I snorted, Lindsey rolled her eyes and finally Jodi cracked a smile. "Okay, so we're all fruitcakes."

"And Greg's a self-proclaimed head case, and now that he's in the picture, Will's going to get messed up," Lindsey said. "It's a wonder any of us have survived this long."

"Maybe we should rename PWJ, Screwups Incorporated," I said.

"Yeah, maybe," Lindsey said. "Maybe we should."

We were quiet for a moment. I don't know what they were thinking about, but I was thinking about my hip. And my worry about Lindsey. And Jodi. And Will and Greg and all the other screwups in my life. The list was depressingly long, and thinking about it was apparently the fast-track toward squashing the euphoria of successful tester recruitment.

"Let's make a deal," Jodi said. "Lindsey has to limit her activities to ones that have a low risk of serious bodily harm. Paris has to go to the doctor. And I'll let you guys set me up with the guy of your choice."

Lindsey propped herself up on her elbows. "Not just one guy. You need an attitude overhaul. Paris and I are going to take you bungee jumping this weekend. It's a hotbed of testosterone."

"How is bungee jumping a low-risk activity?" Jodi asked.

"Very few people die bungee jumping anymore."

"Very few . . ." Jodi looked at me. "She's insane."

"Apparently. And I'm not going bungee jumping either, so don't worry about it."

"You guys are wusses."

"But at least we're alive." Somehow I couldn't drum up regret at skipping out on bungee jumping.

Lindsey snorted. "You guys consider yourselves alive? You both work twenty-four-seven. You never go out and have fun unless I drag you. Paris is afraid to have a fling with her hot boss even though great sex without baggage is exactly what she needs, and Jodi hasn't had sex since college."

"There's more to life than sex," Jodi said.

I snorted. As if Lindsey would agree with that. "Linds, you go skydiving with a bargain operation that had three people die last year and is currently under investigation for manslaughter."

"So? They need customers. I'm doing my civic duty."

"You went scuba diving last summer in the Cayman Islands with an unlicensed company that is commonly known for having their clients experience 'accidents' when paid enough money," Jodi said.

"So? There's no hit out on me. Why would I worry?"

"You go home with strangers on a regular basis, even if they live in isolated places."

"Oh, so now my sex life is an issue?" She stood up and grabbed her bike. "You guys don't know what alive is, so don't go harassing me for the fact I'm not afraid to live."

"You're not trying to live." I sat up. "You're trying to die."

"We're all going to die. The difference is in how you live before you do. You guys can spend your time being miserable and obsessing about money and propriety and other stupid stuff, but I'm going to have fun. See ya." She and her bike left us on our patch of half-dead grass.

As we watched, she marched up to the softball game, propped her bike against a nearby fence, and sat down on the bench between two of the men. Maybe midthirties, decently attractive, but probably at least ten years older than she was.

"She's going to end up with the wrong guy and be in serious trouble," Jodi said.

"I know." I watched her fix the collar on one guy's T-shirt. "She didn't used to be this bad. I think she's getting worse."

"Me too."

We were quiet for a minute, watching Lindsey get a back rub from a guy she'd just met. Given that she was wearing only a sports bra and spandex shorts, it was a pretty intimate backrub. But she looked happy. Happier than I'd felt in a long time.

Why were we so hard on Lindsey? So she was good at meeting guys. So she took risks. Why was that so bad if it made her happy? "You think she's right?" I asked.

Jodi slanted a look at me. "About what?"

"That we work too hard. Don't live life enough. Look at her face. That's not the expression of someone who's miserable."

"First of all, I don't believe for one second that she's really that happy. If she was, she wouldn't be taking all these risks in search of something."

"Yeah, maybe." But weren't we all in search of something?

"Plus she has one job that pays very well, so she has the liberty of running around and doing fun things. You and I have two jobs and we're busting our asses to make our company work. We're paying dues now so we can roll in the dough in our old age. When we're fifty, we'll be wealthy and happy retirees, and Lindsey will be an aged clown living in gross motels and eating fast food as she follows the circus around the country, wondering how she'll ever have enough money to stop the awful ride she's on."

I watched Lindsey throw back her head and laugh at something one of the guys said to her. "But what if we die tomorrow?"

"And what if we don't die for another eighty years? I don't want to be sleeping on a park bench when I'm thirty because I figured I'd die before then and didn't bother to save any money or have a job."

"Mmm . . ." Maybe it was because Lindsey had what I wanted. Freedom. Independence. Permission to have fun in life. Maybe that was why Will's pressure was chafing me. I wanted to be like Lindsey. Maybe after we sold Sfoam I'd take some time off. Join Lindsey on a cross-country trek as a clown. Maybe.

I looked at Jodi, and there was no mistaking the yearning on her face as she watched Lindsey flirt. Yearning for what? A social life? Men? Someone to rub her back and give her orgasms on demand? Self-confidence?

Maybe we both needed to learn from Lindsey.

Or maybe Lindsey was on the fast-track toward crash and burn.

NINE

On Wednesday night, we had our intro to our new work-place. It was the first time PWJ had gotten together since Greg had signed his contract. It was the first encounter between Greg and Will since Sunday night at my condo. I hadn't seen either of them since that night. Lindsey had managed negotiations with Greg, and Will hadn't called. And now we were all together again.

Had I been dreading it all day? Yup.

Being an expert at avoidance, I'd arrived a wee bit late so I wouldn't have to deal with the pretour chitchat. It had worked: I rolled in just as Orpheus Milkhausen, PhD, was ordering everyone to shut up so he could begin the tour of his lab.

Orpheus was about sixty years old, built like the Pillsbury Dough Boy and wore glasses about six inches thick. Well, not quite, but close enough. He was bald, except for a few lonely strands that he apparently hadn't cut in at least fifteen years. It sort of looked as though he had gray angel-hair pasta coming out of his head. He was wearing old jeans that had years of shoe parts ground into them, and the ugliest pair of leather shoes I'd ever seen in my life. Was that what my future held if I opened my own shoe business?

Suddenly getting thrown off by a mechanical bull while bungee jumping didn't sound so bad.

He gestured at a rack full of shoes that were as heinously unattractive as the ones he had on his feet. Guess the orthopedic market was about function, not fashion. Made me glad I didn't need to wear any. Poor sods. "These are my finished shoes. Don't touch them. Each one is specially made and costs between one and five thousand dollars depending. You get so much as a thumbprint on one of them, and you pay me."

Yeesh. If I was going to pay that much for shoes, they'd better look at least moderately decent.

"This is the machine for molding the outsoles." He pointed to a thick metal slab with a hole carved out of it in the shape of the rubber bottom of a shoe. "You have to make your own molds, or else pay me for each use of mine. Molds are expensive."

Next up. "Sewing machines."

Greg snorted. "I don't sew."

I rolled my eyes at him. "You don't get to do anything, remember? You're a bank, and that's it."

Jodi ran her fingers over the sewing machine. "Looks new."

"It is. And it's expensive, so don't break it."

She pulled her hand back. "I wasn't planning to."

"She uses expensive machines every day," I reassured Orpheus. "She knows how to handle them."

He harrumphed at her, then moved to a big table with

leather and textile parts on it. "This is the cutting table. I do all my cutting by hand."

Ouch. That would take forever. No wonder his shoes cost so much.

He moved toward a big metal unit. "Lasting machine. I used to last by hand, but I got this old machine when a local shoe company upgraded. It's very temperamental and I can't afford another one, so you mess it up and you pay for it."

"What's lasting?" Greg asked.

Orpheus gave him an exasperated look and held up a form that looked like a fake foot made of plastic, without any details like toes or ankle bones. "This is called a last. You put the upper around it . . ."

"What's an upper?" Greg had a clipboard out and was jotting down notes. Not the actions of a man who was planning to adhere to a contract that said he had no input on any business operations.

"The upper is the leather part of the shoe. Or the nylon or mesh or whatever you're making it of." Orpheus gave Lindsey an annoyed look. "I thought you said they knew what they were doing."

"They do. Greg's the money. He knows nothing, but we can't kick him out, you know?"

Greg nodded. "I'm rich. It's my one redeeming quality at the moment." He shot me a meaningful glance.

What was that about? It wasn't my fault he was a loser. Will moved next to me and slung his arm around my shoulder and glared at Greg. Tension, anyone? As soon as Greg looked away, I shrugged Will's arm off my shoulder and gave him a scowl.

He shrugged and mouthed "your funeral" to me. Then he turned away.

This really wasn't going well.

"So continue with the lasting lesson," Greg said.

Orpheus scowled, but his eyes were excited. I had a feeling that despite his grouchiness, he was enjoying having a group of admiring pupils to impress. "You put the last onto the machine like this. . . ." He wedged it on. "Then you set the upper in the machine like this. . . ." He fastened the unattached upper on. "And then you hit this button. . . ."

Glue poured. Steam whistled. Metal arms clanged and yanked the upper around the foot form and glued it together. Then a press swung up and smashed them tight.

Impressive.

"Don't want to get your hand stuck in that, huh?" Greg wrote down "safety hazard" in his little notebook, followed by "employee waiver form."

Orpheus sighed and gazed dreamily at his machine. "I've been doing that by hand for years. Isn't that amazing?"

"Incredible," I agreed.

"Very impressive," Will said.

"Awesome," Jodi said.

Lindsey looked over Greg's shoulder. "Add 'liability insurance' to your notes."

Yeesh. Could they get any more uptight?

Orpheus continued the rest of the tour, showing us how he roughed up the lasted uppers, spongy midsoles (the middle part of the shoe that goes under your foot and provides cushion) and rubber outsoles (shoe bottoms), and then glued them together. He had some cool machines for stuff like rivets, but all the lace holes were punched by hand. It was quite the operation, and I had to admit, far more mechanized that I would have expected given his solo operation.

Then again, according to Lindsey, the business had been in his family for several generations and they did charge a fortune for the shoes. I supposed they could afford to acquire some machines over the years.

After he finished the tour, he stopped and eyed our group as if we were five sorry excuses for human beings. "So who's going to actually use the machines?"

Will and Jodi raised their hands.

"You two come with me. I'll show you how to work them." He glared at the rest of us. "No one else is allowed to touch anything."

I held my hands up. "Scout's honor."

With a final intimidating glower that was somewhat lessened by the bit of dinner still on his shirtfront, he left us disorderlies to our own devices while he took Will and Jodi off for a little private tutoring.

Greg frowned at me. "How are you going to manufacture shoes here? It costs Orpheus a thousand dollars a shoe because this is an archaic setup and everything has to be done by hand. I'm not footing the bill for a thousand bucks a pair. It doesn't make financial sense, not when we'd have to sell the shoes for a hundred bucks a piece at most."

I resisted the urge to make a little face to accompany his whining. "You may remember me as nothing more than a runner who went to classes only so she didn't lose her scholarship, but believe it or not, I actually have a brain and I use it."

Lindsey coughed and turned her back to us, but I noticed she didn't walk away. Why would she? She wouldn't be able to eavesdrop if she got too far away.

111

Greg made an irritated noise in the back of his throat. How many times had he directed that sound at me before? Too many. I didn't need to take it anymore. I punched his arm not so softly. "If you don't like it, go home and write the checks from your office. We'd all prefer it."

He sighed with feigned pain. "I'm not trying to insult you, Paris. I simply want to make sure you have a plan."

"We're going to buy sneakers, then rip off the bottoms. We'll remove the inch-thick spongy midsoles, replace them with our one millimeter of Sfoam, and then put the shoes back together. So all we really need to do is tear apart and reattach."

"Oh."

I waited for him to tell me how brilliant I was.

Instead he wrote something down on his clipboard.

I was beginning to hate that clipboard. "What's up with all the notes? Can't you remember everything?"

He gave me a smooth look. "My therapist recommended I record everything that happens to me while I'm here. You never know what little incident may spark something."

"Ah."

He held out a piece of paper. "Care to try it? You might find it soothing."

"I don't need therapy."

"No?"

"No."

"Then why are you spinning your wheels on a business that will never fly, just because it was the dream you had with Seth?"

I got right up in his face and shoved him hard. Then I

did it again because I enjoyed the look of surprise it engendered. "First of all, don't ever say PWJ won't fly. Second, you don't know anything about my relationship with Seth, so back off."

"I know nothing? I was his best friend while you were dating. I was the one you married after his death because we were both too insane to realize what we were doing. I was there, Paris. And that's why I'm back."

I felt hands settle on my shoulders and knew Will had abandoned Orpheus and returned to me. He said nothing, simply stood behind me and offered silent support through his touch. I didn't want support. I didn't need support. I wasn't weak anymore, not like I used to be. But I couldn't make myself step away from him. I clenched my fists and glared at Greg. "You think the reason we got married was because we were both insane? That's it?"

"Of course it is."

"You're a bastard." How about, we got married because we loved each other? Or at least had a bond that brought us together? It wasn't simply that we'd been insane. It couldn't be. We'd had something.

His eyes narrowed. "Don't be angry with me. You're just as responsible for the wedding as I am."

"But I didn't take off without an explanation!"

"You want an explanation? I'll give you one—"

Lindsey stepped between us. "Save it for when we're not guests in someone else's office."

I bit my lip and looked at Orpheus. He was staring at us with a mixture of disgust and morbid fascination. I think the disgust trumped, though.

"Are you quite finished? I don't have all night." There was sweat dripping down his forehead, and his upper lip had beads of perspiration on it. Apparently this was common for him, because he whipped out a dingy, grayish handkerchief and mopped it up. Nice. "I suggest the rest of you leave while I give a tour to your scientists." He gave Jodi a smile that was much warmer than what he'd been giving the rest of us. What was that for? I was the one who was into shoes! They were only along for the ride.

Orpheus the pompous jerk. He was judging me just because I got into a screaming argument with my ex-husband instead of listening to him talk. How dare he?

"Good-bye," Orpheus said pointedly.

"Fine." I spun around, and Will dropped his hands from my shoulders. "I'll see you later."

Will stopped me. "I'll come by afterwards. I'll stay over tonight."

He made the comment just loudly enough for Greg to hear. I might have thought it was a fluke or that I was being overly sensitive, except that he was staring at Greg while he said it, giving him a smug look that said, "I get to play with Paris's booty and you don't."

"Fine." I was really getting tired of Will staking his claim while Greg was around. I didn't want to get mad at him in front of Greg, but if he kept it up, I was going to snap. He knew I didn't like to advertise to the world who was sleeping in my bed. Public displays of ownership weren't my gig.

But that was a discussion to be had in private.

"You coming?" Orpheus scowled across the room.

"Yep." Will gave me a not-so-quick kiss that made me want to pull away; then he gave Greg a very male look and jogged across the lab. Or he jogged two steps before

Orpheus yelled at him not to run in the lab.

Greg got the last laugh as Will slowed to an obedient walk.

This was so not going to work.

Will didn't get to my place until almost two in the morning. I was already in bed, my earliest bedtime in months. A fluke? Not so much. I was practicing avoidance.

I tensed when I felt him slip under the sheets.

I tightened even more when he wrapped his arms around me and buried his face in my hair.

After a moment, he released me and rolled away. "What's up, Paris?"

"How was the tour of the lab? Will it work?"

"Should be fine, since we don't have to manufacture shoes in large quantities." He laced his fingers behind his head and let his breath out in a long groan. "What's going on?"

There was no sense in pretending I didn't know what he was talking about. We'd known each other for too long for stupid games. So I rolled over until I was facing him. The light from the streetlights outside cast a soft glow on him, enough that I could see his expression.

His brow was furrowed, his lips pressed tight together.

I trailed my finger over his forehead, trying to smooth the wrinkles. "This thing with Greg. I don't think it's going to work to have him part of PWJ."

He gave me a slanted look. "Too late for that."

"Yeah." And yes, I did notice that he didn't disagree. "He's making you push too hard."

This time, Will turned his head so he looked right at me. "What are you talking about?"

"You're feeling threatened by him, so you're pushing me. I can't handle relationship pressure. You know that."

He sighed and rolled over so he faced me. Our noses were almost touching, our hands nearly brushing the other's chests. "I don't like it either."

"Then why are you doing it?" How many nights had we lain like this talking? There was something so comforting about talking in bed in the dark. Something safe.

"I don't know. When I'm around him and I see him trying to check out your butt, I get pissed. He lost that right when he ditched you."

Greg inspected my body when I wasn't looking? I wasn't sure what I thought of that. No, it was good. I wanted him to think about what he'd given up.

"Look at you. You're pleased that he thinks you're hot." Could Will sound more annoyed?

"It's a girl thing. I want him to know what he can't have."

"But can he have it?"

"No." Crud. I'd hesitated. Had Will heard it?

His lips tightened and I knew he had. "I'm worried about you, Paris."

"You're not my boyfriend. You can't act like one."

I felt his body tense. "I'm not acting like your boyfriend."

"Yes, you are. You get all pissy if he so much as talks to me. You have to get over it."

"Maybe I'm acting like a friend who cares about you."

I shook my head. "You basically told Greg tonight that you were going to have sex with me. Since when is our sex life public?"

Will cursed softly, rolled onto his back and flung his arm over his face. Then he cursed again.

I'd rattled him, and he was vulnerable. I was taking advantage of the moment. "You've been concerned about money lately. What's up with that? When I mentioned it to Jodi, I got the feeling that you'd been discussing the situation with her, and not me. What's up?"

He looked at me with a darkness to his gaze. "You're upset that I'm telling Jodi things that I'm not sharing with you?"

"Well, yeah, a little." Okay, a lot.

"You want distance, but you also want me to confide. I want space, but I can't deal with Greg's hands on you. This is getting too complicated."

I sighed. He was right. Our relationship was no longer the straightforward sexfest it used to be. "I miss us being relaxed and having fun. Isn't that what we promised it would be?"

"We also swore that if it stopped being that way, we'd end it with no hard feelings."

I felt my belly clench. "You want to end it?"

"Do you?"

"No."

He rolled over until he was facing me, then laid his hand on my cheek. "Do you want it to continue like it's going?"

I swallowed. "No." But to let go? I didn't want that either. I wanted it to be like it used to be. Damn Greg for coming back into our lives and changing everything. Damn him!

Will kissed my forehead. "I don't want to lose you as a friend. I don't think we're heading in the right direction anymore. It might be best if we cooled it until this thing with Greg is sorted out. Until he's gone." He rubbed his thumb against my cheek. "We always knew it wouldn't last. What we had couldn't last. It would either have faded or gotten too complicated. We both need space." He sighed. "I need space."

I pressed my lips together. Will was right. I'd known it wouldn't be forever, but I hadn't been ready for it to fade so soon.

Except that our relationship was different now. Negative. Destructive. It would destroy our friendship.

What did I need more? Sex or friendship? Mmm . . . tough one.

I could get sex somewhere else.

But there was only one Will in my life. Only one friend who could give me what he did.

Not much of a choice.

I flattened my hand on his bare chest, digging my fingers in. "It's time to take a break."

He nodded. "I agree."

I bit my lip hard, fighting back the tears.

He gently kissed each cheek, and then my lips. It was a gentle kiss. No tongue action at all. A farewell peck between friends. "I'd better go."

I nodded. Didn't want to talk. It was the right thing to do. Calling it quits would keep Will in my life. Keeping him in my bed wouldn't.

But damn, I'd liked waking up in his arms.

I watched him get dressed, knowing it was the last time I'd see that muscular chest disappear under his holey T-shirt. I really liked his chest. I was going to miss that chest. It made a very comfortable pillow.

He shoved his wallet in his pocket, picked up his cell phone and keys, then sort of stood there. "I'll, um, pick up the rest of my stuff some other time."

I nodded. "You'll be back. As my friend."

He managed a smile. "As your friend, I'll always be there for you."

But as he walked out, I wondered if he was right. And if he wasn't, if Will my friend was going to slip away soon after Will my lover had left, what would I do then?

TEN

At six o'clock in the morning I started crying.

At seven, I dragged myself out of bed to the shower. By the end of the shower, I was feeling good. I was free. Free to find out what I wanted. No more dating responsibilities. This was great!

At eight, I had just splurged on Starbucks coffee when I realized Will would never be in my bed again. He wasn't my special Will anymore, not even part-time. I started crying again.

At nine, I locked myself in my office and decided ending it with Will was a good thing. It gave me time to focus on work and PWJ without tying myself down with girlfriend obligations.

At ten, I realized I was a total loser and I was going to be like Ike Isenhauf and have no one at my funeral except the garbageman. That's when I really started crying.

And that's exactly when Thad walked into my office.

He caught me heaving sobs and blowing snot like there was no tomorrow. My eyes were bloodshot, my face puffy and makeupless (even the most waterproof makeup can't withstand that kind of assault). The tissues had been black with mascara for the past hour, but by now, I'd pretty much wiped it all off.

And let me tell you, I looked lovely.

We stared at each other for a long minute, during which I hiccupped three times and had to blow my nose twice. Then I did one of those choking breaths that you take when you're trying to regain control after sobbing uncontrollably for much too long.

I thought for sure he'd leave. What guy wants to deal with a blathering woman?

"We're going for a walk."

I stared at him, then hiccupped. "What?"

"Get up. We're leaving."

"I'd rather not." Sob, inhale, choke. "Can you please close the door?"

He folded his arms across his chest, and I didn't even have the energy to think about what a nice chest it was. It wasn't Will's chest, and that thought made me want to cry again.

"No. I'm your boss. You come with me now or I'll fire you."

"You're a jerk."

He grinned. "Whatever it takes."

I hiccupped again.

Thad waited.

Dani popped in her head, took one look at my face and ran off.

Maybe it would be better if I left.

But not because I was taking orders from a man. I didn't like men enough at the moment to take orders from one. Scowling at Thad, I grabbed my purse and followed him out of my office, using him as a shield so that no one could see my face. Unfortunately I couldn't really hide the wheezing of my sobs as I tried to hold them in.

I think he figured out what I was doing, because he shifted to his left as we passed his boss's office, blocking me as he said hello.

What a guy. If he hadn't been a guy and my boss, I'd probably have kissed him for that. But seeing as he was both, he had to settle for me not kicking him in the head for all the wrongdoings of his species.

We didn't talk until we were out of the building.

Actually, we didn't talk even then.

I was still trying to dampen down the hysterics, and he was giving me space. Where was he taking me? If he tried to push me into Boston Harbor, I was so going to be pissed.

But he didn't. He walked into Fanueil Hall, bought two gigantic ice creams from one of the street vendor carts, and then sat down on one of the benches. I sat next to him, figuring it was the only way he was going to give me the ice cream.

We sat in silence while I licked my cone and thought about how I would never wrap my tongue around anything belonging to Will again. Eventually, my sobs subsided, leaving me looking like your stereotypical cover girl model.

"Ex-husband issues?" he asked.

"Ex-semi-boyfriend issues." I sucked a bite of double-chocolate fudge ice cream off my waffle cone and blinked really hard. I would not cry anymore. Would not. Would not. Would not. Why was I crying? We hadn't even been dating seriously anyway. I didn't love him. He didn't love me. So what the hell was the big deal?

I frowned at that very good question.

"Care to share?"

Good thing he'd already explained that his concern for me was merely as a boss and not as a potential lover. Otherwise, in my desperate state, I might have clung to his kindness as some gift from heaven and started having fantasies about him and me.

Oh, wait. I already did that.

Except now I was completely free to turn them into reality. Like I was in the mood for sex with anyone at the moment.

"You break up?"

I sighed. "We had this casual relationship, you know? No commitment, no baggage, just sex when we wanted it." A mom hustled by, hollering at her wayward kids as she balanced three shopping bags and a baby.

Thad's face was carefully neutral. "And that's a bad thing?"

"No! That's good! But since Greg showed up, things have been getting tense between Will and me, so last night we decided to hang it up. From the start we said we'd stay together only as long as the relationship stayed easy." I shrugged. "It stopped being easy."

"So why were you crying? You like him more than you thought?"

I scowled. "I was wondering the same thing. I definitely don't want to get serious with him. I mean, he was starting to bug me with his pressure."

"So it's that change sucks."

I raised my brow. "You an expert on change?"

"I took a management course on change in the workplace when I took over in this job. The goal was to help me understand how the change in management would affect my staff. Apparently people get upset about change, even if it's a good change."

I pursed my lips. "I have had a lot of change lately." That made more sense than thinking all those tears were about losing Will as a lover. I mean, he was a great lover and all, but it wasn't as if I'd expected our arrangement to last forever. He'd needed sex with a normal person to recover from his She-bitch-from-hell episode, and I needed to get warmed up for the dating scene again. Did I mention Will was the first person I'd slept with since Greg had left? It had been almost as long for me as it had been for Jodi. Now that was a scary thought.

He nodded. "Plus you're losing out on some regular sex. That could upset anyone."

I eyed him over my ice cream. Correct me if I'm wrong, but this wasn't sounding much like boss-employee talk to me. "Uh-huh."

Thad's cheeks got a little pink. "Sorry."

"About what?"

"Sex talk. That's crossing the line." He cleared his throat and made a move as if to stand up and end the conversation.

I laid my hand on his forearm. "Don't worry about it." Oh, wow. Was this the first time I'd ever touched him? I couldn't remember, but I sure hadn't noticed it before. The result of being partnerless? Hmm . . . "I can handle a racy discussion. Trust me, it's fine."

He studied me for a moment, then he relaxed. "All right, then."

Oops. My hand was still on his arm. He hadn't moved away and neither had I. Oh, wow. The fantasy about

Thad in his thong popped into my mind. I'd always been a boxer girl, but there was something about Thad that made me wonder what he'd look like in his bow tie and a thong.

"Take the rest of the day off. Don't you run or something? Go for a run. Endorphins are great for working things off."

He talked endorphins? I hadn't talked endorphins with anyone since Seth had died and I'd been forced to stop running competitively. Will lifted, but he didn't run. And you already know about Jodi and Lindsey. "How do you know I run?"

"I've seen you out running after work."

"You have? When?"

He shrugged. "Around. I run too."

"You do?" My fantasy lover was a runner? It figured. I'd always had a thing for athletes, especially runners.

"Yeah. You run, what, a seven-minute-mile pace?"

"Yep." Wow. He could tell how fast I ran just by looking at me. He was a real runner. "You want to be a shoe tester for our business? We need testers."

He looked thoughtful. "Maybe."

Maybe.

Then he sort of cocked his head. "Ever get tired of running by yourself?"

I caught my breath. "Sometimes."

"Maybe we should hook up."

Hook up? There was more than one interpretation of that word. "Sure."

He glanced at his watch. "I have to get back to the office. You take the day off." He hesitated. "I'm out of town all next week, but would you be interested in meeting for a run the following weekend? Maybe Sunday afternoon?"

I eased my breath out between my lips. "Sure. That'd be cool."

He nodded. "I live close to work. Want to meet at my place? Maybe you could change there afterwards and we could grab food?"

Oh, wow. "Um, sure." My heart was starting to accelerate. Why? He was my boss. Doing his personal bonding thing with his staff. Trying to keep a subpar employee from going off the deep end. Nothing personal. It wasn't as if he wanted me to shower at his place with him.

"Two o'clock?"

I nodded. "Two."

"Great." He pulled out his business card and jotted a street address on the back. "That's where I live." He folded it into my hand. "Take the rest of the day off. I don't want to see you until tomorrow."

"What about my probation at work? My new schedule?"

"Starts tomorrow."

Wasn't going to argue that one. Maybe there was something to letting your boss know your personal problems. And that you were single.

He stood up. "See ya." And then he left, his catlike gait carrying him across the cobblestones.

Holy cow. I had a running date with my fantasy lover. And I was totally single. And he knew it.

But he was my boss.

And I had an ex-husband in town.

And I had a former lover with whom I worked and socialized.

And I had a business in trouble.

Bottom line, I had too much on my plate at the moment to even think about getting down and dirty with Thad.

But there was something appealing about Thad. He wasn't a part of my history. He wasn't a part of PWJ. He didn't know any of my friends. He was totally separate, and I liked that. Plus, he wasn't interested in getting serious. I really liked that.

I was so going to meet him for that run. Maybe it would be platonic. Maybe not. I didn't even know what I wanted. All I knew was that I wanted to escape from my world, and if Thad was offering an invite into his, I wasn't going to turn it down.

I took advantage of my free afternoon by visiting a discount sporting goods store, buying thirty-five pairs of sneakers and hauling them to Orpheus's lab.

I tapped lightly on the door with my toe, holding a towering stack of boxes in my arms. I hoped Orpheus wouldn't be there, and I could slip inside and drop off the shoes for Will and Jodi to start tearing apart later tonight. I didn't feel like running into anyone today, especially Will and Jodi.

"Go away! I'm working!"

Apparently Orpheus was there. Lucky me.

"It's Paris. I need to drop some things off for tonight."

Silence.

Should I take that as a reinforcement of his orders for me to disappear, or should I interpret that as an invitation as long as I had my own key?

I used my key, and when I opened the door, Orpheus was fighting with the lasting machine. He was sweaty, and I could smell him from across the room. His stained T-shirt might have been white at one point, but now sported yellow armpits and numerous black and gray marks. Baggy army-green pants covered in dust and dirt completed the look. His belly was hanging over his belt, and I had a feeling plumber's butt was in high fashion for him. Plus his shoes were still monstrosities. Fashion god he wasn't. "Good afternoon, Orpheus."

He glared at me and went back to working on his machine.

I scooted to the back of the lab and dumped the stack of boxes. Two more trips, and I was done.

I was going to sneak out, but then I noticed that Orpheus had lowered his bulk to a stool and was sprawled in an exhausted heap. His eyes were even closed. Heart attack?

I sidled over to him. "Orpheus?"

Nothing.

I nudged his foot with my toe. "Orpheus?"

"I'm thinking."

Good. Not dead. "Sorry. Thought you'd died."

He opened one eye. "Why are you here?"

"Because I had to drop stuff off."

He opened the other eye. "But you aren't supposed to be here until after nine at night."

"Yeah, well, I got the day off. Won't do it again."

His sweaty fingers caught my wrist as I turned away. Yuck-o. "What's with the boxes of sneakers? I thought you were making shoes, not buying them?"

I twisted free. "We're putting foam in running shoes. We figured we'd test it in existing shoes before trying to make our own. Cheaper."

He lifted a brow. "What kind of foam?"

My pride won out over the protests of my nasal passages, and I retrieved a sample of Sfoam from the cabinet Orpheus had let us set up in the corner. "This."

I handed it to him and waited for him to smother me with admiration.

He pressed it between his fingers, sniffed it, licked it (interesting), then shoved it inside his shoe and stood up, bouncing on it. Then he sat back down, pulled it out of his shoe and tossed it to me. "Useless."

I blinked. "Excuse me?"

"That thin piece of garbage? What good is it?" He picked up a particularly clunky pair of orthopedic shoes and pointed to the midsole. "I adjust the thickness of the foam depending on the stability, flexibility and support needs of the foot. My footbeds are contoured to the foot, like custom orthotics. You can't do any of that with that little piece of material."

"Sfoam provides cushion, dispersing the weight so there are no pressure points and—"

"Who needs only cushion in performance shoes? You need to do more." He shook his head. "It's crap."

Um, crap? My dream for the last four years was being called crap by someone who has been in the biz for over thirty years? My gut sank.

Not good. Must go on the offensive immediately. I glared at him. "What do you know about running shoes? All you make are these orthopedic monsters."

"Hey!" He sat up, his belly rolling out of his way. "My priority is making shoes that perform. I can't worry about looks. It's a choice my grandpappy made, and then my daddy made it and now I'm following in their footsteps. My family has been doing this for eighty-three years and we're the best, so back off and don't insult my shoes."

I got up in his face. "Then don't insult mine."

"But yours are crap."

"Yours are ugly."

He glared at me.

I glared back.

Then he grinned, slapped me on the shoulder so hard I actually stumbled, and gave a howl of laughter. "I like you, Paris Jackson. You're all right."

"Thanks, I guess."

He was still grinning. "You're right. My shoes are the ugliest damn things I've ever seen."

"Doesn't that bother you?" I rubbed my shoulder, wondering how big the bruise would be.

"Not when I see someone walk without a limp for the first time in five years."

Oh. Good point. "Well, when someone wins the next Olympic marathon wearing shoes that have Sfoam, I'll feel good too."

"It'll never happen."

I scowled. "I thought we were friends now." Well, maybe not friends, but at least not enemies. I hadn't been planning on insulting his shoes again, at least not for an hour or so.

He shrugged. "It still won't work. It might provide cushioning, but you can't adjust the foam to affect stability or flexibility. Any performance shoe worth its salt needs to be fine-tuned to that level."

I pursed my lips. He did have a point, damn it. Hmm . . . "We'll adjust stability and flexibility through other means. Like with plastic plates under the foot."

He rubbed his chin. "That's a thought. What kind of research have you done with plates?"

"None yet. We're working on the foam first." Shit. Plates? We had to do stuff with plates now?

"Don't you think the research ought to be concurrent?"

"No." Ack! As if we could handle another research project. This was wrong, all wrong.

He cocked his head, his triple chin jiggling. "How much do you really know about shoes?"

"A lot. I was a runner my whole life."

"I meant about making them."

I shifted. "That's why we're planning to sell the technology. We're experts in Sfoam. Let a footwear company figure out how to make it work." Yeah, I wasn't feeling very optimistic about the idea of opening our own footwear company at the moment.

Orpheus mopped his forehead. "Tell you what. If you pay me for my time, I'll help you guys out. Without me, you'll be a mess." He sighed deeply, making it clear what a huge sacrifice it was for him to offer to spend any more time in our presence than was totally necessary.

Pay him? As if we had money for that, even if I wanted to add Orpheus Milkhausen to our employee list. "I appreciate the offer, but we're fine. We're only tearing shoes apart and putting them back together right now. Even I can manage that."

He gave me a long look riddled with disgust and disappointment. "I don't offer my expertise lightly. You'd be a fool to turn it down."

"I'm sure you're right, but we're going to try it this way." As if I were going to let him attempt to convince us ugly shoes were the way to go? Not so much.

Orpheus lumbered to his feet, then wiped more sweat off his brow. "How come you aren't working in the lab with Jodi and that boy? You're never here."

"They're the scientists."

"Well, they don't know jack about shoes or biomechanics. They're going to screw it up."

I frowned. I'd known they weren't into this technology for the sports angle, but I hadn't worried about it. I'd figured their rocket-scientist IQs would atone for any lack of interest in running. Maybe it had been enough when their project was Sfoam. Now that we were dealing with actual shoes, maybe we needed a shoe expert. . . .

"All they do is argue about the molecular structure of that damn foam. They had no idea what I was talking about when I mentioned the need for stability and flexibility." Orpheus studied me. "You knew what I was talking about." He waggled a flabby finger at me. "You need to be here every night working with them."

"Ha."

"Why not?"

"Because."

He narrowed his eyes. "Lover's triangle?"

"What? No. Don't be ridiculous."

He harrumphed his disbelief. "This is why I work by myself. No need to deal with people." He gestured broadly to his lab. "This is my world. I'm in charge and no one tells me what to do. It's just the way I like it."

I glanced around the lab, and suddenly noticed how dismal it was. The machines were old. Shoe parts were everywhere. The floor was marked with adhesive and shavings from midsoles. The air was musty. Lighting was poor. Walls were gray. Floor black. Ceiling tiles missing.

Sort of reminded me of the PWJ offices, actually.

The difference was that the PWJ offices were temporary, and whenever I was there, I was with my friends and we were having fun. To work in this environment day after day all by myself for thirty years? I would definitely end up like Ike Isenhauf, if I didn't kill myself first. "Yeah, well, if it works for you."

"It does."

"Great." I made a point of looking at my watch. "I have to go. Sorry to bother you."

He shrugged and turned back to his lasting machine.

All the way home I thought about Orpheus and his ugly shoes. How could that man really be happy?

ELEVEN

Despite my protests, I showed up at the lab just after midnight. I couldn't sleep. Couldn't stop thinking about Sfoam in the hands of two people who didn't care about running. My baby. My dreams.

I couldn't leave it alone.

When I walked in, Jodi and Will were sitting with their feet up, drinking coffee and eating pizza. And laughing. Bonding. Looking happy.

I felt like an outsider with two of the people who had been closest to me for the past five years of my life.

It wasn't a good feeling.

I cleared my throat. "Hi."

They fell silent immediately and looked at me.

There was a pause before anyone spoke. There'd never been a pause before. I wasn't sleeping with Will anymore. Shouldn't that take all the tension away? But it hadn't. It was worse. Maybe I should jump his bones and try another tack.

Then Jodi grinned. "Come on in, partner. What are you doing here?"

I looked at Will. He managed a smile as well. So I stepped inside. "I thought I'd check in and make sure things were going all right. See if you found the shoes."

Will raised a brow. "How could we miss thirty-five boxes of shoes?"

"I don't know." I walked over and picked up a shoe that had the bottom ripped off. It looked as though it had been shredded by a hyperactive Labrador. "How's it going?"

"Bad. We can't figure out how to get the bottoms off without destroying the shoe," Will said.

I frowned. "Did you ask Orpheus how to do it?"

"Why would we ask him?" Jodi asked.

"Because he knows what he's doing when it comes to shoes." I ran my fingers over the torn-up shoe. The edge was ragged, and there was no way they'd be able to reattach the bottom, seeing as how it was in three pieces.

The door opened, and Orpheus waddled in. "I told you you'd need my help."

I jumped a mile and so did my partners. Was he psychic? "What are you doing here?"

He glared at me. "It's my lab and I can do whatever the hell I want. Plus I've been watching you through the security camera." He pointed to a camera mounted in the corner, then grabbed the shoe and held it in front of my face. "See what I mean? Heathens."

Will gave me a questioning look.

I gave him a blank, innocent smile, as if I had no idea what Orpheus was talking about, and that his claims of heathenism being practiced by Jodi and Will had nothing to do with why I'd appeared there tonight.

Will didn't buy it, and the tension went up another notch. He knew I was questioning his competence, and no man ever responds well to that.

"This is what you need to do." Orpheus took the shoe over to an oven that was rusty and tilting slightly to the right. "Heat the adhesive first. It makes it much easier to disassemble." He stuck the sneaker in the oven, shut the door and then gave us all a pointed look. "I don't make mistakes, but sometimes my shoes need tweaking that I can't do without taking them apart." He pulled out a gray piece of material and mopped his brow. Why did the man wear jeans and long-sleeved shirts if he was always hot? At least he didn't smell tonight. Probably just got out of the shower. Lucky us.

Apparently capitulating to his expertise, Jodi took some Sfoam over to Orpheus and started discussing tactics of putting it in the shoe, leaving Will and me alone on our side of the lab.

It was the first time we'd been together since we'd decided to stop riding the hobby horse.

Awkward silence, anyone?

"So, um, how was your day?" he asked.

I shrugged. "Fine. Yours?"

"Fine."

I nodded.

He shifted. "Want a piece of pizza?"

"No, thanks. Already ate."

He picked at the torn-up shoe.

I opened a bottle of adhesive and sniffed. Could I get high off it? Might be worth a try.

"You here to check up on us?" he asked.

Since when was he threatened by my appearance? This

YES! 🔲

Sign me up for the **Historical Romance Book Club** and send my THREE FREE BOOKS! If I choose to stay in the club, I will pay only $13.50* each month, a savings of $6.47!

YES! 🔲

Sign me up for the **Love Spell Book Club** and send my TWO FREE BOOKS! If I choose to stay in the club, I will pay only $8.50* each month, a savings of $5.48!

NAME: _____

ADDRESS: _____

_____

TELEPHONE: _____

E-MAIL: _____

🔲 **I WANT TO PAY BY CREDIT CARD.**

🔲 VISA   🔲 MasterCard   🔲 DISCOVER

ACCOUNT #: _____

EXPIRATION DATE: _____

SIGNATURE: _____

Send this card along with $2.00 shipping & handling for each club you wish to join, to:

Romance Book Clubs
1 Mechanic Street
Norwalk, CT 06850-3431

Or fax (must include credit card information!) to: 610.995.9274.
You can also sign up online at www.dorchesterpub.com.

*Plus $2.00 for shipping. Offer open to residents of the U.S. and Canada only.
Canadian residents please call 1.800.481.9191 for pricing information.
If under 18, a parent or guardian must sign. Terms, prices and conditions subject to change. Subscription subject
to acceptance. Dorchester Publishing reserves the right to reject any order or cancel any subscription.

wasn't good. At all. "I'm here because you shouldn't be the only one working on this at midnight."

"Oh."

Silence.

"You want a piece of pizza?" he asked.

"Still no." Gee, you think we were scavenging for conversation? I wanted to take my bottle of adhesive and leave. This wasn't how it was supposed to be after we broke up. We were supposed to be back to the old Paris/Will relationship.

"Forgot I already offered," he said.

"No problem."

After a moment, he looked at me. "This is weird, huh?"

I felt a wave of relief soar through me. It wasn't just me. "Yeah. Big time."

"It'll get better."

"If it doesn't, maybe we should start having sex again." I was only partially kidding.

He laughed, and I relaxed at the sound of his laughter. "If it's this hard to split up after only six months, I don't think it would be smart to start up again."

I felt a little tug at my gut. "Yeah, probably not."

He patted Jodi's vacated chair. "Sit."

I sat, and he didn't try to touch me. I didn't touch him. I missed touching him. Maybe we'd get that back someday. I hoped so. It was a fine time to realize I needed Will's touch to keep me happy. I'd have to get over it, at least for now.

"You talk to Greg today?" he asked.

I frowned at the fake casualness in his voice. "No. Why?" Was he checking up on me already? Wanted to see if I'd run to Greg's arms the first moment I'd become a free woman? I immediately tensed. *Don't pressure me!*

"You might want to check in with him. He came by earlier tonight and was trying to tell Jodi and me what to do. He thinks our approach isn't going to work." He scowled. "He seems to have forgotten that his contract gives him no authority over how his money is spent."

Great. "I'll talk to him." Or better yet, Lindsey could talk to him. Wasn't that what lawyers were for? Reining in the scum of the world?

He nodded. "Good. I tried to, but he seemed more interested in trying to piss me off than listening to me." He hesitated. "I didn't want to ask you."

"Why not?"

"I feel uncomfortable asking you to spend more time with him." He narrowed his eyes and quickly added, "Not because I'm jealous, but because I don't trust him."

Some of the tension eased out of my shoulders. Despite the awkwardness, our relationship hadn't changed. Will still cared about me. I smiled. "I appreciate your concern, but I have to be able to work with him while he's here."

He studied me, then nodded. "You'll tell me if you decide you can't deal with him?"

"So you can be my rescuer?" I teased.

"If you need one."

For a moment, I felt myself wanting to accept his offer, and I scowled. The only reason I'd survived Greg's abandonment was because I had resolved to stand on my own and found my own strength. Six months of shagging Will and I was half tempted to lean on him and stop relying on myself?

Crap. I was in deeper trouble than I'd wanted to admit.

I lifted my chin. "I am perfectly capable of managing my own life."

Will lifted an eyebrow at my slightly defensive tone. "Chill, Paris. Greg's being an ass, and I was looking out for you, not trying to fight your battles."

Ah, he knew me so well. Knew exactly what was bugging me. Maybe that had been the problem. How do you keep a sexual relationship casual when you both know each other so well? Apparently you don't.

Jodi sat down on the table, her butt smashing the mangled shoe. "Oh, relax, Will. Greg was just trying to be supportive." She looked at me. "It wasn't a big deal. Don't talk to Greg. I think it's great that he's interested. He's a business genius and has some excellent ideas. Besides, he was in such a bad place after his wife left him, I think we need to help him focus on something more positive, like PWJ."

"You've been talking to him about his ex-wife?" What was up with that? Why was she being so chummy with my ex-husband? And why did I care?

"Yeah. I went to lunch with him today. He's really in tough shape. We need to support him."

"Um, hello? Since when did Greg get on our emotional aid list?"

Jodi set her hands on her hips. "He's always been a part of our group. Sure, he lost his way for a while, but he came back for a reason. So we could all help him." She glared at Will. "You certainly weren't helping tonight with all your little remarks. Could you have made him feel more unwelcome?"

"He is unwelcome," Will said.

"He's our friend."

I stood up. "He's not my friend." I wasn't sure he'd ever been my friend, even when we were married. Certainly he'd never been a friend the way Will and Lindsey were.

Will nodded his agreement. "He mistreated Paris and ditched all of you. How can you support him?"

Jodi hesitated for a moment, and I realized she looked nervous. Almost guilty.

"What's up, Jodi?"

She shook her head. "Just give him a chance. He's an all-right guy."

Will raised his eyebrows at me, and I shrugged. I had no idea why Jodi was being loyal to Greg, but it had been that way since he'd walked into my condo that night. But with any luck, her loyalty would alienate Will, and then their little alliance might fade, and then I could stop feeling petty and excluded.

She touched Will's shoulder in a way I didn't dare do anymore, and I felt a twinge of jealousy. "Will, I know you're protective of Paris, but you never met Greg before this. Try to forget the jealous boyfriend thing and give Greg a chance."

Hah. Will would never put Greg over me.

But he grimaced. "I'm not acting like a jealous boyfriend."

"Sure you are. You judged Greg instantly, even though he hasn't done anything wrong since he returned. It's been five years, and he already apologized to Paris and is putting a lot of money into PWJ just to make amends to her. Doesn't that warrant a second chance?"

Will glanced at me. "I'm not acting like a jealous boyfriend."

"Then prove it," Jodi said. "Give him a break."

Will shifted in his chair, and he wouldn't look at either of us. "Yeah, maybe." He stood up and walked over to Orpheus. "That shoe ready yet?"

Jodi and I looked at each other. She spoke first. "Give Greg another opportunity, Paris. Maybe you'll rediscover love."

"He tracked me down because he tried to commit suicide with a safety razor and his therapist ordered him to face his past. No reconciliation there." As if I was going to risk falling for him again. No way.

"Maybe he's back because he wants to try again."

I felt something flutter in my gut. "Did he say that?"

She gave me a mysterious smile. "Maybe."

And then she got up and walked over to Orpheus and Will.

Shit. I really didn't need to be thinking about Greg in that way. Not again.

Please, not again.

I practiced avoidance after that. Didn't see Greg. Didn't see Will. Didn't see Jodi. Lindsey had taken a week off from work to go to a race car driving school at a company that was offering discounts after a student had had a fatal crash a month before, so I hadn't seen her either. I went to work at the bank. I thought about my upcoming date with Thad on Sunday. I vetted emails my mom forwarded to me from her various personal ad respondents and rejected her requests for my company at three different funerals. Worst—or best of all, I'm not sure—I had sex fantasies about a hot garbageman I'd seen outside my building. I dreamed he was an undercover professional assassin using me to get to Greg so he could take him out. I was happy to be used for such nefarious purposes, so I let him have his way with my body as much as he liked. Ike Isenhauf left his legacy to a garbageman. So why couldn't I have fantasy sex with my professional killer garbageman?

We handed out shoes to testers on Thursday, with orders to run in them twice over the next two days. I was totally bummed to learn that Jodi and Will hadn't made an extra pair of eights for me. After four years of waiting, I couldn't even run in the sneakers we'd designed! Torture of the worst kind.

Was it a fluke that they hadn't made a pair for me? Or a sign I was already being forgotten? Or a burgeoning mutiny?

On Thursday and Friday, I sat at work and counted the hours until our discussion group on Saturday, when we'd finally gather proof that Sfoam rocked.

Saturday afternoon finally came. My moment of victory. I couldn't wait.

I clapped my hands and beamed at my roomful of testers. Six men and seven women were all that had shown up, even though we'd handed out thirty-one pairs of shoes.

Still, it was our first tester session. I was so pumped. "Is everyone ready to begin?"

A few mumbles and grumbles and the room settled into relative silence. They were sitting around our picnic table, but we'd spruced up the office with a few plants and a paper tablecloth with stars on it. I'd added a couple air fresheners to try to overcome the native odors of our building, and Jodi had splurged on a new coffeemaker. Her job was to keep making coffee so the delicious scent never faded from the room.

Will was sitting at the back of the room, his arms folded over his chest. He looked so gorgeous in his jeans and old T-shirt. But when he caught me staring, he didn't even react. Just met my eyes for a second and then looked away.

My throat immediately tightened up.

Greg leaned over my shoulder. "Problems with you and the boyfriend?"

"Shut up." I stepped away from Greg, who was in charge of recording the session, and raised my voice to the group. "I'm Paris Jackson, and I think I've met most of you already. . . ."

A guy raised his hand, and I nodded at him. "Yes? You have a question?"

"Is Lindsey going to be here?"

The scab on his forehead identified him as one of the testers Lindsey had "recruited" at the park. "Sorry, but she's only a legal consultant." I didn't mention that she hadn't reported in from driving school and we were quite certain she'd had a fatal encounter with a guardrail and would never be heard from again. Well, not really, but I hoped she'd call soon so I could stop worrying. "She did leave the waiver forms, which I assume you've all signed?"

The guy stood up. "If she's not going to be here, there's no point in hanging around. See ya."

He was gone before I could recover enough to block the exit.

Crud. Down to five male testers and seven females. We couldn't afford to lose any more.

A woman raised her hand. "How much are we being paid for this?"

"Your reward is knowing you are changing the future of running shoes. And getting free shoes. And, um . . ." I could tell by the pout of her lips that she wasn't buying it.

She lifted her eyebrows. "No money?"

"It's volunteer." That's why it was in the contract. So we didn't waste time with people who couldn't live with the terms.

She leaned over to the girl next to her. They whispered, and then stood up in tandem. "It's too nice of a day to spend my Saturday afternoon cooped up in this dump. Sorry."

And then there were ten.

Will gave me a concerned look, Jodi frowned, and Greg circled the room with his camera. People were starting to get restless, shifty, uncomfortable. I was losing them.

I nodded at Will. "Pizza will be arriving shortly."

He frowned, gave me the "we can't afford pizza" look. I scowled and gave him the "we can't afford to lose our testers even more" look. So he shrugged and gave me the "it's coming out of your pocket" look and got up to go order it.

I turned back to the room just as Greg moved past me, his arm brushing against my shoulder. Made me freeze. When was the last time I'd touched Greg? Had he touched me on purpose? Was Jodi right that he wanted to get back together?

Forget about it. Focus on testers. "So you've all had a chance to run in the shoes twice. Why don't you go ahead and start sharing your thoughts. Please remember that we're focusing only on how it feels underneath your foot. Cushioning, impact protection, stability. I don't care about fit or appearance or any of that. Who wants to go first?"

A guy I'd recruited raised his hand. His name card identified him as Les. "Les? Go ahead."

"They look like shit. No one is going to buy them."

I smiled. "Yes, I'm aware that they look rather sloppy. They're prototypes put together only so we have a way to test the performance of the technology. What did you think of the cushioning system under your foot?"

"It looks too thin. No one is going to buy it."

I clenched my teeth. "Again, we're not talking about looks. How did it actually feel?"

One of the women picked up a pair of shoes from the table and stuck her hand inside the shoe. "Feels soft."

"I meant, how did it feel on your foot while you were running?"

She frowned. "I got a blister on my little toe, so I couldn't wear them."

"Okay, thanks." Getting useful feedback from testers was apparently more difficult than I'd anticipated. I nodded at a man with a name tag that said Bill. "Bill? What did you think?"

"They're great."

I beamed at him, and at Jodi and Greg. "Excellent. What was great about them?"

"Everything. They were just great."

"Well, was the cushion firm or soft or in between?"

"It was great."

I took a deep breath and leaned on the table. "I'm glad you liked it, but I need you to describe it. Like saying chocolate is creamy and smooth instead of simply saying it tastes good. Do you understand the difference?"

He nodded. "Got it."

"Excellent. So can you describe how much protection from impact you felt?"

"It was great."

I felt my left eye begin to twitch. "What about rocks? How much protection from rocks did the shoes provide? And please describe it. For example, did you feel the rocks when you stepped on them, or did you feel like there was a shield between your foot and the rocks you landed on?" He nodded. I prodded him. "So, can you describe for me how the shoe handled rocks?"

He nodded again. "They were great."

My fingers began to curve into a ball, and the twitch in my eye increased. "Bill. Can you describe how it felt? Not how much you liked it, but how it felt. Was the cushion hard or soft? Firm? Stable? Unstable? Lumpy? Smooth? Resilient?"

"It was great."

Me, frustrated? Yeah, uh-huh.

No, I had to focus. Stay calm. There had to be a way to get information out of this numbnut. "Can you use another word to describe the shoes other than great?"

He hesitated, then smiled again. "Really great."

I pressed my hand to my cheek to hide the out-of-control twitch and spun toward Jodi. "Can you please start writing down the names of who we will not invite back for another round of testing?" I kept my voice low, kept beaming at the roomful of total idiots to distract them from my whispering.

"Yep."

Greg stuck the camera in my face, and I swatted it away, but not before I caught a scent of his aftershave. Like I needed a flashback to days when that scent made me want to jump his bones. "Get out of my face."

"You're being recorded."

"No kidding." I walked back to the table and surveyed my testers for someone who looked at least moderately intelligent. "You. Kaitlyn. What do you think?"

She shrugged. "Honestly, I was afraid to really wear them. There's no cushioning at all. I mean, it's just the top part of the shoe and a rubber bottom stuck on. I have a race next weekend and I was worried your shoes would injure me."

I ground my teeth. *Then why did you agree to test, you*

wuss? But I nodded empathetically. "Did you happen to at least wear them around the house?"

"For a few minutes. They seemed fine, but I didn't dare work out in them."

My hands set themselves on my hips, and I surveyed the rest of the room. "Did anyone actually run in the sneakers?"

A two-hundred-fifty-pound man named Butch spoke up. "I ran three miles in them. My feet and ankles were killing me. There was no protection and no stability. It was like running barefoot."

I frowned. "What shoes do you usually run in?"

When he described some heavily reinforced running shoes, I realized his problem. Butch was so big and heavy that he probably blew right through the cushioning, same as he'd do in any regular running shoe. Good thing to learn. And yes, it did imply that Orpheus's comment had some validity. There might, just might, be some issues with Sfoam. "Well, thanks, Butch, that's very helpful." Not welcome, but helpful. I nodded at a slight woman who couldn't have weighed even a hundred pounds. "Jessica?"

"I didn't actually get hurt, but I was really nervous the whole time. I mean, there was no protection under my foot. I was afraid I was going to strain my arch or bruise my feet. I gave up after about a half mile."

Ack! Wasn't anyone enlightened enough to actually try to wear the shoes? Another hour of frustrating interrogation revealed, that no, no one was. No one had run in them and liked them. Most of them had refused to even try them because they "looked" like they wouldn't work. Others were so biased by the appearance of the shoes that I could tell they hadn't given them a legit shot even if they had actually worn them.

I sent the testers on their way, fat and happy after munching on pizza they hadn't earned, then flopped down on the abandoned picnic table bench with the rest of the team.

Greg set down the camera, and they all looked at me. And waited.

TWELVE

I noticed Jodi was sitting close to Will. Guess they made up from their little disagreement about Greg. So good to know.

"They hated it," Will said.

"They hated it before they even wore it," Jodi added. She dropped her head onto the tabletop. "I can't believe it. All those footwear companies who turned us down were right. Sfoam sucks."

"No, it doesn't." I smacked my hand down on the table. "It was a perception problem. It looked like there was no cushioning, so they assumed there wasn't. We need to blindfold them next time and have them judge it based on feel."

Greg eyed me. "But isn't perception a real issue? No matter how well a product performs, if people don't believe it'll work, they won't even try it in the first place. Consumer acceptance is critical."

I frowned at him. "What do you know about running shoes?"

"I own a venture capital company. My job is to evaluate companies and to know business." He shrugged. "It's a pretty basic concept, actually."

Just what I needed: my ex-husband talking down to me. Yeah, he really sounded like he was back to win my forgiveness. More likely he was here to grind his heel into my throat as hard as he could.

Jodi cleared her throat. "I think he's right. We can't change people's biases."

Will nodded. "I agree with Jodi."

Of course he did. There was a time when he used to support me. Maybe this was good. Maybe I'd been getting too dependent on him. Dependency was bad.

"Sfoam isn't going to work in running shoes," Will said. He wouldn't meet my eyes. "We need to think of another application for it, or give up. It's not a viable option for running shoes, either from perception or actual performance."

"Yeah," Jodi said. "You heard Butch. He didn't have an issue with its looks, but it didn't work for him. Unstable, no protection." She shrugged. "I know it feels great when we stick it in our shoe and walk around the lab in it, but it's not the same thing as running in it."

Spoken like a runner. Hah.

"We're not going to use it for something else," I snapped. "It'll work for running shoes. Maybe we just have to tweak it. Overcome perceptual bias."

Will faced me, sympathy heavy in his eyes. "Paris, it's time to let it go. It's not working." He touched my arm, like the old days. "I'm sorry. I really wanted it to succeed, and I know how much this means to you, but it's over. Sfoam isn't going to fly in running shoes."

"It will work!" I didn't want his pity. I wanted him to believe in me. I wanted them all to have faith in my vision.

Jodi frowned. "Listen, Paris, I want this to work too. I've put four years into Sfoam, and it's great stuff. There's nothing wrong with changing our focus and putting it in something else."

"But our goal was running shoes, not the foam. We made Sfoam for running shoes. If it won't work, then we'll think of another technology that will make the ultimate running shoe." My words were slurring together. "It's about running. It's always been about running."

"To you, maybe," Will said. "Not to us. PWJ isn't about running. It's about innovation. It's about Sfoam."

I blinked. "You know it's always been about running. You *know*." How could he pretend he didn't? Why was he playing the enemy now?

"I know it's been about running for you, but it can't be anymore. If you want PWJ to go forward, you have to let go of the running part. You have to."

I stared at Will. "How can you ask me to do that?"

Greg leaned forward, and I felt his hand on my shoulder. "Listen, Will, you don't know Paris from back then. I understand how she feels about running. Why don't you take off for a bit and give me a chance to talk to her? I know what's behind this."

Will's face tightened, and for a minute I thought he was going to punch Greg right in the face. Then he shoved back from the table and stormed out.

Jodi sat there for a moment, as if she was unsure who to go with. Finally she touched my arm. "I'm sorry, sweetie. I got caught up in what Will was saying, and I forgot how important the running thing is to you."

I shrugged and stared at the table. "It's fine."

"No, it's not." She walked around the table, sat down next to me, and wrapped her arm around me and rested her head on my shoulder. "Greg's right. I should have been more sensitive."

I finally hugged her back. "It's okay."

"I'm going to go after Will. Make sure he's okay."

Oh, really? She's going to cheer up my ex-lover? I pulled back from her. "Fine. Go."

She gave me a speculative look. "I think we need to have some girl talk. How about tonight? I'll call Lindsey and we'll meet up. She's supposed to get back this evening."

"Maybe." I wasn't really in the mood for Jodi to tell me that she'd had another deep chat with one of the men who used to share my bed.

She lifted a brow. "No maybe. I'll leave you a message with the place and time." She glanced at Greg, who gave her a warm little smile. "See you."

And then she left me alone with my ex-husband, whom I hadn't been alone with since our dinner that had gone oh-so-well.

The moment the door shut behind her, an awkward, smothering tension settled over the room. Then I caught a glimpse of Greg's thoughtful face as he scribbled something on his clip board and decided that maybe I was the only one feeling the tension.

Lucky me.

He set the page down in front of me. He'd drawn little stick figures with lines between them. One of the stick figures wore running shoes. "That's you," he said.

"I figured. Is this a trick your therapist taught you?"

"Yes." He apparently missed the sarcasm in my tone. "See, that's Seth, and that's me. Solid line between Seth and me. Solid line between you and Seth. Dotted between you and me." He drew a large shoe and made a solid line to both Seth and me. "You and Seth shared running as a passion, with your plans to go to the Olympic trials together."

Yes, I was aware of that. "This has nothing to do with PWJ, so can we drop it?"

He ignored me. "Then the car accident. Seth dies. You break your pelvis. I get completely fucked up over survivor guilt." He drew a black cloud over the head of the stick figure that represented himself.

In case you hadn't guessed, Greg had been driving the car that night. The accident hadn't been his fault, but that hadn't changed the fact that he'd killed his best friend.

"So what do you and I do?" He filled in the dotted line between us. Now it was solid. What an artist. "We cling to each other, as the only ones who understand what the other is going through. You know, we were both in the car, we both loved Seth, yada yada yada."

It was the first time I'd heard the worst period of my life referred to as "yada yada yada." "Is that proper psychiatric lingo?"

He set down the pen. "Want to know why I left?"

Yes. "No. What does this have to do with the fact that our testers were a bunch of asinine fools?"

He gave me a condescending look. "Everything we do is connected to everything that has ever happened to us."

Yawn. Time for some coffee and leftover pizza. I helped myself while he continued to drone. I wasn't sure why I was letting him talk. Maybe it was because it was better than having to do any active thinking myself.

"I left because I couldn't deal with the situation," he said.

"Apparently." Yuck. Someone's hair was on that piece. I threw it out immediately. Then washed my hands three times.

"I thought marrying you would make things better. Get rid of my guilt by taking care of you the way Seth would have wanted." He shook his head. "It just made things worse. Like I was trying to move into Seth's place. I couldn't deal, so I took off and tried to pretend none of it had ever happened."

I stared at him. For the first time, was I really hearing the truth about why he'd left me? Why he'd married me? Out of guilt?

"Your reaction to the accident was to latch onto that which you'd lost: running and Seth. I was the surrogate for Seth and Sfoam was the surrogate for running. Seth was your running partner and your lover, plus you couldn't run anymore because of your hip. From America's next hope in international distance running to a has-been."

I frowned. "And how is this supposed to be making me feel better?"

"It's not. Pain must come before healing. You used Sfoam to create a way to have Seth and running in your life. And now it's time to let go."

"I liked you better when you were a butthead who refused to talk about anything personal. And you were no prize back then either." I didn't like all this touchy-feely stuff. I didn't want to know that I'd been nothing more than part of the healing process to him. That he'd never cared about me. I'd loved him, and I wasn't going to let him belittle my feelings for him or my company into some therapeutic psychobabble.

He finally looked irritated. Good. About time I got to him. It was bugging me that he was so okay with everything while I was *not* having a good day. "This is the deal, Paris. You've clung to your past with this dream. You think if you can create the ultimate running shoe, then maybe it will make up for all the bad stuff that happened back then."

"That's ridiculous. I love running. I care about running. Nothing deep about that."

"I tried to get rid of the pain from the accident by clinging to unrealistic dreams. It doesn't work. But you can break away." He picked up a piece of Sfoam. "Look at this stuff. It's incredibly innovative. It's brilliant. So it won't work for running shoes. If you can embrace what you've accomplished and look with an open mind, you'll see new paths for yourself."

I didn't want a new path.

He held out the foam, and I took it. Sfoam was for running. It was made for running.

Seth would have liked it.

Seth. We never talked about him anymore. Certainly Greg and I had never talked about him, even after we got married. It was weird to talk about him. Sort of sad, I guess.

Greg was quiet for a minute. "You named it after him, didn't you? The S in Sfoam is for Seth."

I nodded.

"You ever think about him?"

"A lot."

"Me too." He sighed. "You ever think about that night?"

"I try not to."

He nodded. "Maybe it's time we stopped hiding from our past. You and I, we need each other."

I pressed the foam between my thumb and index finger and watched it spring back. "Is that what your therapist told you?"

He set his hand over mine. "No. It's what I realized the minute I walked into your office."

Uh-oh. Didn't like that tug at my gut. Didn't like it at all. I carefully extricated my hand. "I think you should leave."

He put his hand back over mine. "I don't."

Warning bells! I pulled my hand away again and tucked it under my thigh. "Your only role is to be a bank for PWJ. Not to give advice and interfere."

He propped his head up, elbow on the picnic table, and studied me. It was such a relaxed pose, much more like the old Greg than this new Greg. I wanted to run my hand through his hair, rub my fingers over his whiskers.

"I've changed my mind," he said. "I don't want to be only a bank."

"You suck when you change your mind." Amen to that.

He grinned. "I think Sfoam has great potential to make money. Since my business is venture capital, I've decided to stick my nose in. It's what I do."

"I thought leaving was what you did." Okay, so I was a little fixated on that incident. Was it time to get over it? Maybe.

He shrugged. "And now I'm back." He reached for my hair, and I pulled back out of his reach, even though what I wanted to do was close my eyes and let him comfort me with his touch. "I like how you've changed. You're stronger now," he said.

"I know." How strong was I? If I were really strong, I

wouldn't be responding to him like this, would I? If I were really strong, I wouldn't feel so wobbly now that I didn't have Will in my bed anymore. I wouldn't be so cranky that I had to stand on my own again.

"I've changed too," he said.

"Not enough."

He grinned. "You'll discover you're wrong."

"I don't think so." I couldn't deal with this anymore. With our past, with him trying to make me believe Sfoam was the therapeutic equivalent of him leaving me. I pushed back from the table. "Take a hike, Greg. I have work to do."

He grabbed my wrist and stood up, his face mere inches from mine. "I came back to clear up my past so I could move on. But my agenda has changed."

I tried to get free, but he wouldn't let go. Maybe because I wasn't struggling that hard. I was being pulled to him by our common past, by our shared pain, just as I had been five years before. Only this time I knew what was happening, and I could stop it if I wanted to.

I meant, I would stop it. Would. Not could. Would. I pulled away this time. "I know your agenda changed. Now you want to get involved in PWJ. Too bad. You signed a contract."

He shook his head. "My agenda is now you."

My throat tightened up. "What does that mean?"

"It means I want you back." He leaned closer, and I leaned back, away from him. "Paris, we got married for the wrong reasons, which is why it didn't work back then. But today it's different. I'm back, and I want you, and I know you still want me. And this time it's for the right reasons."

Was it time for a knee to the jewels? Might be. "I want you to get run over by a truck. Or two."

He moved suddenly, too quickly for me to react, his mouth closing over mine. For a split second, I forgot I hated him. I forgot about all the pain he'd caused me five years ago. I forgot that he was fucking up my life again. All I could think about was how much I loved him, how he'd saved me when I thought my world was going to end, how I knew I'd loved him more than anyone had ever loved anyone, how it was so comforting to be with someone who shared my pain.

And I kissed him back.

Hard.

Held on tight.

Basked in the taste of him.

Sank into his chest.

Relished the safety of his arms.

Forgot about everything but Greg McFee and how much I loved him.

Then I remembered my life, and I shoved him away from me as hard as I could.

He released me and took a step back, his breathing heavy, his eyes dark.

My heart was racing in my chest, my lungs felt constricted and my lips felt ravaged.

For a long moment, we stared at each other.

Then I grabbed my keys and my purse and the pair of testing shoes in my size that had been returned.

And I walked out.

He didn't follow me.

This time.

Next time, I had a feeling he wouldn't let me go so easily. And I was terrified I wouldn't pull away.

THIRTEEN

I threw on the testing shoes and ran. Ran away from Greg. Ran away from Will. Ran away from everything. Thought only about my date with Thad tomorrow. Wondered if Lindsey was still alive. Decided that maybe I'd go with her on her next adventure.

I ended up at my mom's condo ten miles later.

And that's when the bad news hit me.

My feet were killing me.

My arches felt strained.

The ball of my foot felt bruised.

And my hip felt like it was going to explode into a million pieces.

The shoes sucked.

They *sucked*.

I didn't weigh that much. I didn't require stability shoes. I had been predisposed to think they were the best thing ever. And I still hated them.

Shit didn't even begin to describe the moment.

Everything hurt so much I actually took the elevator instead of the stairs.

I limped into my mom's condo, took off the shoes and threw them in the garbage disposal. I wondered briefly if I could fit my head in there too.

My dreams. Gone. *Gone.* I felt so incredibly empty. I had nothing left. Nothing.

At the horrific grinding noise and resulting thunk that indicated I'd broken her disposal, my mom popped her head out of the living room, fully adorned in makeup, her hair cute in a new stylish 'do I hadn't seen before. "Paris? What are you doing here?"

I pulled a bottle of wine out of her fridge. "Sfoam doesn't work and Will and I broke up and Greg is back and he wants to get back together and my hip hurts and Lindsey is trying to kill herself and Will and Jodi have secrets and I'm on probation at work but I have a date with my boss and I'm a mess and I don't know what to do and—"

I stopped as a man in a suit walked out of the living room, a glass of red wine in his hand. "So this must be your wonderful daughter I've been hearing about." He was about five eleven, totally bald, and he looked like an escaped serial killer. I wasn't quite sure exactly what was giving me that impression. Maybe his shifty eyes or the way his hand moved toward me as if to shake my hand, but really I could tell there were little voices instructing him to strangle me and chop me up. "I'm Zach Middleton. Nice to meet you."

I stared at this man who was in my mom's condo. In my world. Was he one of the ex-cons?

My mom nudged me. "Paris, this is Zach Middleton."

I numbly mumbled something and shook his hand.

Zach took a sip of his wine and beamed at us. "Won't you join us, Paris? We were having drinks, and then we were going to go out for dinner."

My mom gave me a look that said I wasn't supposed to accept Zach's invite. Um, since when did my mom ditch me? "I'm having a personal crisis," I said with a meaningful glance at my mom. "I wouldn't be good company. I really just need to talk to my mom."

She patted my arm. "Let's meet for lunch tomorrow, sweetie. You can tell me all about it then."

"Tomorrow? My crisis is now."

Zach just continued to stand there glowing, as if he weren't interfering in a twenty-six-year bond between mother and daughter.

My mom's smile tightened. "Can you excuse us for a minute, Zach?"

"Certainly, my dear. I'll just wait in the living room." My *dear*? He nodded to me. "So nice to meet you, Paris."

Nice, my ass.

My mom shut the kitchen door behind him. "Paris! Why are you being so rude? This is my first date with this man, and I really like him so far. Don't mess this up for me."

I stared at her. Since when did a date take precedence over the utter destruction of my life?

She smoothed her blouse. "Do I look all right? Not too formal, but not too risqué?"

"You're wearing a linen blouse buttoned up to the neck. You look like a librarian."

"Too formal?"

I sighed and unbuttoned the top two buttons. I

161

couldn't believe I was instructing my mom to show more cleavage. What was wrong with this picture? "There. Reveal a little skin, but not too much." I noticed then that my mom's eyes were glittering. Glowing. Hadn't seen that in a long time. My eyes sure as hell weren't glowing, unless it was demonic possession. "Are you sure you have to go tonight? I'm really in a crisis." I shifted my weight off my hip and tried not to wince.

My mom hesitated; then I saw her jaw grow strong with resolve. "You want my advice? Here it is. Marry Greg. Give up on your business. Go to the doctor for your hip. Bring Lindsey along to a funeral I'm going to tomorrow to cure her death wish. Don't sleep with your boss. Get over your insecurity with Will and Jodi." She patted my head. "There. Problems solved."

"That's it?"

"I'm going. You're a big girl now, Paris. You can handle it yourself. Wish me luck." She lowered her voice. "He's been out of prison for a couple of weeks now, and he's ready for a woman. I think his deprivation will make him really value me."

"Prison? Are you kidding? Is he armed?" Maybe I should borrow his gun to keep Greg from breaching my defenses.

"I did a background check on him. He was in prison for a white-collar crime that's really not a big deal. He has a lot more money than I do, so I know he's not after that, and he's very smart. Not afraid to take risks. Funny too. He handled prison very well. He considered it a character builder. It made him appreciate the important things in his life." She beamed. "One of which was the fact that no one visited him while he was there. He doesn't want to

IF THE SHOE FITS

be alone anymore. It's exactly the same thing as my funeral catharsis. We're totally connecting."

I blinked. "You're insane."

"Nope. Just taking charge of my life."

"But you're a lawyer. You can't date a criminal."

"Why not?"

"Well, because." Did I really need to explain?

She grinned and hugged me. "Take a risk, sweetie. You might be surprised at what happens. Let yourself out, and if you decide to stay, don't wait up for me."

"But . . ."

"Bye!" Then she practically danced out of the kitchen, and I heard her hustle Zach out the door before I could do something so dastardly as to interfere.

Well, that sucked.

I thought about going home, but then I remembered that Jodi wanted to bond with me.

And Will and Greg both knew where I lived.

Call me a wimp, but I decided I didn't want to deal. All of them were too tangled up with my past and my present and my baggage.

I didn't want to deal with any of it right now.

So I grabbed the bottle of wine and decided to spend the night in my mom's guest room. That way I could talk to her in the morning before I had to decide how to deal with my life.

Unfortunately my plans got screwed up because my mom spent the night out. By the time I left at noon on Sunday, she still hadn't returned.

I didn't know which was worse: realizing that my mom was a slut who had sex on a first date with an ex-con who was barely out of prison, or realizing that even my biggest crises were less important than an orgasm. So much for two-plus decades of being best friends. Nothing like having your foundation ripped out from under you when things were at their worst to force you to make poor decisions.

Poor decision #1: Keep running date with boss.

I showed up in running shorts and a slightly daring tank top. Thad was wearing shorts and a T-shirt that showed off his body in a way suits never did. He was lean and muscular, all sinewy and strong like corded wire. He was wearing sports shades and a Red Sox hat on backwards.

How could this athletic, sporty guy possibly be a banker? And my boss?

He grinned as I walked into his condo. "Hey there. Ready to go?"

"Yep." He hadn't so much as glanced at my legs or my chest. So that's all it was, then? Just a bonding session with my boss? Shit. I could have used more.

He took my backpack and set it on the couch. "Is this your stuff for after the run? Still up for food afterwards?"

"Yep."

We fell into step as we started off toward the Esplanade so we could run along the Charles River. There were plenty of sunbathing beauties enjoying the summer day, but Thad didn't seem to notice any of them. He was attentive and friendly and cheerful. We talked about baseball and movies and books and bad jokes.

Nothing about dead ex-boyfriends.

Nothing about running.

Nothing about dreams.

How nice was it?

Then we started running harder and we stopped talking entirely. There was just the sound of our feet hitting the ground in perfect sync, our heavy breathing and the sound of traffic going by on Storrow Drive.

There was something about running with another runner that made the world feel right.

It made me realize things hadn't felt right for a long time.

We finished up a couple of blocks from his condo, walking the final few hundred yards as a cooldown. We were only a few houses from his when he cocked his head at me. "Something wrong?"

"Nope. Nothing."

"What's with the limp?"

I immediately stopped limping. "Old injury." I waited for him to tell me to go to the doctor.

"Sucks."

"Yeah."

"Want some ice for it?"

"No." The doctor question would be next.

"So where do you want to go for food?"

I blinked. No pressure? No questions?

Wow.

Nice.

We ended up at a little Italian café down the street from Lindsey's condo. I'd eaten there a few times with her, but it was different going with Thad. For the first time, I wasn't obsessing over the hot Italian waiters.

I was obsessing over the man sitting across from me. No designer shirts like Greg. No ripped jeans like Will. Thad was wearing khaki shorts, a polo shirt, a pair of sandals and another baseball cap.

I didn't know about the thong. Still didn't know if I ever would.

The waiter delivered our wine, and Thad raised his glass. "A toast."

I lifted mine. "To?"

"To a great run on a nice day."

I grinned. "To a great run."

We touched glasses and took a sip. I didn't even notice the wine. How was I going to get Thad to notice me as more than his employee? He was everything I needed. Funny, athletic, no baggage. Just a good time.

"So, Thad . . ." I tore off a piece of bread and dipped it in the olive oil. "You dating anyone at the moment?"

"Nope."

I liked that answer.

"How's the ex-husband thing going?"

"He's an ass."

Thad grinned. "As most ex-husbands are, I assume."

"But he's putting a lot of money into PWJ, so I can't get rid of him."

"And the ex-boyfriend? How's that?"

"Weird. There's too much baggage in my life right now." I eyed him. "I think I need a fresh start. With someone not bogged down in my past."

He met my gaze. "That would probably be a good idea."

"I think so too." Was it my imagination, or did something change in the air between us? "Thad . . ."

"Paris! Where have you been?"

I looked up to find Lindsey and Jodi standing over our table. Crap. The disadvantage of dining at a place two blocks from her house, apparently. "Hi."

Lindsey pulled up two chairs and sat down. "Who are you?"

Nice. "Thad, these are my friends Lindsey and Jodi." Lindsey was wearing a black bra under a white camisole and had a bandage on her forehead, and Jodi was wearing a T-shirt that was too big for her and the wrong color. "This is Thad Wilkins."

Lindsey raised her brow. "*The* Thad?"

Thad shot me a look. "You've been talking about me?"

"Of course I have. You're my boss. I complain about you all the time." Was I a fast thinker or what? I was so suave.

He grunted, and I knew he didn't believe me. Okay, so maybe I wasn't suave. At least he couldn't know for sure what we'd discussed about him. Let him wonder. Women of mystery were very exciting to men, right?

Lindsey picked up my wine and took a sip. "What are you two up to today?"

I glanced at Thad. "We just went for a run."

"You don't look like you went for a run."

"I showered at his place."

Lindsey's eyes narrowed ever so slightly, and Jodi's eyes widened.

"It was just a shower," Thad said. "I'm her boss."

Oh, relax, Thad. It wasn't as if my friends were the sexual harassment police.

"Yeah, we know." Lindsey gave me a thoughtful look. "So . . . you guys want to go out tonight? Jodi and I were thinking of going dancing. Take advantage of the Sunday night 'girls get in free' deal."

Jodi's cheeks immediately turned red. "I wasn't thinking of dancing. I don't dance."

Thad looked at her. "Why not?"

"Because I don't."

"But why not?"

Jodi frowned. "Because I can't dance."

"So?"

Jodi shifted. "So I'm not going to look like a fool in front of everyone else."

"Oh, come on, Jodi," Lindsey said. "All you need to do is show off that body of yours and people will be so busy watching your boobs and butt that they won't even notice whether you can dance."

"Lindsey!" Jodi looked ready to crawl under the table now. "I couldn't do that!"

"I think this evening sounds fun." Thad was grinning now. "I'm in for dancing. Paris?"

Dancing with Thad? Oh, wow. That could turn non-platonic fast. "Um, sure." Did I sound blasé enough?

He grinned. "Great." Then he pushed back from the table. "If I'm going out tonight, there's some stuff I need to get done first. Is it cool if I take off?" At my nod, he stood up. "Call my cell when you guys figure out the time and place. We'll hook up." He nodded at Jodi and Lindsey. "Nice to meet you." He winked at Jodi. "I'm looking forward to seeing you dance." She blushed, but before I could get jealous, he turned his gaze to me, and gave me a long look. "I'll see *you* later."

Oh, wow.

ƆOURTEEN

Lindsey barely managed to wait until the door shut behind Thad. "He's totally hot. Have you slept with him yet?"

"Lindsey!" Jodi groaned. "He's her boss. She can't sleep with him."

"Sure she can. So? Did you?"

"Nope. Don't know if he's interested." I was so impressed with how casual I sounded, because I sure wasn't feeling calm about the situation.

"Are you? Are you interested?"

I shrugged. "Possibly."

Jodi frowned. "What about Greg?"

"He's a jerk. What is your problem with bringing him up all the time?"

"But you kissed him," Jodi said.

Lindsey and I both stared at Jodi. Then Lindsey glanced at me, her face brimming with outrage. "You kissed Greg?"

I didn't look away from Jodi. "He told you?" What was

up with all the men in my life confiding in Jodi? It was really beginning to bother me.

"He's very excited," Jodi said. "He still loves you."

Damn it. I did not need to hear that. "No, he doesn't. It's an ego thing."

Lindsey grabbed my wrist. "You kissed him?"

"He kissed me."

"But you kissed him back," Jodi said.

Lindsey's fingers dug into my skin. "You kissed him?"

"It was a mistake. Because I used to love him. That's it." Heaven help me, I hoped that's all it was. That was one reason why I wanted things to heat up with Thad. To distract me. I twisted my hand free. "I can't believe he told you."

"Well, hellfire and damnation." Lindsey leaned back in her chair. "This is no good."

Jodi shot her an annoyed glance. "Why are you upset? You were just as happy as I was to see him again."

"I was glad to see him as my friend and as a source of income, but if he hurts Paris again, he's not my friend anymore." Lindsey frowned. "This is bad. Very bad." She pointed her finger at me. "You're too vulnerable. He's going to take advantage of that. You need to start sleeping with Will again."

Something caught in my belly at that thought. "It's over with him. Over." Sigh.

"Damn. Then Thad. Sleep with Thad." She sat up. "That's the goal for tonight. Get him to forget that stupid boss/employee thing. We are going to make you so hot his eyes will bug out of his head and he won't be able to stop drooling until he has sufficiently groped you."

"Charming," Jodi muttered. "You don't think that it

might screw up Paris's career a little bit to have an affair with her boss? It's not as if she's going to get serious with him. She'll have sex with him for a month, then dump him, and then what?"

I frowned. It didn't sound like such a smart idea when she put it that way. Because she was right. I wasn't in the market for a serious relationship. Then again, neither was Thad. On the other hand, neither Will nor I had been wanting to get serious, and that hadn't worked out so well, had it?

"She's probably going to get fired anyway, so she might as well sleep with him while she has the chance. Besides, you can't live for the future. You have to live for the present." Lindsey picked up Thad's abandoned wine and took a sip. "Speaking of living for the present . . . What would you guys say if I told you I didn't want to be a lawyer anymore?"

"I'd freak out because PWJ would be dust without you. Why?" As if she'd ever quit being a lawyer. She'd been hankering after the lawyer shtick since I met her freshman year in college.

"Well, law is a little boring."

For Lindsey, I could see that. "So maybe you need some juicier cases. Corporate law probably isn't that interesting." I brightened. "Or did you want to come work for PWJ? Once we get financing, I could put you on the payroll. You could be in-house counsel and take over a lot of this stuff."

She snorted and waved her hand. "No offense, sweetie, but I'd rather get toothpicks shoved under my fingernails than be on the PWJ payroll."

"What? Why?" I mean, yeah, I knew she wasn't that

into our company, but choosing torture over PWJ? That was a little extreme.

"Because it's a pipe dream for you. Jodi told me about the disaster with the testers yesterday. The biz is going in the toilet and fast. I know you need to cleanse your soul or something, and that's great, but it'll never get off the ground. And I'm really not interested in working as hard as you do. Life is too short. I need to have some fun."

"It's not going in the toilet...." Then I stopped. Maybe it was. I didn't know anymore. I'd been avoiding thinking about it since yesterday, but it wasn't looking good. I swallowed my words instead. "I have fun."

She laughed out loud at that one. "Oh, give me a break."

I stuck my tongue out at her. "You'll change your tune when we go public and all become millionaires."

"If you become a millionaire, I'll be happy for you. But I'm not joining your little band of dreamers. I'm going to follow my own dream." Her eyes began to glow, and I got a bad feeling.

"You're serious, aren't you? You're really going to quit the law?"

She wiggled her eyebrows. "What do you think of the name Trisha the Terminator as a pro wrestling name?"

I'm sure I had a look of utter shock on my face, because she tossed her napkin at me. "Don't look so startled, Paris. You know I've always loved watching my brother wrestle."

Did I forget to mention that everyone in Lindsey's family was a cop, except for her youngest brother, who was a professional wrestler who dressed like a cop? He was a total embarrassment to the family, even though they attended every match when he was in town. The son you love to hate. Or hate to love. Or whatever. "You're going to give up a career as a lawyer to become a professional wrestler?" I could see her being a cop, because being a lawyer and a cop were at least in the same genre of jobs. Plus being a cop could definitely be risky. But from a lawyer to a pro wrestler? "You don't even like to exercise. How are you going to get a job that depends on being fit?"

She shrugged. "I could do it if I wanted to. But I might go to clown school and join the circus instead. Still trying to decide."

I stared at her. "Why? I don't get it." I mean, yeah, I knew Lindsey always pushed the limits on every aspect of life, but I thought she'd finally found her niche professionally. Get stability from work. Get insanity from extracurricular activities. If she threw it all away . . .

Lindsey's grin faded and she became serious. "Don't take this personally, but I don't want to end up like your mom."

"My mom? What's wrong with her?" Lindsey worked at the same firm as my mom. Yes, Lindsey had an inside track because she'd known my mom for ages.

"She's almost fifty years old, and she's been living the same dull life for the last twenty-five years. She goes to court every day, deals with the same annoying clients, turns down dates because she has to write up a contract or research a case. Lately she's been looking really unhappy and miserable."

Ah, yes, the funeral thing.

Lindsey rolled her eyes. "I'm sorry, but that's not me. Life has to be about more than work, work, work, you know?"

"But you have to do something worthwhile. You can't just live a frivolous existence," Jodi said. "You already mess around enough in your free time. Why do you have to throw your career away as well? I think participating in something meaningful makes your life worth living."

"I have to do something worthwhile like you're doing?" She rolled her eyes. "Like I said, PWJ is a great goal, but it's not realistic. Either you're going to miss out on the next twenty years of your life trying to get this impossible dream to happen, or else you're going to crash and burn and feel like a total failure."

I stared at her. "And to think I believed you were my friend." Yeah, I was feeling a little betrayed right now, even if there was more truth to her words than I cared to admit.

"Oh, you know I love you, and PWJ's great if that's what you want to do. But it's not my gig. Life is about more than work." She flipped a brochure out of her briefcase. "There's the info on the clown school. You should seriously think about coming with me."

"To be a clown?" I couldn't keep the incredulity out of my voice.

"It's only a week. It might be fun."

"I don't have a week."

"Party pooper. It's not like it's a lifelong commitment. A week of clown camp. Can't you see the possibilities?"

"No. I have to work."

She wrinkled her nose. "You're like Billy Crystal in *City Slickers*. You need a bull to shove its horn up your bum a couple times. Clown camp could be it."

"You're insane." *But wouldn't it be cool to toss aside all my responsibilities and be a clown?* Not that I'd ever do it, but I had to admit, I could see the appeal. But only if I lived in an alternate universe without bills and rent and plans that needed to be fulfilled.

"Yeah, maybe I'm insane. But doesn't it make life grand?"

"No." Who, me, negative?

"The other attendees probably wear shoes. You could use it as a test market."

I eyed her. "You're making fun of me."

"You bet. You're strung way too tight these days."

"Are you really thinking about being a pro wrestler, or were you just messing with me?"

She widened her eyes and fluttered her fingers. "Who knows? I'm always full of surprises."

"Just don't surprise me by leaving PWJ in the lurch and I'll be fine." Just the thought of her ditching us made my skin cold.

She studied me. "Maybe I should do that. Maybe that's what it would take to make you see that you're making yourself crazy."

I was pretty sure my heart actually stopped. "You aren't serious? You're going to leave me?" Good God. I couldn't deal with that. Couldn't deal with one more thing. "You can't do that to me."

When would I have time to find another lawyer? Or to learn how to do it myself? How would I be able to afford to pay someone? What if Greg tried to get more control and I didn't have Lindsey to throw her legal weight around and stop him? What then? What if we got Sfoam to work and we got an offer? Who would negotiate it? Who would do the paperwork? When was I supposed to have time to figure out how to deal with it? When? When? *When?* My head was killing me. My eyes were going to pop right out of my head, propelled by the daggers behind. I couldn't deal. Could. Not. Deal.

"Paris?" Concern clouded Lindsey's features. "Are you going to have a heart attack? You're kind of pale."

Jodi's face came into my view, her brow furrowed. "What's wrong?"

"I don't know." The room was starting to spin. "Did you know there are black spots dancing across your face?" I couldn't breathe. And everything was getting fuzzy. "Guys?"

"Don't panic, girlfriend. Get your head down between your knees." Lindsey jumped up, yanked my chair back and shoved my head toward the floor. "Take a deep breath. Fight it off."

My entire body started to shake and I felt tears running down my cheeks. Omigod. I felt so awful. I couldn't breathe. Couldn't see. Couldn't even hear because the buzzing in my ears was so loud. And annoying. Why didn't it shut up?

Jodi squatted in front me and her mouth was moving, but I couldn't hear her, and she was starting to get really dark. Fading to black.

I woke up to find myself staring at the underside of a table. Lots of globs of gum stuck to the bottom of it. There were hands patting my head, something cold on my forehead. People talking. Some of them sounded familiar.

"I think she's awake." A hand tapped my cheek. "Paris? You with us?"

I turned my head to find Lindsey hovering over me. "Hi."

She smiled, and then Jodi's face appeared next to hers. "How do you feel?"

"Fabulous. How are you?"

Jodi grinned. "Can you sit up?"

Lindsey pushed on my shoulders, holding me down. "Don't get up. The ambulance is on the way."

"Ambulance? Forget it." I struggled to a sitting position, clinging to Jodi's arm to keep my balance in the spinning room. "I just needed a brief nap. All fine now." Suddenly I noticed that our waiter, a chef, and the maître d' were all leaning over me. "Back off," I growled.

They backed.

Using Jodi's shoulder for balance, I staggered to my feet. Then I grabbed my purse, tossed some cash on the table, and made my way out of the restaurant, wavering only slightly in my path. The room was still spinning, but it wasn't black yet.

I caught my toe on a piece of dust and almost did a header, but Jodi and Lindsey kept me upright. They got me all the way to the curb, at which point I felt sufficiently recovered to sit down and take a break.

So I sat.

They sat too.

"Paris?"

"Don't say it."

"You're scaring me," Jodi said.

"What time do you want to meet tonight for dancing?" The cars across the street were coming into focus now. Much better.

Lindsey frowned. "Don't you think you should take it easy tonight? I mean, you did just collapse."

I glared at her. "You want me to have fun. Dancing is fun. I'm going. When and where?"

She eyed me. "Nine-thirty? Meet at Hot Stuff?"

"Fine." I stood up. "See you there."

I started to walk away when Jodi caught my wrist. "Paris?"

"What?"

"What about PWJ? Did you think about that—ow!" She eyed Lindsey. "Why'd you hit me?"

"Because Paris just had a freak-out. The last thing she needs to do is think about PWJ right now. Don't you workaholics have any sense of limitations?" Lindsey stood up and threw her arm around my shoulder. "Don't worry about PWJ, sweetie. It's not going anywhere. Go home, take a shower, buy some slut clothes and we'll see you to-night." She kissed my cheek. "Bye!"

I nodded and stumbled off. What was wrong with me? Too much stress. Too much pressure. Too much work.

I needed a break.

Dancing.

Fun.

Thad.

And maybe clown school.

FIFTEEN

Sex kitten I wasn't, but I was doing my best imitation of one. Black lace thong, no bra under my cute little sundress (okay, so it had a built-in), break-my-ankle heels (and I wasn't even wearing my ankle brace), body wash that smelled like seduction (according to the saleswoman) and I'd copied an article in *Cosmo* about creating "come hither" eyes with artfully applied eyeliner and makeup. Not bad for a Sunday night, don't you think?

Either Thad would pull me off into the coatroom and do me right there or I'd be arrested for soliciting. I hoped for the former.

Lindsey was the first one I saw at Hot Stuff. She stopped about ten feet from me, lifted one eyebrow in a slow, deliberate motion, then did a stroll around me, checking me out from all sides.

Then she sidled up to me, put her arm around my waist and leaned into me. "Will you go home with me?"

I grinned. "It works?"

"That it does, baby. That it does. If I was a lesbian, I'd

179

be willing to risk our friendship for a night with you." She tucked her arm through mine. "Thad won't be able to resist you. You'll be sharing his bed by the end of the night."

I grinned, and then suddenly got really nervous. Was I really trying to seduce my boss? Was that really a good idea? Ah . . .

"Holy shit, girl! You clean up good!" Lindsey exclaimed, staring past me with a big grin on her face.

I turned to see Jodi walking up to us, wearing snugly fitting black jeans, a camisole and some makeup. I felt my jaw drop. "You're dressed like a woman."

She looked a little embarrassed. "I got tired of the harassment I get from you two, so I decided to buy clothes that fit. You like?"

"Well, *yeah*." Lindsey tucked her other arm through Jodi's. "I can't believe my friends are the two hottest chicks in here. This deserves a celebration." She headed over to the bar and beckoned to our favorite bartender, Rex.

Hot Stuff was a new dance club/bar that had opened about six months before. The bar food was passable, the beers cheap, the cover charge low, and the music was great. The lights stayed dim, so you could hide in the corner without anyone knowing you'd been there. We'd gone out dancing here a few times, and I'd spent more than a little time making out with Will on the dance floor. I frowned and elbowed Lindsey as she headed toward a table near the door. "Why'd you pick here?"

"So you could develop a new association with this place." She sat down and put the pitcher of beer on the table, along with four glasses. "Time for a new future."

We'd just raised our glasses when Lindsey elbowed me. "There's Thad. Go greet him."

Jodi spun around. "He doesn't look like a banker."

I followed her glance and nearly choked on my beer. Thad was wearing black jeans, a collared shirt unbuttoned just the right amount, and a thin gold chain around his neck. His hair was gelled so that it stuck up a little bit, and he was freshly shaven. He looked like a guy who'd spent a little time getting ready, and he looked hot.

Wow.

"You think he's still going to insist on that dance with me?" Jodi asked. "I mean, I don't want to dance with him, you know?"

Lindsey and I exchanged a glance. "Do you have the hots for him?" Lindsey asked.

Jodi's cheeks immediately turned red. "Of course not. I was just wondering. Paris, go talk to him. He's your date."

My date. Hah. I stood up, took a deep breath and then headed over to the door.

He saw me when I was about ten feet away. His gaze flicked over my outfit, quickly and subtly, but there was no doubt that he had checked me out. My stomach did a little jiggle, and I walked up to him. "You look good," I shouted over the music.

A smile curved his mouth, and I realized he had a nice mouth. "I like that dress," he yelled. Then he leaned forward, his lips next to my ear so I could hear him, and he lowered his voice. "I like it a lot."

A shiver caught me at the feel of his hot breath on my neck. Was I getting in over my head?

Probably.

And it felt great.

"Jodi and Lindsey are here," I managed, pointing to them.

He gave them a wave, but made no move toward the table. "Want to dance?"

"Sure."

He grabbed my hand and led me across the room, a man who'd apparently arrived with one thing on his mind: to get his hands on me.

We reached the dance floor and started dancing. It was a fast song, but Thad was one of those guys who still managed to touch while dancing. A shoulder bump here, a hand on my back there, a finger to tuck my hair behind my ear a few times. Each time he touched me, I felt something sizzle in my belly. Each time he came near, I caught his scent of soap. It was a good smell.

And he was always smiling, grinning at me as though I was the sole reason for his good mood. His eyes were laughing, his lips curved, his teeth white. He kept leaning forward and whispering comments into my ear. Making fun of the bad dancer next to me. Telling me how much he liked a song. Laughing about his dancing ability, which was actually very good. Turns out Thad had a little bit of silly goof in him, and he was quite hilarious.

After a while, I was laughing too. Having fun. Just fun. Nothing heavy. Just a good time. A great time.

Then a slow song came on.

We both stopped dancing and sort of looked at each other.

Uh-oh. Awkward moment there. I felt as if I was thirteen again. Didn't know what to do. "Um . . . want to get a drink?"

He held out his arms and lifted his brows in invitation.

He wanted to slow dance with me. As in, wrap his arms around me and hold his body against mine.

This was my boss. Slow-dancing with him wasn't part

of the employee/boss bonding, was it? I guess it could be. I didn't know what he was thinking. Or planning. Or feeling.

Crud.

I wasn't ready for this.

But I moved into his arms anyway.

My arms slipped around his neck as his hands went to my waist, settling on the very thin fabric of my dress. Not much between my skin and his. Then he moved his hand around to my lower back. A gentle tug, and my body was against his. I turned my head so my face was buried in the curve of his neck.

Did I mention he smelled good? Even better up close.

I felt him nuzzle my hair and then rest his cheek against my head.

Oh, wow. My heart was racing. Thudding.

I hadn't been this close to anyone but Will in five years.

It was scary. Exciting. Exhilarating. Liberating.

Thad lifted his head, and I could tell he was looking at me.

So I did the same, and met his gaze.

Our faces were less than an inch apart, his mouth so close to mine.

He was looking at my lips, and it wasn't a boss/employee kind of look.

Oh, wow. Was I ready to cross that line?

Yes. I was.

I lifted my chin as he began to close that final distance. I was so going to do this.

"Hi, Paris."

We both froze at the sound of a familiar voice right in my ear. I turned my head slightly, away from Thad's oh-so-appealing lips. Sure enough, there was Will, with his face practically between us. "Will."

"Want to dance?" he asked. His voice was tense, the tendons in his neck twitching.

Surely he was insane? "I'm already dancing."

Will stuck his hand between us. "I'm Will Foster. And you're Thad Wilkins, right? Paris's boss?"

Thad released me and stepped back to shake Will's hand. "Yep. You a friend of Paris?"

"That I am," Will said.

"Was," I muttered. "He was a friend."

Will's gaze narrowed. "May I have a word with you, Paris?"

"I'm busy."

Thad moved closer to me and put his arm around my shoulder. Protecting me. What a hunk. "Can she chat later? We're sort of busy."

"No. It's important."

At that moment, a leggy blonde with a fake rack wrapped herself around Will, shooting me an evil look. "Will, honey, I'm thirsty. Why are you talking to her?" She pursed her collagen lips in a full pout, then She-bitch-from-hell turned her full hostile glare right on me.

For a moment, I was in shock and unable to respond. I couldn't believe it. Simply couldn't believe he'd gone back to her. I gaped at Will, giving him my "Are you kidding with the She-bitch reappearance?" look.

He gave me a "Are you a total idiot to be making out with your boss?" look right back.

Thad touched my arm. "Paris? Everything all right?"

Will peeled She-bitch off his arm. "Dance with Thad for a minute. I need to talk to Paris."

I glanced at Thad. "I'll be right back."

And I followed Will off the dance floor, right back to our corner. In the past, we'd used it for making out. Tonight it was for something else. We had barely made it there when Will swung around and faced me. "Are you insane? If you have an affair with your boss, you can kiss your career good-bye."

I slammed my hands against his chest. "You're dating She-bitch again? She cheated on you, stole money from you and ruined you for other women. How can you take her back?"

"She didn't steal any money from me, and I'm not taking her back. She called and wanted to go out as friends, and I agreed. I'm not getting back together with her."

"Then why was she wrapped around you?" I shoved at his shoulders. "Will, don't you get it? She makes you miserable. You can't go back there." How could he be with her again? How? How? *How?* "You deserve so much better."

"It's my business what I do with her. What the hell are you thinking with your boss?"

"I'm not thinking anything. I haven't even kissed him!"

"Only because I interfered." He ran his hand through his hair. "God, Paris, what's wrong with you? You kiss your ex-husband, you start an affair with your boss. What are you thinking?"

"Oh, so Jodi told you about Greg?" What the hell was up with Jodi? Why was she interfering in my life like this?

He looked shocked. "So it's true? You really did kiss him?"

"For one second. That's it." I turned away and stared at Thad and She-bitch slow dancing. I had to get back there. Defend my turf. But I also had to protect Will. She was everywhere, her tentacles glomming on with ruthless evil. "Are you with her because we broke up? Is that why? If that's why, then you'd be better off with me. At least I won't hurt you." To save Will, I'd take him back. I was such the loyal friend. I should be sainted.

Will grabbed my shoulders and turned me toward him. "Forget about Christine. I can take care of her. It's you we need to be concerned about. Why are you being so self-destructive? You're falling apart, and I'm worried about you."

I pushed his hands off my shoulders. "I'm not falling apart."

"Then what about the restaurant today?"

"Jodi told you about that too?" Can't a girl have an anxiety attack and not have it posted all over town?

Will shook his head. "She asked me to come tonight. She was worried about what you might do with your boss." He fluffed my bangs the way he used to do when we could touch each other. "I'll always be your friend, Paris. That's why we broke up, so we could be here for each other. I think you need me now."

"You're the one who needs me. She-bitch is a bad idea, Will. What are you thinking?" I simply couldn't focus on my own problems. I was too upset about Will getting back together with She-bitch. It was just wrong. Not because I was jealous or anything like that. I wasn't. But I loved Will as a friend, and I couldn't stand to see him hurt.

He dropped his hands. "What I do with her is my business."

"As your friend, it's my business too. At least as much as who I kiss is your business."

He ground his teeth, and I lightly smacked his jaw. "You aren't supposed to do that. Cut it out."

He caught my hand. "Listen to me, Paris. I'm worried about you."

The intensity of his gaze hit me hard. The caring in his expression caught me right in the heart, and my anger about She-bitch crumbled. "I'm worried about myself too," I whispered.

"What can I do?" He tightened his grip on my hand. "Tell me, and I'll do it."

"I don't know." I shook my head. "Nothing. There's nothing you can do. I have to figure it out for myself."

He touched my cheek, and I wanted to bury myself in his safe arms. So I stepped back. Five years before, I had fallen for Greg because I was too weak to fight on my own. I wouldn't make the same mistake again, relying on someone else to help me survive. I was going to do it myself this time.

I took a deep breath and turned away from Will's offered comfort. She-bitch was massaging Thad's biceps now. Time to send her packing. "I gotta go."

He caught my arm. "You were damaged when I met you, and you're not anymore. Don't go back there."

"Pot. Kettle. Black. Ditch She-bitch, Will."

"She has a name."

"I know. Doesn't mean I'm going to use it." I pulled away. "Thanks for your concern, but maybe Thad is exactly what I need." He was easy, light, and he wasn't Greg. If he kept me from going back to Greg, it would be worth it.

"Damn it, Paris." He caught up to me when I was only a few feet from Thad and She-bitch. "You can't go around sleeping with every guy you think is hot. It won't make your problems go away!" He yelled it loud enough that Thad and She-bitch heard it. And everyone else in the room, I think.

I ripped my arm free. "Shut up," I hissed. He knew damn well I hadn't slept with anyone except him in the past five years.

Thad moved between us. "I think it's time to go." He tucked me under his arm and gave Will a flickering look. "Nice to meet you, Will."

I let him lead me off the floor. I didn't even look back to see if Will had wrapped himself around She-bitch. Let him ruin his life. As if I cared.

Thad leaned close to me. "Was that ex-boyfriend or ex-husband?"

"Ex-boyfriend. But not really a boyfriend. It was never serious." I sighed. "We've been friends for a long time. That's what the whole scene was about. Not our relationship."

"Ah." He escorted me back to the table where Lindsey and Jodi were sitting. "Good evening, ladies."

Jodi turned pink and tugged at her camisole straps, and Lindsey gave him a flirty grin. "Hey, Thad," she said.

Thad touched Jodi's shoulder, and she jumped. "I know I threatened to dance with you, but can we take a rain check? I think I'm going to head out."

While Jodi tried to form a coherent sentence while being blinded by Thad's apparent sexuality, Lindsey and I exchanged frantic looks. Thad was leaving? Without me? Not if I could help it. I slid next to him and wrapped my arm around his. "You want to go get something to eat somewhere else? Maybe coffee?"

He shook his head and extricated himself from my grasp. Yeah, I felt stupid. "We both have to be at work early tomorrow. I'll see you then. You stay and have fun. Bye, Jodi. See ya, Lindsey." Then he waved and took off.

He waved.

He'd been a millimeter from giving me a kiss, and I'd ended up with a wave instead.

Jodi sighed. "He's totally cute."

Lindsey rolled her eyes. "Go after him."

"You think?"

"Without a doubt. Go. I'll deal with Will if he tries to pursue."

I blew her a kiss. "Thanks." I was going after him.

Sixteen

I headed for the door, moving as fast as I could in my heels, but just as I was nearing freedom, a heavy hand came down on my shoulder. Will again? I spun around, ready to tell him off.

But it wasn't Will.

It was Greg. Immediately I could taste our kiss again, and my heart leapt. I thought of Jodi's claim that he still loved me. I recalled him saying that he was in town to get me back. I felt the room begin to spin again, just as it had that afternoon. So I stepped back and folded my arms across my chest. "What are you doing here?"

"Heard you needed me."

Over his shoulder, I saw Jodi watching us, a pleased expression on her face. I glared at her, and she gave me a smug look that said she wasn't feeling overwhelmed with regret.

Then Lindsey leaned forward, and I saw her notice Greg. Her face darkened, and she started to get up.

Jodi grabbed her arm and hauled her back down, leaning over and whispering with great animation.

Lindsey frowned and she yelled something at Jodi, who shouted back.

Then Greg moved into my line of vision. "Want to dance?"

"No." I slung my handbag over my shoulder. "I was just leaving."

He grabbed my arm. "Stop running from me."

I leaned forward, pressing my face toward his. "Don't you get it? You don't have a place in my life anymore. Go. Away." Being around him was too tempting. I wanted to fall into his arms, let him take care of me the way he had before.

But that wasn't me anymore. I was independent and I didn't need anyone. I certainly didn't need a man who made me want to revert to the needy, spineless wuss I used to be. I turned away, caught Lindsey's gaze and jerked my head toward the door to let her know I was leaving.

She nodded, and I could see the regret on her face . . . just before she turned back to Jodi and started gesticulating wildly.

At least I knew Lindsey was on my side.

As for Jodi? I had no idea what was up with her. We were going to have a serious chat. Very serious.

"Paris, don't leave." His hand came up to cup my elbow. Not likely!

I ducked out of his reach and bolted for the door. Ran carefully down the steps into the street. Looked right. Looked left. Repeated both actions.

Thad was gone.

I felt my shoulders sag. Yeah, I could probably follow him to his house, since I knew where it was, but that dripped of a desperation I didn't feel I'd sunk to just yet.

So I went home.

I made it about half a block before I kicked off my stupid heels and hooked them over my handbag. I walked the rest of the way in bare feet. I wasn't in the mood to break an ankle. Or rather, I wasn't in the mood to break my ankle. Offer me someone else's to break, and I might have a different answer.

An hour later, I was in my pajamas, huddled over my computer, trying to brainstorm what was wrong with Sfoam. Anything was better than thinking about the men in my life. I'd come so close to kissing Thad, and I didn't know whether it was good or bad that Will had stopped us. I was furious at Will and terrified of Greg, of what he made me feel.

Focus on the shoes. I could handle shoes. Maybe I should call Orpheus. Would he know? He'd certainly predicted everything so far.

I sighed and closed my eyes. I couldn't come up with an answer. Was that it, then? Was it over?

A light knock sounded on my door.

After midnight on Sunday night.

It had to be Will. Probably afraid to use his key now.

The knock sounded again.

I was so going to let him have it for interfering in my life. I shoved back my chair and ran for the door. I flung it open to find Greg in the hall.

I slammed the door shut, and he stuck his foot in the way. Even as I tried to use my hip to crush him with the door, he shoved past me and walked into my apartment. I stood in the doorway and glared at him. "I'm really not in the mood to deal with you," I said.

"Are you ever?"

"No." Involuntarily my hand went to my hair. I'd taken all my makeup off, shoved my hair up in a rat's nest on top of my head. I was wearing long underwear bottoms and my pink Bugs Bunny tank top that was about a hundred years old. Not exactly my outfit for slaying men.

Not that I cared about Greg, but as an ex-husband, I wanted him to realize what he'd lost.

Oh, well. Too late for that.

He sat down on my couch. "Here's the deal."

I folded my arms over my chest and leaned against the doorjamb, leaving the door open. "I'm not getting back together with you."

"I want to talk about PWJ."

"Oh." Why didn't he want to talk about us? Didn't he want me anymore? "What about it?"

He leaned forward, resting his forearms on his legs, cuffs rolled up to reveal strong wrists and an expensive watch. He was wearing gorgeous slacks and his shoes were highly polished. His tie was subtle and classy, and his button-down shirt was perfectly pressed. Not the man I married at all. "Running is in your blood," he said.

"Everyone knows that."

"How many people know you cried every day the Olympics were on television that summer?"

I swallowed. The Olympics had been on while Greg and I were on our honeymoon. It had taken all his powers of persuasion to get me out of my tears and down to the beach to forget about the fact that I should have been there, but I never would be. It was only his stubbornness that had saved the honeymoon. At the time, I thought it was because he loved me. In retrospect, it was more likely that he didn't want me to ruin his vacation.

He stood up and walked over to me, but didn't touch me. "Who sat with you when the doctor told you your career was over forever?"

I chewed my lower lip. Greg and my mom had been there. The news that I would never make it back from my injury had been devastating.

"Who held you while you cried that night?"

Greg had.

He put his hands on my shoulders and rubbed softly. "Seth was my best friend. My roommate. I sat there day after day while the two of you talked about your plans for the Olympic trials. While you debated whether to go pro or finish your college career. I heard your dreams. Every single one of them was about being a runner." He brushed his thumb over my cheek, and I didn't stop him. "I know what you lost that night. Not just Seth. Your entire world. Your identity."

I realized I was nodding. I immediately stopped and lifted my chin. "Since when did you become so insightful?"

"Since my ex-wife left me. Made me do a lot of thinking."

He didn't stumble over the "ex" part this time. Was that significant? "I can't believe you married someone else."

He gave a sad sigh that tugged at my heart. "I needed to escape."

"Me?"

He slid his hands down my arms and took my hands. I didn't pull away. "Not from you. From myself." He tightened his grip, and his eyes darkened. "I killed Seth. I destroyed your career. It was all my fault." He blinked hard, and his eyes got shiny. "Damn it, Paris. I tried to fix it. I thought if I could somehow fill in for Seth, I could make it all okay. Help you get running back in your life. Be the lover Seth had been for you. Make you whole."

I stared at him, willing myself not to believe him. He'd given me this line before, after the tester fiasco, but this time, I sort of believed him. But I didn't want to. I didn't want to put my heart at his mercy again. Now would be a good time for the building to burn down, before he stripped away my final defenses. "There's no way you had all those thoughts back then. You weren't that nice of a guy."

He grinned. "Well, yeah. I realize now that's what I was doing. At the time, I was running on instinct. Be with Paris. Marry her. Take care of her." His thumb was doing circles on my palm. "But when school started again and we walked back into that house we'd all rented, and I saw Seth's empty room . . ." He shook his head. "I couldn't take it. Couldn't ignore what I'd done to my best friend." He looked at me. "What I'd done to the woman I'd always loved."

I pulled away and walked over to the couch. "You didn't love me. Not then. Not now." He didn't know what love was. There was nothing between us. Nothing. Our past didn't mean we had a future together.

But it felt so good to connect like this. He was saying all the right words; it was exactly how I'd dreamed it would be for years after he'd left me. I closed my eyes and tried to find the strength I claimed to have.

He sat down on the easy chair. "I loved you while you were with Seth. For a long time, I wondered if some subconscious urge of mine had killed him so I could have you."

I opened my eyes. "That's insane."

"I know. Guilt will do that to you, though." Regret and grief lined his face, and I wanted to reach out and hug him. Take away his pain.

But I didn't. Good for me.

He pushed himself up and slid next to me on the couch, his arm behind me. "Did I mention I have a brilliant therapist?"

I couldn't help but laugh. I needed to laugh. Lighten the heavy air around us. "Either that or she's been brainwashing you. Hypnosis, maybe?"

He grinned. "Probably."

Laughter faded into silence. I became very aware of how close he was to me. Of the fact that the only light in my condo was coming from the bedroom. The living room was dark. Quiet. Just us.

I cleared my throat. "So, um, is that why you came by tonight?"

He raised his hand as if to touch my face, and then let it drop to his lap. "I know how much running is a part of your soul. I really know you. Don't I?"

I shrugged. I didn't want to admit it, but he was right. He'd been my world when all those horrible things had been crashing down around me five years before. That's why I'd been so devastated when he left. Too many losses in too short of a time.

That's why I could never forgive him, remember?

Except how could I be so heartless as to punish a man who carried so much guilt?

"I know you want to keep your running and Seth alive, through Sfoam in running shoes. But the fact is, Sfoam is a long way from working for running." He put his hand over my mouth when I opened it to protest. "As a good businessman, it's my job to get the business side right. It makes no sense to drain funds into running when it's not succeeding. Don't give up on the running application, but focus on something that can infuse funds now."

I pulled his hand off. "Like what?"

"Dress shoes."

I started laughing. "Dress shoes? Like heels and stuff like that? Like I know anything about that."

He wasn't grinning. "I'm serious. Think about it. Dress shoes are uncomfortable because looking good is most important. What if you made shoes that were aesthetically pleasing but also fit? Throw some foam around the pressure points and you've got it made. You don't need to figure out the stability or flexibility concerns for dress shoes."

My amusement faded. "But if we sell Sfoam technology for dress shoes, then we won't own it anymore, so we won't be able to make running shoes."

"So make your own dress shoes. Make an exclusive designer brand where you don't manufacture many, but have great profit. Like Orpheus does with his orthopedic business. Sell some high-end ladies' shoes, then use the profits to keep working on the running application."

My first reaction was to shut him out, but his honesty about the past, his willingness to make himself so vulnerable to me, had breached my defenses. I listened. I considered it. Make dress shoes instead of sneakers. The idea had merit, except . . . "But I don't know anything about designer shoes. I only own one pair of heels, and I nearly broke my ankle in them."

"So? Lindsey knows about them. Go to stores. Do research. All you need to do is learn about fashion. You already know how to make a good shoe."

I rolled the idea around in my head. I didn't have to give up on making running shoes. Just find another way to finance it. Hmm . . . "It's an idea. . . ."

He touched my cheek. "It's a way to keep your dream in sight, but without crippling your business."

I pulled his hand away, and he entwined his fingers in mine. "Why do you care?"

"Because I committed a lot of money to PWJ. I have a vested interest in seeing the company succeed."

"And that's it?"

He shook his head. "You know it's not. But I'm trying to keep my PWJ recommendations separate from how I feel about you."

I pressed my lips together and stared at our entwined hands. "You devastated me when you left."

He made a soft noise and slipped his free hand behind my head, twisted his fingers in my hair. "I'm so sorry, Paris. I really am. That's why I came back. To make amends."

I met his gaze. "How do you make amends for running out on me when I needed you the most?"

"I don't know. But I'm trying." His gaze flickered to my mouth. "Give me another chance. Please."

All I had to do was lean forward and our lips would touch. My bed was in the other room. There was no one to stop us.

Except me. I could stop us.

"Paris." His voice was a whisper of hot breath on my mouth.

"Don't kiss me." I couldn't kiss him. Not Greg. How

could I trust him? The man he was today was nothing like the guy I'd married. He couldn't change that much. Or could he? He'd killed his best friend. That could change a man, couldn't it?

He framed my face with his hands. "I have to kiss you."

Our lips were almost touching.

"I have to be with you again, Paris. Five years ago, we were too screwed up. Today it's different. I won't leave you again. I promise. Being with you again has made me realize what I lost when I left five years ago. I won't lose you again." He stopped talking and touched his lips to mine.

So gently. So softly. Not the arrogant, demanding kisses of five years ago. It was tender and caring. Hesitant. Even his kisses had changed.

He smiled. "You'll always be a runner to me."

That was all it took. He had me. I didn't want to let go of my past. It was who I was, and to be with someone who understand what I'd gone through, who understood why I was the way I was . . . It was what I wanted.

So I threw my arms around him and kissed him back.

The kiss went from tentative to sizzling in less than a millisecond. Five years of longing and remembering and wishing went up in flames. Greg was back in my arms. And I wanted him there.

I tugged his shirt out of his pants, freed the buttons, yanked off his tie (had I ever been with a guy wearing a tie? I didn't think so), squirmed as his hands slipped under my tank top. His fingers were hot against my skin, familiar yet exciting.

My phone rang just as I was undoing his belt.

As if I were going to answer that.

My shirt was on the floor now; his chest was bare. Skin-to-skin with the man I'd married.

"I missed you," I whispered.

My machine clicked on.

"I'm here." He crushed me against the couch, his body pressed against mine. Like the old days, only not. "I'm back, Paris McFee, and I'm not going anywhere."

"My name isn't McFee anymore."

"It will be."

What?

Lindsey's voice rang shrilly into my condo. "Paris Jackson, pick up the phone immediately! Jodi's been in an accident and I'm on the way to the hospital!"

I nearly threw Greg into the coffee table as I flung him off me. "Oh my God! Jodi!" I grabbed my shirt and bolted for the kitchen as Lindsey continued to scream into the machine. I yanked the phone off the hook and slammed it to my ear. Ow. Too hard. "I'm here, Lindsey. What's happened? Is she okay?"

Greg was on his feet behind me, shrugging into his clothes. "What's wrong? What happened? Where are they taking her?"

"Is that Greg I hear? Did he really show up there?"

I yanked my shirt on. "Yeah, he's here. What happened to Jodi?"

"Were you fooling around with him?"

"Lindsey! What's wrong with Jodi?"

"I gave her a bloody nose. Do you realize she told Will and Greg to show up at the dance club and then sent Greg over to your house? What a bitch! Tell me you weren't sleeping with Greg when I called. Were you?"

"You gave her a bloody nose? Are you serious?"

"No, I'm not serious. I'd never hurt her, but she deserves it. Damn it, Paris. Get Greg out of there now before you do something you'll regret."

I looked at Greg, who was fumbling to get his shirt buttoned while still trying to mouth questions at me about what had happened to Jodi. I narrowed my eyes. "Did anything happen to Jodi?"

"No, of course not. But how else was I going to get you off the couch with Greg?"

I hung up on her. Adrenaline overload, anyone?

Greg frowned. "What's wrong?"

"She lied. She figured we were about to have sex and decided that was the only way to stop us."

He gave up on his cuffs and dropped his hands. "Seriously? Jodi's fine?"

"Yes."

"Were we about to have sex?" he asked.

I licked my lips. How exactly does one answer that when standing under the very unromantic fluorescent lights of a kitchen?

His shirt was still untucked. He looked adorable in a rumpled sort of way. Like a combo of the old Greg and the new Greg. "And now?" He held out his hands in invitation. "Be with me, Paris."

Um . . .

SEVENTEEN

The phone rang again.

"Lindsey," he said.

"Probably." I tilted my head. "She hasn't forgiven you for what you did to me five years ago."

"I figured that out." He made a face. It was a cute expression for him. He looked vulnerable. I liked it.

"Why has Jodi forgiven you?"

"I don't know." He shrugged, but something changed in his face. As though he was closing a part of it off. As though he had a secret. As though he wasn't telling me something.

That was all it took for my defenses to shoot back up. "Get out."

He blinked. "But . . ."

I walked to the door and opened it. "You eviscerated me when you left before. I'm over you now and I'm not going back there." Yeah, right! "Leave." The answering machine clicked on.

Instead of walking toward the door, he caught my wrist and leaned toward me.

I leaned back. "No."

"You still love me."

"Not a chance."

He grinned. "You forget. I know you. And I know you love me."

"Same old arrogance. You haven't really changed, have you?"

The smug look faded. "Yes, I have."

"I don't believe you. Out."

Lindsey's voice rang through the apartment. "Paris Marie Jackson, answer the damn phone."

"I have to take that."

"This isn't over," he said. "We connected tonight. The bond is still there." He kissed my cheek before I could stop him, and then left.

"Paris! Answer the phone! You're going to regret this in the morning! You know I love you. I'm right. You have to listen to me! Answer this damn phone!"

I shut the door and leaned back against it, my heart thudding dully. Damn it. How could he still affect me like this? If Lindsey hadn't called, we would have had sex. And I still wanted to.

I wanted Greg back in my life. For good. He knew me. Knew my past. Understood what drove me. Understood that running was so deeply entrenched in my body that I could never walk away from it.

He was the only one who really understood.

Should I go after him?

"Paris! Stop kissing him this minute! Put your clothes back on! Don't you remember how he treated you before?

He doesn't deserve you!" Her voice nearly broke. "Come on, sweetie. Please don't do this to yourself."

I'd give myself until tomorrow. If I still felt like this, I was going to stop fighting it. I levered myself off the door and picked up the phone. "Never lie to me like that again."

"Oh, Paris," she sighed. "It's too late, isn't it? You slept with him."

"He's gone. And no, I didn't sleep with him. You called in time."

"Really?"

"I swear."

"Thank God. Are you mad at me?"

"Of course I am. You scared the crap out of me." I opened my freezer and surveyed for chocolate. Nothing. Damn. "Want to go shopping with me tomorrow after work?"

"You know I do. For what?"

"Shoes."

"What kind?"

"Expensive ones. Designer shoes. High heels. Those kinds of things."

Silence. "Are you dressing up for Greg?"

"Not a chance. I'll fill you in tomorrow." I hesitated. "And thanks. Not for giving me a heart attack, but for . . . well . . . caring enough to call."

"No need to thank me. That's what friends are for, sweetie. Sorry about scaring you, though. The thought of you sleeping with Greg scared me far worse, so I think we're even. I'll see you tomorrow. Love you."

"Back at you." I hung up and tossed the phone on the counter.

I really needed to have a chat with Jodi. What was

wrong with her? Why had she sent Greg and Will to the club tonight? Why was she so set on getting Greg and me back together?

And then it hit me: I'd almost slept with my ex-husband. I shuddered.

I'd almost made a huge mistake . . . right?

I walked into the living room and clicked on a light. Greg's tie was on the floor where I'd tossed it. I stared at it for a while.

Then I left it there and went to bed.

Alone.

The next evening, I met Lindsey at six at the mall. I should still have been at work at the bank, but since Thad had been "out of the office" all day (yeah, right, like that wasn't suspicious and as if I weren't completely paranoid now), I'd decided to cut out early.

The moment I walked up in my sneakers and business suit, she rolled her eyes. "Oh, come on, Paris. That look is so out."

"My hip's a little sore after running in the Sfoam shoes. I have to wear my sneakers as much as possible."

Lindsey frowned. "I have a one-word response to that: doctor."

"Shut up."

She shrugged and changed the subject. "So what happened with Thad today?"

"Called in sick."

"Oh." She shot me a look as she led the way to the most expensive department store in the state, a store I had never bothered to enter. "That doesn't bode well."

"You don't think he's really sick?"

"Do you?"

"We didn't even kiss. He wouldn't bail on his job just because of one dance. He might blow me off or something, but he wouldn't bail." Or so I'd been telling myself all day. In truth, I was glad for the respite. In the light of day, with Greg's tie still on my floor, I was feeling more than a little embarrassed about what had almost happened between Thad and me. I was pretty sure I was glad we'd been interrupted, but I was happy for some time to think before I actually had to face him and address the situation.

"Maybe." She paused outside the shoe department. "So, what are we looking for?"

"Inspiration."

"For?"

"PWJ. I'm going to put Sfoam into women's dress shoes and charge a bazillion dollars for them to keep income coming in while we work on designing the perfect running shoe."

Lindsey raised an eyebrow at me. "You're serious?"

"Yep."

"Wow." She blinked. "Wow."

"So show me what we need to compete with, show me the most expensive brands."

"Right." She took a sharp right and headed toward another part of the store. "The shoes you want are in a specialty section." She eyed me as we walked. "I think it's a great idea. Sfoam could make heels so much more comfortable."

"Yeah, I think so too." It wasn't designing running shoes, but if it could salvage PWJ, it was worth it. Maybe. Somehow I couldn't get excited about fashion. It wasn't me.

"Who talked you into it?"

"Can't you just give me credit for seeing the light?"

"Not after what Jodi reported happened on Saturday. You wouldn't even consider it." She lifted a brow. "Greg?"

I shrugged. "He said some things that made sense. Doesn't mean I'm going to take him back." I frowned, recalling his claim that my name would once again be Paris McFee. How presumptuous was that? Can you even imagine?

I could.

I could very easily.

And that really scared me.

She gave me a look. "What's up with you and Greg?"

I sighed. "I don't know. We would have had sex last night if you hadn't called."

"And?"

"And it might have been the right decision."

Lindsey sighed and put her hands on her hips, studying me closely. "He broke your soul last time."

"I know."

"You really want to go through that again?"

"Of course not. But he swears he won't do it again. I'm different now. So is he."

She cocked an eyebrow. "Is he?"

"You've seen him. He's different."

"Different enough?"

I shrugged. "How do I find that out ahead of time?"

"I don't know, sweetie. I just don't know." She sighed. "I don't know what to tell you."

"You keep telling me to live. To take risks. Maybe this is what I need to do."

"I was thinking more along the lines of having an affair with your boss and doing naked bungee jumping. Getting

back together with your ex-husband is in a whole different hemisphere. It borders on self-destructive, if you
ask me."

I slanted a glance at her. "Looked in the mirror lately?"

"You calling me self-destructive?"

"Fits, don't you think?"

She glared at me. "No, I don't think. Here I am trying
to support you and you give me that old spiel again?"

"Right. Sorry. My life is the screwed-up one right now."

"Damn right it is." She stopped in front of a display
and picked up a pink shoe with a four-inch heel and all
sorts of wacky beads hanging from it. "This one."

"It looks like a call-girl shoe."

She flipped it over and showed me the price.

I nearly croaked. "Eighteen-hundred dollars? Are you
kidding?"

She picked up another shoe. This one was black with
sleek lines and a string of pearls around the open toe.
"Two grand."

I held it up. "It's a shoe."

"By a very special designer. And real pearls."

A sales associate flitted into earshot. "May I help you?"

Lindsey held up both pairs. "We'll try both of these in
a size eight."

"Of course." The sales woman gave Lindsey's suit a
nice smile, then frowned at my sneakers.

Whatever.

I picked up the hooker shoes and inspected them carefully for construction, materials and design. By the time
the saleswoman came back, I was inspired. These fancy
shoes weren't that difficult to make. Sure, the materials
were expensive and the designs a little outrageous, but I
was pretty sure I come up with something to compete.

The saleswoman was carrying six boxes. "I brought a few other pairs of similar taste that might be of interest to you." She beamed at Lindsey. "Shall we?"

"Certainly."

Lindsey led the way to a chair, then shoved me down. "Paris is trying them on. Not me."

I almost laughed at the look of dismay on the saleswoman's face. I guess I didn't exude the right aura for those types of shoes. I gave her a haughty look. "Can we hustle? My driver will be back in forty-five minutes. I can't be late for my meeting with my attorney."

"Oh, yes." Her face brightened up considerably. "We wouldn't want to keep your driver waiting." She pulled out the prostitute shoes and slipped them on my feet. "They look lovely on you. Really accentuate your slender feet."

Hah. My feet were so not slender. She was totally lying to me for a sale.

Impressive. I should hire her.

I stood up, took two steps, then almost passed out from the pain. Holy shit. It was like there was a vise in the front of the shoe trying to crush the bones in my toes. "Are you kidding with these?"

Her eyes widened. "What's wrong?"

Lindsey cleared her throat. "They're wonderful, don't you think?"

I limped over to the mirror for a closer inspection. My feet looked about an inch wide. No wonder my toes hurt. I lifted my right foot to inspect the heel and promptly tipped over. Only Lindsey catching me prevented my knocking over an entire rack of shoes. Guess that's what happens when the base of your heel is about one millimeter wide.

The saleswoman looked a little annoyed now, as if she was beginning to suspect I wasn't a legit customer.

I flashed her a blinding smile. "So what do you think is the biggest reason women select a specific shoe to buy?"

"The designer name and the look."

"Not comfort?"

She frowned. "Comfort doesn't matter. It's all about how you look. Who you're wearing."

Hmm . . . Any shoes with my name on them wouldn't exactly qualify as a "who," would they? "If two shoes were identical except for comfort, would they choose comfort?"

"All our shoes are one of a kind. That would never happen."

"Humor me. Does comfort play into choices in any way?"

"Of course not. Fashion has no bounds." She narrowed her eyes. "You aren't going to buy any shoes, are you?"

"Eventually. Maybe not today."

"I work on commission." She set her hands on her hips. "Do you realize how rude it is to take up my time when you aren't going to buy shoes? I might have missed other customers because I'm standing around with you. Do you even have the money to afford this kind of shoe?"

Lindsey stepped forward. "I do."

The saleswoman glanced at her feet. "Obviously you don't spend your money on shoes." She nearly yanked the shoes off my feet and scooped up her boxes. "Please don't waste my time in the future. It's incredibly rude and insensitive."

She left me in my stocking feet standing by the mirror. *I'd say that went well, don't you think?*

* * *

I ended up buying three pairs of cheap heels and heading to the lab all by myself. It was only eight o'clock, and Orpheus was still there. No one else was.

"Hi, Orpheus."

"Go away."

I dropped my shoes on the table. "Didn't want to talk to you anyway." I pulled out a pair of candy-red heels and studied them. How to stick Sfoam in there? Hmm . . . I picked up a piece and cut it to fit. Laid it inside. Might work.

Orpheus was suddenly leaning over my shoulder. "What are you doing?"

"Trying something. Got any glue?"

"Adhesive." He handed me some.

I felt a little self-conscious with the smelly shoe guru watching me, but I managed to spread glue—oh, sorry, *adhesive*—on the Sfoam and wedge it into the front of the dress shoe. Some under the forefoot. Two pieces around the tops of the toebox.

"Looks ratty," Orpheus said.

"You're one to talk, Mr. Ugly Shoes." I slipped off my socks and put the doctored shoe on my left foot and the undoctored one on my right. Then I closed my eyes and walked around. I tripped three times, but managed not to crash into any machines. My left foot felt way better. Yeah, the shoe was a little tighter, but it felt much more comfortable.

I opened my eyes and beamed at Orpheus. "It works."

"You can't do split-pair perception."

"What?"

"Your left and right feet are different shapes. Different

sizes. The morphology is not the same, so you can't compare them. You need to compare left to left and right to right."

We both studied my feet. "So I should rip out the foam?"

"You should have two pairs of shoes. A control pair and an experimental pair. Don't you know anything about testing?"

"Not enough, apparently." I'd bought three different pairs of shoes so that I could test the foam in each. I didn't have identical pairs so I could have a proper experiment.

Oh, well. I was still pretty sure it would work.

Orpheus gave a disgusted grunt. "What's up with the ladies' shoes anyway?"

I sat down on a bench. "You were right. There are stability and flexibility issues with Sfoam. We need to do more research. So we're going to throw Sfoam in some dress shoes in the interim." I sighed. "I was going to design some shoes that we could sell for a bundle, but have you seen what kind of merchandise they carry in those stores? You need a designer name and you need some fancy-shmansy design that looks like something a prostitute would wear." I sighed. "All I know is sneakers. Jodi and Will know as much as I do about designer shoes. And none of us can draw." I cursed and dropped my head into my hands. God, my head hurt.

Then I realized I was being that wimpy loser I no longer was. So I lifted my head. "Never mind. I'm totally capable of designing competitive shoes. This will work."

Orpheus didn't say anything, and when I looked at him, he was lacing up a pair of his monstrosities, totally ignoring me. Granted, it wasn't as if I'd really expected support from him, but I thought maybe we had the shoe bonding thing going on.

Guess not. "So, I'll see you later," I said.

No response.

Great.

When I got home, I went for a run to clear my mind, but I had to quit after two painful miles. I limped all the way home. Not good. Even three rounds with the ice pack and anti-inflammatories didn't help.

I spent the rest of the night brainstorming, trying to figure out a new strategy. By morning I was sure I had an answer. I sent an email to the PWJ team to meet at the PWJ offices at eight that evening. I'd provide the pizza. All they had to do was show up.

EIGHTEEN

When I walked into work that morning, Thad was sitting at my desk.

He looked totally cute. Was his gold chain still on? I couldn't tell with his shirt buttoned up and his bow tie on. "Hi, Thad." I guessed he wasn't avoiding me if he was at my desk.

He looked up from the note he was writing. "Hey."

I eased into my office and sat down in my client chair. "How was your day off?"

"It's nine-thirty. You're just getting in?"

"I worked from home this morning. Visited a potential client on the way here. Looking good." I was such a liar, and I hated it.

"You left early yesterday."

I narrowed my eyes. "Spying on me?"

"It's my job. I'm your boss." He sighed and leaned back. "Listen, I'm sorry about Sunday night. I got way out of line." His cheeks turned pink, as if he was embarrassed.

"It's totally cool," I said. "It was fun hanging out with you."

He cleared his throat. "About when we were dancing . . ."

"Nothing happened." How could I have been thinking about having an affair with Thad? He was my boss. He didn't know me. Not like Greg did. I wanted someone who knew me. Really knew me.

So I guess that was my answer, then. I wanted Greg. Relief, excitement and fear rushed through me.

He lifted a brow. "Something almost happened."

I felt my cheeks heat up. "Yeah."

"Regrets?"

I met his gaze and realized he really was cute. Regrets that we'd crossed a line with all the dance-floor fondling? Regrets that we'd gotten interrupted? Regrets which way? "I have no regrets."

He nodded, and I couldn't tell how he interpreted my reply. "All right, then. We're cool?"

"Very cool." But cool in what way? This conversation was too cryptic to be useful.

"Yeah. So. Work on your hours, okay? My boss was the one who told me you left early yesterday. She wants to see your loan documents when you turn them in, and she wants an accounting of your hours." He stood up. "Help me out, Paris."

"I'm on it."

He paused in the door. "Want to go for a run this weekend?"

"A run?"

"Just a run."

"Maybe."

215

He nodded. "We'll be in touch."

"Right."

I watched him walk out the door and had no idea what we'd just agreed upon.

I met the gang at PWJ at eight. They were all there, including Lindsey and Greg. My stomach did a little jiggle when Greg walked in and brushed against my shoulder as he passed me.

I handed out the designs I'd spent all night working on. They were every bit as good as the shoes we'd seen yesterday. I'd even surprised myself. Did I rock or what?

"What's this?" Will asked.

"Design boards."

"For what?"

"Shoes."

Greg gave me a wink as he leaned over Jodi's shoulder to look at her stack.

Will frowned and so did Jodi. Greg looked thoughtful. Lindsey was studying me, not the designs.

Finally Will looked up. "I don't get it."

"Dress shoes. We'll put Sfoam in dress shoes, manufacture them, and sell them to get a cash influx while we work on the technicalities of Sfoam in running shoes. It's what you guys wanted, right?"

Will set down his board. "You want to manufacture dress shoes?"

"Yes."

"Why not sell Sfoam to a dress shoe company?"

"Because then we'll lose the rights to it. We won't be able to make running shoes."

Jodi sighed and set down her boards. She looked at Lindsey, then down at her hands.

"What's wrong?" I asked.

Silence.

I was getting really tired of these silences. Why weren't they excited? This is what they wanted, right?

Then they all exchanged glances.

"Um, hello? What's with you guys?"

Lindsey set down the board and folded her hands across the table. "This is the deal, sweetie. Your drawings are . . . well . . . they aren't so good."

"They what?"

"These designs aren't going to get you any sales. Not even close."

"I knew I'm not the best artist, but they're innovative and stylish. . . ."

Lindsey set her hand on my shoulder. "Paris, hon, I love you, but you're a total fashion flop. These are too ordinary. They'd never sell in the exclusive stores. There's a reason those designers make a lot of money. It's not just the materials they use. They're brilliant with their vision." She patted my arm. "You aren't."

"But . . ."

Will interrupted. "I'm really glad you're willing to go for other uses for Sfoam. But maybe you should be thinking about trying to license the technology to a shoe company. Even if you had great designs, it'll take a while to make any money from it."

"But . . ."

"We could try to limit the license for use only in dress shoes," Lindsey said. "But it probably wouldn't work. We have to count on giving up all our rights."

"Or hire a new designer," Jodi said. "Someone with talent. Someone with a name."

Will shook his head. "No. This all is taking too long.

Either we sell Sfoam to a dress shoe company or I'm out. I need to get out."

"Why do you need to get out so badly?" I asked. "Sure, Jodi knows, but how about enlightening the rest of us." Oops. Was my sarcasm too obvious? Darn it.

He met my gaze. "Later."

Later? That didn't sound good. "I want to know." I was still mad at him, remember? "And do you have a date with She-bitch later? You couldn't keep her waiting, I'm sure."

He narrowed his eyes. "We'll talk after this. Alone."

"About your need for money? Did you knock her up or something?"

"Paris!" Lindsey gently hit my shoulder. "Chill."

I pressed my lips together, my gut dropping ever so slightly. I had a bad feeling about what Will wanted to talk about, especially with Jodi suddenly getting interested in picking lint off her jeans. What did Jodi know that I didn't? And why was I getting so cranky about it? I didn't own Will. He didn't owe me explanations.

"So, are we all agreed that manufacturing our own dress shoes is a bad idea?" Jodi said.

Everyone nodded. Except me. Even Greg nodded. I looked at him. "You're not supposed to vote."

He laid his hand over mine. "This process is gradual, hon. Trial and error. I hadn't thought through the designer shoe angle. It's a tough market. I think licensing is best. You can still work on running shoe ideas after you get some money coming in."

Will snorted and muttered, "Hon," under his breath.

Yeah, I'd noticed it too. Made my belly go all jiggly.

Greg kept his hand over mine, rubbing gently as if to take the sting out of his words. He addressed the whole group. "So, I'm thinking that our next step is to make a presentation to footwear companies who specialize in dress shoes." He looked at Lindsey. "Can you draw up a sample licensing agreement? Try to limit it to use in dress shoes only."

I sank back in my chair, watching as Jodi collected my design boards and put them in the trash. The trash. I'd spent all night working on those. And now my friends thought they belonged in the trash. And they were planning to sell Sfoam for dress shoes. Dress shoes. My dream. Seth's dream. It was all going to amount to nothing but dress shoes.

I felt someone watching me, and I looked up to find Will looking at me. He gave me a sad smile and my heart got tight. Greg might say he really knew me, but it was clear from the look on Will's face that he actually felt the pain I was going through right now. Greg, on the other hand, was actively leading the discussion about how best to present Sfoam. Whether to do some tester research first. He didn't seem too worried about me.

But that's what I'd asked for, right? For no one to take care of me and defend me. I wanted to take care of myself, right?

I spent the rest of the meeting trying to figure out what I was doing wrong. Why did it feel as if every decision I made ended up with me questioning myself and feeling worse than I had before?

I don't even know what they decided.

They didn't need my input.

And I could tell they didn't want it.

It was if they'd finally wrested control of PWJ away from me, and they were afraid to give it back.

And I was too tired to fight for it.

* * *

Greg followed me home from the meeting.

I didn't realize it until I parked my car and he parked his very expensive little convertible next to me.

The value of my car was about equal to the value of his floor mats.

He met me at my rear bumper. "Tough day at the office, huh?"

I nodded and headed into my building. I wasn't in the mood to talk about it. He'd let me down, changing his mind after talking me into making dress shoes.

He was the old Greg, and I didn't trust him.

He fell into step beside me. "I know how hard it is for you. But you can work on the running shoes afterwards."

"Whatever." I shoved my key into the lock and walked inside. I didn't wait for him, but he caught the door before it closed and followed me inside, up the stairs and into my condo.

I kicked off my shoes, walked over to the couch and sat down. Tonight was the kind of night where I'd watch television without ever turning it on.

The couch moved under his weight. His arm slid behind me, and his fingers started massaging my neck. "You all right?"

"No."

"Are you mad at me?" He turned me so my back was facing him, giving him full access for his massage.

"Last night you told me to design the shoes. Today you change your mind in front of everyone. How could you do that?"

He sighed and dug his fingers into my back. "I'm really sorry. I didn't realize you'd see it that way."

"How else would I see it?"

"That I love you and I'm trying to help you find a way

to save your company in whatever way I can. I gave you bad advice last night, and it would have been wrong if I hadn't corrected it."

Oh.

Did he just say he loved me?

Did he mean it? Really mean it, in the way I'd dreamed of for so long?

"Still mad?"

I sighed. "I guess not. I mean, this is it, right? This is the way it has to be." I couldn't design shoes. And we had to get money. Had to.

He leaned forward, his breath hot on my neck. "You'll get your running shoe, hon. This comes first. That's all."

I nodded. "I was thinking of talking to Orpheus about the stability problem. Maybe he has some ideas for plates—"

"We have to work on the new proposal first. There's time for the running shoe stuff later." He ran his fingers through my hair. "I know you did the presentations yourself last time, but I'd like to help. I've done a lot of them. I know some tricks."

I chewed my lower lip. PWJ was mine. I ran the business side while Jodi and Will did the technical stuff.

I didn't want to let go.

I didn't want to take direction from somewhere else.

I didn't want to lose the focus I'd worked so hard on.

I didn't want to make the presentations a team effort.

But I didn't want to fail either.

I hadn't done so well on my own, had I?

He kissed the nape of my neck. "Paris? You there?"

I sighed. "Yeah."

He gently clasped my shoulders and turned me to face

him. "I know you're upset about this redirection of focus. I understand what running means to you, don't I?"

"So you say."

"More than anyone?"

"Maybe." I would have agreed before that night's meeting. It had seemed as if Will was the only one there who'd really known what I was feeling. Not that he'd said anything to stop everyone else. He was leaving it to me, and I'd sat there in silence. Because I was a wimp, or because I knew they were actually right?

Greg kissed the tip of my nose. "Don't worry, hon. It'll work out. Someday you'll have those running shoes. In the meantime, we'll get rich first."

"You already are rich."

"You can never have enough money." He put his hands on either side of my face. "I love you, Paris McFee."

"My name isn't McFee." *And I don't want to make dress shoes.*

"You'll always be a McFee in my mind." And then he kissed me. My heart jumped, and I wanted to kiss him back. His kiss felt like coming home after years of being on the run. "Let me help you with the presentations, hon." He kissed me again. I sat on my hands to keep from grabbing his shirtfront. I didn't want to need him. To trust him. To believe in him. But I did. "I'm really good at persuading people of things," he said. "It's my specialty."

I frowned. "Is that why you're kissing me? Because you're trying to get me to agree so you can make more money?" I was clutching at straws, but I was desperate.

He immediately pulled back, his elegant eyebrows furrowed into a frown. "They're totally separate. I love you because you're you. Because of your dreams and our bond and everything that brings us together. Even if you refuse to go with the dress shoes and send the company into bankruptcy, I'll still want to wake up naked with you every day for the rest of my life."

I blinked. "The rest . . ." A little noise popped out of the back of my throat, and I felt the last bit of resistance wash away. He wanted me forever—only this time, he meant it.

It was what I'd wanted ever since he left. And now he was offering it to me. The man I'd loved finally loved me back. Why was I so upset about how he'd run the PWJ meeting? He was only trying to do right by me and the company, right?

"Yes." He moved closer again and kissed me. Heart-melting. "Jodi told me how you won't commit to anyone. I know you're gun-shy, and that's okay." He kissed both cheekbones and then my forehead. "I'll wait." He grinned. "It's the least I can do, since it's my fault in the first place."

I closed my eyes and tilted my head back as he trailed his lips down my neck. "What about your ex-wife? The one who broke your heart?" I clutched at his shoulder, unwilling (or unable?) to let go. "What about her?"

"What about her? She was part of my healing process, like Will was yours. They were necessary for us to get where we are today." He kissed the top of my breast, at the edge of my V-necked T-shirt. "Be with me, Paris. Like it once was."

I opened my eyes and looked into the gaze of the man I'd loved so hard for so long. The man who was saving my business. Giving me a chance at my dream, even if it was the long road. The man who truly understood why I was the way I was.

He was waiting. For me. Finally.

I reached up, wrapped my arms around his neck and pulled him down on top of me.

Tonight nothing would come between us.

NINETEEN

I dreamed of Seth that night. Of the day Greg, Seth and I had rented mopeds and taken them to the beach in Maine. We'd spent the day lying in the sun and drinking wine coolers and the night huddled up in a big pile under blankets on the beach, watching the stars. Listening to the ocean. Snuggling. Two boys, one girl, no sex. A Paris sandwich, we'd called it.

I woke up to a familiar scent that sent warmth and safety through my soul.

I woke up to a heavy arm around me.

To the heat from another body pressed up against my back, the kind of heat that only skin-to-skin contact can generate.

Greg.

I smiled and snuggled tighter against him as he mumbled my name and nuzzled my hair.

It had been the right decision.

And to think I'd almost ended up with Thad, certain I wanted someone who had nothing to do with my past. I'd been wrong. I needed someone who had everything to do with my past.

A light knock echoed from the front of my condo.

I frowned and glanced at the clock by my bed. It wasn't even seven on a Wednesday morning. Who could possibly be there?

"Ignore them," Greg mumbled. "Stay here with me, McFee."

I grinned. "Works for me. But my name isn't McFee." Once we'd gotten hitched, Greg had gotten a kick out of the fact that I had the same last name as he did. McFee had become his pet name for me.

It didn't feel as if it fit anymore. I mean, he fit, but it was different now. I wasn't Paris McFee, and I didn't think I'd ever feel as if I was.

Then I heard keys jingle and the door open. "Paris? Are you here?"

Oh, shit. Will.

I threw back the covers. "I'll be right out!"

Greg propped himself up on his elbow while he watched me throw on a T-shirt and sweats. "You'll be getting that key back from him, won't you?"

"All my friends have keys." I glanced at myself in the mirror. Crud. I looked awful.

"He's an ex-lover, not a friend. Take the key."

I shot him a look as I grabbed the doorknob. "You don't control my life, Greg."

His face immediately softened. "I'm not trying to control it. I'm just making suggestions. Sorry."

"It's okay." I pointed at him. "Stay in here."

He lifted a brow. "Why?"

"Because I asked you to."

I left while he was still staring at me, shutting the door

carefully behind me. Will was sitting at my kitchen table, helping himself to a bowl of cereal as he'd done so many times in the past. "Hey," I said.

He grinned. "Nice bed-head."

"Thanks." I eased into the seat across from him, suddenly very aware of the fact that I wasn't wearing a bra under my T-shirt. Yeah, he'd seen me in far less many times, but it felt different now. "So what's up?"

"About last night. At the offices. You okay?"

I shrugged. "Fine."

"No, you're not." He leaned forward. "Listen, I know you don't want to do dress shoes. If I didn't need the money, I'd tell you to screw the idea and keep on with your dream. But I can't."

I tried to untangle my hair with my fingers. "Why do you need the money?" I felt sort of bad about the knocked-up remark. Maybe I should apologize, I thought. I was mad at him, but he was still my friend, even if we hadn't been too friendly lately. "Sorry about the comment I made last night. It was unnecessary."

He shrugged. "No big deal. You were stressed. It's okay."

I smiled. "Thanks."

He smiled back, and I felt better. "So, um . . ." He set down his spoon. "I've decided to go to medical school."

"Medical school? Are you serious?"

He grinned. "Yeah."

"That's so awesome! You're going to be a doctor?"

"I want to do cancer research. Experimental treatments. Forward-thinking kind of stuff." There was a fire in his eyes I hadn't seen before. "That's what I'd really like to do. Innovative, cutting-edge treatments. Research to make a difference."

"Will! That's so cool!" I jumped up and hugged him. "I'm so excited you figured out what you want to do with your life! You'll make a great doctor. You're so brilliant and caring and dedicated." I sat back down, my heart nearly bursting with pride. "That's incredible. I'm so thrilled for you."

His smile reached his ears, he looked so happy. "I'm so glad you're okay with it. I wasn't sure if you would be."

"Why wouldn't I be? It's the best thing in the world to realize what your dream is and go after it." I sighed again, still grinning. I was so proud of him. "This is great."

"Well, I thought maybe you'd be mad because I won't be able to help out with PWJ anymore."

My smile dropped off my face. I hadn't thought about that. "Oh." *Oh.*

"I didn't want to tell you, because I knew I couldn't keep working on Sfoam and go to med school at the same time. I didn't want to let you down." He shrugged. "But school starts at the end of August, so I had to tell you now." He leaned across the table and took my hand. "I'm so sorry to let you down, Paris. I really am. If there was any way I could do both, I would, but I have to do this for myself. Medical school's what I want to do."

"I understand." I did. I knew what it was like to have a dream. He had to follow it. But if he was starting school in August, that meant he'd already taken the GMATs and had interviews and everything. How had I not known about it? Was I that self-obsessed I hadn't even noticed him redirecting his entire life? "How long have you known?"

"I've been thinking about becoming a doctor for a while. I mean, I love the research I do, but I don't want to do it forever. So I started considering other careers in the science field. Medicine seems like a good fit."

"Wow." I leaned back in my chair and studied Will's happy face. "I had no idea." How could I have had no idea? We'd been best friends for a long time. "This is your dream, and you were afraid to tell me?"

"Well, not afraid. I just didn't want to upset you."

I tried to shake off the need to cry. "Am I so obsessed with PWJ that you thought I couldn't be happy for my best friend?" God, I was a horrible person. He'd told Jodi instead of me, because I wasn't a good enough friend.

He took my hand. "It's not that. I was just trying to protect you."

I blinked hard and nodded. "I'm happy for you. I just wish you'd told me. I wish you'd felt you could tell me."

"I'm sorry."

We were silent for a moment; then I forced a smile on my face. "So you're going this fall?"

"Yep. School starts in a few weeks."

A few weeks? He was leaving Sfoam in a few weeks? I tried not to panic. "What school? Where are you going?"

"Stanford."

"Wow. Stanford. That's an amazing school." And it was in California. Three thousand miles away. My Will. Leaving PWJ. Leaving me. *Don't cry. Be happy for him. Prove you're the friend you claimed to be.*

He nodded. "I'm still wait-listed at Harvard, but Stanford is my first choice. It has some programs I'm really interested in."

I managed a bright smile. "Two great schools. I'm so impressed."

He grinned. "When we were still dating, I was holding

229

out for Harvard. But now that we're not . . . there's no real reason for me to hang around." He frowned. "Honestly I would have been disappointed with myself if I'd chosen Harvard just to stay around for us. We weren't going anywhere, but this is my future."

I let my breath out in a long sigh. "Wow." So it wouldn't have mattered if we'd still been dating. Because that's all it had been. Casual dating. You didn't select your med school based on the city you were having sex in. We simply were never that serious. I mean, I'd known it, but a part of me had always felt comfortable with Will, felt I could have him if I wanted. Guess what? I was wrong. He didn't want me. Hadn't then. Didn't now. Wow. I was a little emotional right now.

He peered at me. "Are you upset?"

I shrugged. "A little. I'll miss you. But I'm so happy for you that it doesn't matter."

"Are you mad at me?"

I met his gaze. I wanted to be mad, but how could I? How could I fault him for following his own dream? And he was right. He had no obligation to me or to PWJ. I finally shook my head. "I wish you'd told me before, but I guess that's my fault, not yours."

His whole body relaxed and the light shone from his eyes. The passion for his new future. Which didn't include me. "Thank God. I was so worried. Jodi said you'd be fine, but I didn't believe her."

Jodi again. "Why'd you confide in her?" What was it about Jodi that made these men trust her the way they didn't trust me? Was I really that messed up?

"I had to tell someone, and I knew my secret would be safe with her."

"How did you know she'd keep your confidence?" Why

hadn't she told me? Lindsey, Jodi and I always put each other first.

"Because she owes me."

I tilted my head. "How so?"

"I've kept a secret of hers for a long time, so I knew she'd hold mine."

Another secret I wasn't privy to? "What secret?"

He shook his head. "Nope. You'll have to ask her."

"Do I know it?"

He hesitated. "No."

"Would I care?"

"Ask her. I'm not getting in the middle." He met my gaze, and I knew he believed I would care very much. My gut tightened. I was really tired of secrets.

"You already brought it up. Finish it."

"I'm moving to California in three weeks. I'm flying out there this weekend to look for apartments."

Well, that was certainly an effective change of subject. I pressed my lips together. "That soon?"

He held out his hands and I put mine in them. "I'll miss you," he said.

"I'll miss you too. A lot." God, life was going to be weird without Will around. "Who else is going to stay up and watch Nick at Nite with me?"

He grinned. "And burn the popcorn?"

I laughed. "You're the only person I know who has a zero success rate in popping microwave popcorn."

"It's because I'm distracted by your witty conversation and hot rack," he said. "I can't think straight when I'm around you."

"And who's going to keep me from being too serious and morose? You're the only one who has kept me sane for the last five years."

His grin faded and he took my hand. "I'll have a cell phone. You can call me anytime."

I nodded. "But it won't be the same as crawling into your lap and having you wrestle me out of my bad mood."

He rubbed his thumb over the back of my hand. "Even if I was still here, I don't know how much we'd be doing that anymore."

"I miss it."

He looked up at me. "Miss what?"

"You touching me. You being around all the time. Our bond."

His grip tightened around my hand. "I miss you too."

For a long moment, we stared at each other. For a split second, I wondered if our relationship could have ever developed into something more serious.

He cleared his throat. "I'm leaving."

I nodded. "Yeah."

Another long moment of silence. What if I told him I didn't want him to leave? What if I asked him to go to Harvard? But I couldn't. You didn't ask that of someone who was your friend and former lover. It simply wasn't fair.

"What are you going to do about PWJ?" he asked finally. "I'd love the money from the sale of the technology, but I'm already doing the paperwork for loans. If you don't want to sell out for dress shoes, don't do it. Be true to your dreams, Paris. I'll find a way to get by. I can't put in any more money, but even though I won't be here to help you with PWJ, that shouldn't stop you. You can call me anytime and . . ."

"Good morning, Will."

I cringed at the sound of Greg's voice. Will's gaze

flicked over my shoulder. He looked surprised for an instant; then his face closed off. "Is that how it is?" His voice was low, for my ears only.

"She still loves me." Greg walked into the kitchen, wearing only his boxers. Silk, by the way. I was way too embarrassed to enjoy the sight of his naked chest, not with Will sitting there. "Mine now, Will."

Will's gaze narrowed and he pulled his hands away from mine. "She belongs to herself."

"And me."

Will glanced at me. "You're taking that?"

I slanted a look at Greg. "I'm not yours."

"Sure you are. Always were." Greg pulled out a chair, flipped it around, and straddled the seat backwards. "And to answer your question, we're going forward with the licensing of Sfoam to a dress shoe company. You'll have your money."

Will's gaze flickered between us. "Don't do it for me."

"I'm not. I'm doing it for me," Greg said. "And for Paris. She deserves to have some money."

"She deserves what she wants," Will said. "And it's not money."

"I'm the one who knows her," Greg said. "Not you. You were a filler, and you've done your job."

"Greg." I smacked his arm. "Don't be an ass. Will's my friend. He was never a filler. I love him."

"He's your ex-lover who's bailing on PWJ when you need him. Doesn't sound too loyal to me." He gave me a cool look. "And you don't love him. Not like you love me."

Will shoved his chair back. "I'm outta here."

I hit Greg in the head with the cereal box and followed Will into the corridor outside my condo. "I'm sorry, Will."

He pulled the front door shut behind me, his eyes blazing. "Don't fall for him again, Paris. Just don't do it."

"It's not that simple."

"He's a jerk. He's trying to control you and PWJ."

"Do you really think I'm going to let him?"

"He thinks you will. He's falling back into his old ways of controlling you, and you're letting him. He hasn't changed."

"How do you know? You didn't even know him back then."

He snorted. "I know enough. He said he owned you, and you didn't stop him. What's up with that? If I so much as indicated that we were dating, you were pissed at me for a week."

"I corrected him."

"Hah. Hardly." Then his eyes darkened. "Or is that the difference? With him you're ready to be owned?"

"I will never be owned, and don't be a jerk. Can't you be happy? He was my true love and now he's back. He cares about me. He knows me. It feels good."

"Does it?"

"Yes." My voice held a conviction I didn't feel in my soul. I couldn't even think about Greg right now. I was too upset over the thought that Will was leaving. Possibly forever.

His eyes were glittering. "Then I'm glad for you. I hope it works." He paused. "Ask Jodi her little secret. You need to know."

"What secret?"

"I'll see you later." And he left me standing in the hall. Left me with a big hole in my heart.

He was leaving. Forever. And I might never see him

again once he was gone. Not if we weren't even friends anymore.

I couldn't stop the tears from spilling over my cheeks.

The door opened behind me. "Want some breakfast before you go to work?"

I took a deep breath and turned to Greg. "Why did you have to be such a jerk to him? He's one of my best friends, and he deserves respect."

"I'm sorry." Greg brushed his finger over the tears on my cheeks. "Come back inside before the neighbors realize there's a show going on."

I let him take my wrist and pull me back into the condo. "I'm not the same person I used to be. You can't walk all over me and treat my friends badly."

"In some ways you're the same. In some you aren't. It's a good combination." He dumped Will's cereal bowl and put it in the dishwasher. It was the first domestic task I'd ever seen him do. "I've changed too."

He searched various cabinets, found the necessary items and started the coffeemaker. Then he folded his arms over his chest and leaned against the counter. "I'm not trying to own you. If it came out that way, I'm sorry. I felt threatened by Will's presence. Maybe I pushed too hard. When I walked in and saw your hands in his . . ." He shrugged. "It sort of threw me. I just got you back. I don't want to lose you already."

"You don't have me, Greg. No one has me."

He studied me. "Someone can have you without it affecting your independence or your freedom. It's not a bad thing."

I shrugged. "Maybe." That sounded like the advice my mom would give me now that she'd lost her mind.

He levered himself off the counter and walked over to me. He slipped his hands around my waist and tugged me against him. After a moment, I relaxed and rested my head against his chest. I closed my eyes and inhaled his familiar scent.

He kissed the top of my head and held me. "I'm sorry for being an ass."

I smiled into his chest. "Which time?"

"All of them. Including five minutes ago." He pulled back so he could look at me. "This isn't easy for me, either. I don't want to screw up again. I'm trying to do it right." His fingers tightened around me. "I'm sorry for killing Seth. I'm sorry for destroying your running career. I have to live with that forever. I'll never forgive myself."

I laid my hands on his rough cheeks. The thick stubble was the first sign of anything less than perfect I'd seen on him since he'd gotten back. A few whiskers made him human. "We were all stupid back then."

"But I was driving. It's my fault."

It occurred to me then that maybe he really hadn't left because he hadn't loved me. That maybe he'd had issues he'd had to deal with. Issues that were even deeper than mine. I took his hands. I couldn't say I forgave him. I couldn't take away the responsibility. But I could show him it didn't matter. Not anymore. "I'm going to take a shower. Want to join me?"

His kiss was his answer.

TWENTY

The next evening, I found Jodi hunched over Orpheus's workbench in the back of the lab. And to my amazement the fine owner of our new office space seemed to be milling around as well. Since when did Orpheus stay until ten o'clock at night? I'd thought he bailed at six. "Hi, Orpheus."

He looked up. "How is the designer shoe business going?"

An actual greeting from Mr. Antisocial caught me by surprise, and it took me a moment to form a response. "Um, not so hot."

"Paris!" Jodi glanced up. "You have to see this!"

I sidled past Orpheus and went over to Jodi, trying to figure out how I was going to bring up the subject of her little secret and all the other machinations she'd been operating of late.

I forgot everything when I saw what she was working on. "My designs?"

She bobbed her head enthusiastically. "After everyone

went home last night, I pulled them out and took another look. Then I researched some styles on the Internet, and I realized you had some interesting ideas. I mean, yeah, I'm not into running shoes, but fancy shoes . . . Well, they're kind of fun." She held up the basic model of a dress shoe. "So I was sort of playing with the idea, trying to put one together to check out the basic structure. I think you're onto something. I think . . ."

"What is that monstrosity?"

We both glanced up to find Orpheus leaning over our table. "They're women's shoes," I said. "Designer ones."

"Designer my ass. They suck."

I rolled my eyes at Jodi. "Orpheus, you're not exactly the fashion king. So—"

He yanked one of my drawings off the table and held it up. "See that curve? That's completely incorrect for a woman's foot. It'll hit at the wrong place and make that bone on the top of her foot stick out. And this heel? Are you serious? It's last season's style. You need to make it flare out like this." He grabbed a marker and drew over my picture. "And the beads will fall wrong if you leave them there." He scribbled new ones. "See? If you place them here, then they move with the foot instead of working against it. And this way they'll elongate the leg instead of drawing the eye to the beads and making the shoe appear clunky." He shot us a disdainful look. "Women don't like their legs or feet to look fat."

"Yeah—"

"And the toebox is the wrong shape. That pointed thing? It only works if it fits with the rest of the shoe. The way you did it makes it look like someone stuck an arrow on the end of a shoe. It has to blend like this." He fell silent while he sketched.

I leaned closer and Jodi did the same. Before our eyes, my design was transformed into a classy, stylish high-heeled shoe.

Orpheus finished and held up the drawing. "Doesn't that look better? Surely even you two can see the difference?"

I nodded. "Oh yes."

"Definitely," Jodi said.

I looked at Jodi. "Are you thinking what I'm thinking?

"Without a doubt."

We both looked at Orpheus, whose smug mug faded under our scrutiny. "What?"

"Didn't realize you knew how to make good-looking shoes," I said.

He shrugged and tossed the board on the table. "Just because I make ugly shoes doesn't mean that's all I can do. I inherited the business, and I stay loyal to the direction my grandpappy and daddy put forth. My customers value function over form, and I cater to them."

Jodi and I followed him as he eased back across the lab toward his riveting machine. "How do you know about fashion?" I asked. "You don't seem like the fashion type."

"Just do." He bent over and focused on the ugly black shoe he was working on.

"Do you go to fashion shows?" Jodi asked.

"Go away. I'm working."

I stuck my face up close to his. "You're a designer."

He glared at me. "Back off."

"Will you design shoes for us?"

"No. Go away."

"Imagine going into an upscale store and seeing women fight over your designs. We'll call them Orpheus. That has a ring to it, don't you think?"

Jodi nodded. "Definitely. Everyone will want their own Orpheus."

He finally groaned and looked up. "I make orthopedic shoes. I'm not a designer. I would never be a designer."

"Why not?" I perched on the edge of his machine, rendering it useless unless he wanted to rivet my butt.

"Milkhausen men make orthopedic shoes. It's what we do." He cleared his throat. "No Milkhausen man would design ladies' shoes. Ever."

Jodi and I exchanged glances. "You've been making orthopedic shoes for thirty years, right?"

"Thirty-two. Get out of my way."

"Don't you think you've paid your dues? Why not try to design? We won't tell anyone."

Orpheus's lip twitched. Had I hooked him with the promise of anonymity?

"We won't even put your name on them," I said. "You'll be the mystery designer. Only Jodi and I will know. It'll be a secret."

He looked at me.

Then he looked at Jodi.

I could see the gleam in his eyes.

"I don't like drawing pretty things," he said.

"Of course not."

"I don't even like drawing."

"I didn't think you did."

He frowned. "But you guys are a total loss when it comes to making shoes."

I grinned. "That we are."

"So I guess I could help you."

"Help us. Please."

"I'd help you make the shoes. Dress shoes. Because you'll pay me."

"A cut of the profits is all we can afford right now."

"Fine." He took out a rag and wiped his forehead. "And you do the designs."

I narrowed my eyes. "How about I work on them in my off time, when no one is around? Like maybe I leave the design boards here and pick them up later."

He studied me. Looked at Jodi. We gave him our "we can keep a secret" smiles.

Finally he nodded. "I'll do it for the money."

"For the money," I agreed.

He shoved back from the riveting machine and walked over to the design boards. "Maybe I'll take a look at these. Make some changes so they're a better-quality shoe." He glared at us. "Not for fashion reasons. Just because you two don't know shit about making shoes. The design needs to be sound from a biomechanical perspective."

"Of course."

He tucked them under his arm. "I'm going home. I'll drop these off tomorrow. Structurally they'll be perfect."

He gave us a final hostile glare, then stormed out, the design boards clutched to his chest.

The door slammed shut behind him, and Jodi and I looked at each other.

"Where do you think he got that talent?" Jodi asked.

"Years of working in shoes. He's brilliant."

"But fashion?"

"I don't think he'll ever tell us. He won't even admit it."

"Still. He's amazing."

I grinned. "He is, isn't he?" For the first time ever, I was starting to feel a gleam of excitement about the dress shoe angle. If we could keep Sfoam in-house, then I didn't risk losing out on the running-shoe technology. And I couldn't deny the swell of excitement I'd felt when

I saw Orpheus create something so beautiful. "I think we should hold off on trying to license Sfoam to a dress shoe company. Let's see what he comes up with."

Jodi grinned. "I agree."

We gave each other a high five and went out to celebrate.

I wasn't in the mood to bring up her secret.

Not tonight.

My cell phone rang as I drove home. "It's Mom," she announced when I picked up.

"Mom." Wow. I hadn't thought about her in days. It was almost one, but we often talked at that hour. It wasn't as if either of us would be sleeping when we had work to do. "What's up? How's the ex-con?"

She cleared her throat. "Yes, well, we need to talk."

I frowned as I cut through a gas station to avoid a red light. "Yeah, we do. Want to meet for lunch?" Did I have stuff to tell her or what? "There's so much going on in my life."

"I got married tonight."

I almost hit a fire hydrant standing rudely in my way. "What?"

"Here, talk to him." There was a scuffle and then a man's voice came on the phone. "Paris?"

"Who is this?"

"Zach Middleton. We met at your mom's place last week."

The ex-con serial killer?

"I want you to know that I love your mother and I will do right by her."

I pulled the phone away from my ear and stared at it. The phone. Not my ear. Were they kidding?

I put the phone back.

". . . and I know you already have a dad and I won't try to replace him, but I will love you like my own daughter and . . ."

Please. This was disgusting. He was totally up to no good. Manipulating son of a bitch. "Can you put my mom on?"

"Sure." A little more shuffling and then my mom chirped, "Isn't he wonderful?"

"Exactly how many days have you known him?"

"I feel like it's been my whole life. I've been waiting for this forever. It's so wonderful."

"Did you sign a prenup?"

"Of course I did."

"You did?" If he didn't want her money, what was he after?

"When can you meet for dinner? I want us to start to be a family."

"A family? With a serial killer you just met? Have you lost your mind?"

Silence.

Uh-oh.

"Paris Marie Jackson. This is the man I love. I expect you to treat him well and welcome him to our family. I will tolerate nothing less from you."

Oh, wow. Fine, then. I guess I knew where I stood. "Fine. He's welcome." Until I found out his secret, of course. No way was I going to let another man use marriage to destroy a Jackson woman.

"Don't be sarcastic with me, young lady . . ." There was a lot of muffled noise, and then Zach came back on the phone. "I know this is difficult for you, Paris, but I'm not going anywhere. We'll work through this. I've been looking for your mother my whole life, and I'm the luckiest man ever to have found her. Come to dinner at her condo a week from Sunday, after we return from our honeymoon. We'll start to get to know each other."

"Honeymoon?" My mom on a honeymoon? That was so against the natural order of things.

"Yes, honeymoon," Zach said. "It's very important to your mom that you support our marriage. I'll do my best, but you need to meet me halfway."

"Yeah, sure, whatever you say, Zach." Since when had my mom let a man fight her battles for her? Since when had she wanted to get married? Since when had she believed love was anything more than a woman's excuse not to take responsibility for her own future? "Can you please put my mother back on?"

Another round of phone tag, and then my mom was on the line again. "I love you, but I love Zach as well. I need both of you in my life."

"If you need me so badly, why did you get married without telling me?"

"Because I didn't want to give you the chance to talk me out of it. This is my life, my choices, and I'm happy. But it won't be complete unless you're part of it."

Crap. I could hear the tears in her voice. What kind of a bitch was I to make her cry when she'd been so happy? "Fine. I'll be there."

"Thank you."

"I look forward to getting to know you better, Paris," Zach said. What, were they sharing the phone or something? Too cute. "See you next weekend."

"Can't wait. Have a great time on your honeymoon." I really tried not to sound sarcastic, but I wasn't sure I'd managed. I hung up the phone and realized I'd driven to Will's house.

Past one in the morning, and I was sitting in my car outside Will's ready to cry because my mom had left me.

Why hadn't I driven to Greg's?

Well, for one, I didn't know where he lived. Was that weird? I was sleeping with him and letting him call me McFee (well, not really), and I didn't even know where he was staying while he was in town?

But I could call him on his cell.

I was in danger of having a major meltdown. My mom, my best friend, my other half, had gone and gotten herself hitched, flying in the face of everything she'd preached my whole life. Leaving me on my own.

As strong as I was (yeah, right), I needed a little help on this one.

I stared moodily at Will's building. Why had I driven here? I could have gone to Jodi's. Or Lindsey's.

But I was here.

And now I was going to go home. Maybe Greg was there waiting for me. Except he didn't have a key. I should get my key back from Will.

A light knock on my window scared the crap out of me. I screamed, jumped sideways, nearly decapitated myself on the seatbelt and then passed out.

Well, almost.

After I regained function in my body and got my pepper spray out of my purse, I looked out the window.

Will waved at me. Relief and happiness surged through me. I was so glad to see him. I rolled down the window. "Hi."

He frowned. "What's wrong? You look upset."

245

I saw a leggy blonde slide out of the shadows and let herself into his building. My gut dropped. "Are you sleeping with She-bitch again? Because I don't think you should. I mean, you're leaving and everything. Wouldn't be fair to do to her." Oh my God. He was totally back together with her. Pain slammed into my chest and I hunched over. I couldn't deal with this right now. I really couldn't.

His frown deepened. "What happened?"

"Why would you think anything happened? I'm fine." I had to get away. I couldn't cope with She-bitch in Will's life. "I have go." I fumbled for my keys to turn the car back on, but I couldn't seem to make my fingers work.

He squatted and rested his forearms on my car door. "Why won't you talk to me?"

Why indeed? "Maybe because you're leaving and I have to figure out how to get along without you." Yes, that was it. It had nothing to do with the fact that at this very moment, She-bitch was on her way up to Will's apartment to get naked and play with strawberries and chocolate. I was the one he was supposed to do that with. Had he taught her my games? "Did you give her a key?" I sounded way too whiny on that question.

"You're sitting in front of my building at one o'clock in the morning. Something's wrong. What is it?" Understanding and sympathy lit his features. "Did you talk to Jodi?"

"No. Yes. Well, not about that." I gripped the steering wheel. "You know what? Forget it. I shouldn't have come. You have company."

He reached inside and pulled my keys out of the ignition. "You're more important."

I stared at the dashboard, and my lower lip started to

tremble. Why was I so upset? It wasn't as if anything really bad had happened. So my mom had gotten married. Without telling me. So she had a new best friend. So she'd violated every pact we'd ever made. Why should that upset me? It wasn't as if I needed her anymore. I mean, my life was great and I didn't even see her that much anymore. "Things are really looking up for PWJ."

The tears started falling, and I sniffled. "It turns out Orpheus has an amazing flair for fashion. He's going to design some dress shoes for us and we're going to make some samples. Try to manufacture them."

I started crying harder and used my T-shirt to wipe my eyes. "I'm really excited about it. It's going to be really fun and I'm going to learn a lot and then we won't have to sell the technology so I can do the running shoes and stuff." I inhaled in a heaving sob. "So, basically, it's just really good news and I'm thrilled and I thought you should know. We won't ask you for any more money, but you'll get income and stuff. So it's great news." I stopped to bawl really hard for a minute. "So that's what I wanted to tell you. Drink some champagne. It's really great news. Do you have any tissues?"

"There's some in your glove box."

"There is?" I fumbled around and found a sleeve of pink Kleenex. "How'd you know?"

"I put it there a couple of weeks ago when you used up your stash."

"Oh." What was I supposed to do after he left? Who would replenish my tissue supply? My life was over. Over! I blew my nose hard, wiped my eyes and tried to stop gasping for breath. Not so easy. "So anyway, that's what I wanted to tell you."

He took a tissue and wiped my cheeks. "Anything else going on?"

"Nothing major. My mom got married. That's about it." *And you're leaving me and you won't be around anymore and even if you weren't leaving, you'll still shacking up with She-bitch and I'll never be able to come to your house in the middle of the night again because I might find her naked in your bed. Sob.*

He stopped wiping my tears, let his hand fall from my face and looked at me. "Married?"

"Yeah. So what do you think about Orpheus being a designer? Pretty weird, huh?" Focus on Orpheus. He didn't make me cry. I had to get it together.

"Since when has she been dating?"

"She met this guy through a personal ad a few days go. Or a week? Maybe two. It sort of blends. He just got out of prison, but apparently he's a really great guy." I took a deep breath. "So anyway, I have to go to dinner with them next Sunday. Do the bonding thing. You know. One big happy family. I'm excited about it. I've always wanted a dad and stuff."

"You're such a liar."

I stopped sniffling long enough to give Will a haughty look. "I am not."

"You're terrified that you're going to lose her. You're freaking out that she's done a one-eighty. You're the most marriage-averse person I know, and to have your mom suddenly get hitched has got to be shaking your foundation."

I sniffled. "Well, maybe a little."

He shook his head. "You guys have an unshakeable bond. A man isn't going to change that."

I blew my nose again. "You don't think?" *What about us? What about our bond?* I'd always thought it was unshakeable, but I was scared now.

"Not a chance." He hesitated. "You, um, want me to go to the dinner with you? Lend some moral support?"

Fresh tears surged. "You'd do that?"

"Of course I would. I'm supposed to be in California, but I could schedule around it."

I started to cry again. "Why do you have to be so wonderful?"

He smiled. "Sorry. I could try to be a jerk if you'd rather."

"I wouldn't rather. It's just that when you're so nice and understanding and supportive, then I don't want you to leave and I realize how important you are to me and I know I won't survive when you leave and I wish . . ." I stopped. What exactly did I wish?

Will's face had gone expressionless. "You wish what?"

"Um . . ."

He leaned forward, his face close to mine. "What do you wish?"

I looked at his face, at his lips, at his beautiful eyes that were so loyal. "I wish you and I . . ." I wish what? That we would be together forever? I wasn't ready for forever. Not with anyone. And neither was Will. "I wish things hadn't changed between us."

Something flickered across his face. "So you're officially back together with Greg?" His voice had an edge to it that I hadn't heard before.

I put my hand over Will's just as he was pulling it away. "Please understand, Will. He's good for me." *And you're leaving.* Not that that mattered. Even if he was staying, we were still no longer an item.

"Whatever you say." He slipped his fingers free of mine and stood up. "Christine is waiting for me."

Christine. I'd forgotten She-bitch's real name. "I thought you weren't dating her."

"She likes the fact that I'm going to med school."

"So you weren't good enough for her when you were a scientist for a start-up company, but now that you're going to be Doctor Will, that's enough for her?"

"Yep. She might move out to California when I go."

I blinked. "Are you serious?" Why hadn't he asked me to move with him? I would have gone. Whoa. Would I have? Not that it mattered. He hadn't asked.

"She is."

"But that's so shallow. She should love you for who you are, not what your job is."

"I never said she loved me."

"But that was the problem before. She said she did and she didn't but you did and then . . ." Then I scowled. "And you don't want to get serious with anyone. If she moves out there, isn't that getting serious?"

"Maybe."

"So it was me you didn't want to get serious with, then."

He raised his eyebrows in surprise. "What? Did you want to get serious?"

"No, of course not." I hesitated. "Did you?"

"No, I didn't."

I nodded. There it was, then. Neither of us had changed. Too bad for me if I was going to miss him. Like really miss him. I grabbed my keys back from him. "I gotta go. Greg's waiting for me." Lie.

His face tightened. "Yeah. Wouldn't want to keep your ex-husband waiting." Then he turned and walked off.

* * *

I watched Will until the door to his building swung shut. He never looked back. His choice was made.

Okay, that's the way it was. Fine. I could handle it. I had my own new life to lead. I sighed, attached the headset and stuck it in my ear and dialed Greg's cell. He was the man in my life now. He loved me. Sure, he'd left me once for another woman, but he was back now. Unlike Will, who had Christine in his bed and would soon be on the other side of the country. We weren't a couple, never had been and never would be. So I needed to quit acting like a petty ex-girlfriend and get over it.

Greg answered on the first ring. "Hey, hon. What's going on? Why'd you call at this hour?"

"Got plans for next Sunday night?"

"Why, you want to work on the presentation? I have some great ideas about—"

"No, Greg." I started my car and headed toward my condo. "Dinner with my mom and her new husband. Will you go with me?" He'd spent time with my mom before. Like Will, he'd realize that her unexpected marriage would be traumatic for me.

"Oh. *Oh.*" Silence.

"Greg?"

"Yeah, I'm not thinking that's such a good idea."

My heart thudded. *But I need you.* "Why not?"

"Because she hates me."

"Well, yeah, she did, but she has other things on her mind right now. She got married tonight and wants me to bond with her new husband."

"Yeah, I'm still not sure it's a good move. Why don't you go without me? I'll work on PWJ stuff."

"She's really in a pretty pro-marriage mood, actually. She'll probably be glad to see you because you managed to snag me once. Besides, if we're really going to start dating again, you're going to have to interact with her eventually."

"Yeah, I know, but . . . I think it would be better to wait until we're a little more solid. I don't want to lose you, and getting your mom involved, well, it could change your mind. She has a lot of influence over you, you know. Yes, I think it's better if I don't go. But thanks for the invite. Anything else?"

I scowled and took a corner a little too fast. "Greg. I'm pretty upset here. I was looking for your support on this." Um, hello? Where was his empathy? Wasn't he supposed to be all sensitive and in touch with emotions these days? What was all that therapy for, anyway?

"Oh, you were? Sorry. Missed that. What do you need me to do?"

"I need you to come to dinner with my mom and her husband!" Duh!

"Oh. Anything else?"

"How about a little caring and compassion? 'Gee, Paris, I know how close you and your mom are. That must suck to have another person in the picture. I know you're worried, but it'll work out and I'll be by your side giving you all the support you need along the way. Anything you need, I'll do it. Why don't I come to dinner? Maybe I can help smooth things over. Because you know, I really want our relationship to work and your mom might be an obstacle so let's attack this from the first moment. I'm here for you, just like I promised I would be.' Something like that would have worked, Greg. Why don't you give it a try?"

"Shit, Paris. I'm not a mind reader. You expect me to

figure all that out from your one-sentence invitation to dinner with your mom?"

"Well, yeah." Will had. My lower lip puckered, and I knew I was pouting. Well, why not? I wanted comfort, and Greg wasn't giving it to me.

"It's been five years, hon. It's going to take time to get there again. You want me to go to dinner? I'm there. And I think you're great and it'll work out and I'll be by your side the whole time. How's that?"

It just didn't have the same ring with the "How's that?" at the end. "You know what? Forget it. I'll go by myself. It's not a big deal."

"No problem. Whatever you want, McFee. I'm here for you. I'll work on the PWJ presentation instead. More efficient that way anyway. Talk to you tomorrow, okay?"

"Yeah, but—"

And then he hung up before I could point out that he was supposed to reject my offer for him to skip dinner. He was supposed to shove it aside and order me to let him be there for me.

Was it too much to expect him to know that without my telling him? I mean, was being psychic really too much to ask?

Maybe.

I didn't know anymore.

TWENTY-ONE

I was at work at seven o'clock the next morning. Just in time to get a phone call from an irate client.

I answered the phone in my usual sweet way. "Good morning, Paris Jackson. Can I help you?"

"How dare you turn down my loan? I proved my profit is legit and I need the money!"

As if I was in the mood for this. "I'm sorry, I didn't get your name."

"Richard Shipley."

I pulled up his name on the computer. Ah, yes, the owner of the independent hardware store. "Well, Mr. Shipley, according to the documents you submitted, you showed no profits last year."

"That's because I didn't want the damned government to take my money in taxes. The money came in, but then I did creative accounting so they couldn't take it. Nothing illegal about that."

"We evaluate your claim based on your taxes. If you showed no profit, then that's it. No loan."

"But damn it! I was profitable! Just come over here and I'll show you the new computer systems that I bought and—"

"I'm sorry. If you want a loan, you have to do your taxes straight up and admit you made profit. You can't have it both ways."

He exploded into an array of creative swear words.

I held the phone away from my ear and took a long gulp of my coffee. Did I really want to deal with this for the rest of my career? No. I wanted to be my own boss. I wanted to do something I cared about. Were dress shoes better than this?

Yes. Especially when they were as cool as what Orpheus could design.

Maybe it was time to take a real risk. Soon.

The din faded, and I put the phone to my ear again. "I'm sorry, but there's nothing we can do for you. I suggest you reapply next year when you file taxes that show you made a profit. Have a nice day."

I hung up on a fresh stream of curses.

A light knock sounded on my door, and I looked up to find Thad standing in the doorway. "Morning."

"Hi." He looked cute, as usual, but I didn't feel the same heat washing over me. I tried to picture him in a thong, but the image wouldn't come. I no longer needed him as a fantasy lover? Not sure what I thought of that. I was actually feeling in need of a good fantasy boyfriend. One who stood by me and understood my needs before I spoke.

"You're here bright and early," he said.

"Yep."

"So, um, about running this weekend . . ."

Whoops. Forgot about that. "Yeah . . ."

"Let's skip it."

"Really?" Relief and disappointment shot through me. I mean, it wasn't as if I was exactly thinking of dating him anymore, but there were still moments where having a friend who was outside my incestuous college world was more than a little appealing. "Why?"

He cleared his throat and tugged at his tie. "I have other plans."

"All weekend?" It wasn't as if we'd set a date or time or anything. He couldn't find an hour to run? He was a runner. Runners ran. They always found a way. I didn't buy it.

He shrugged. "Yeah, well, I just think it might be better not to get involved." He cleared his throat. "So, um, what's Jodi's last name?"

I frowned. "Harpswell."

"Okay, thanks. So, um, tell her and Lindsey I said hello. I'll, um, see you later. Bye."

I leaned back in my chair. What was that about? Had my fantasy lover ditched me for my asexual friend? As if my ego could handle that at the moment. Best not to think about it.

My phone rang again, and I checked the caller ID before answering to make sure it wasn't Mr. Disgruntled Hardware Store Owner again. It was Jodi. Speak of the devil. "Thad says hello."

Silence. "Really?"

I should have saved it for when I could see her face. I couldn't read anything from her one-word answer. I really didn't need to be blown off by Thad right now. And for Jodi, who already had cozy relationships with the other two men in my life?

What was going on with her? Was she wearing some love potion these days? "Yes, really. He said hi to Lindsey as well."

"Oh, of course he did. Right. That's what I thought. Yeah, anyway, you have to come over to Orpheus's lab right now. He brought in his new designs and they're awesome. I think we should start building samples right now."

I glanced at my empty door. "I'm at work, Jodi. I can't take off." I wasn't immune to the breathy excitement in her voice, however. "Are they really cool?"

"Incredible. He's so talented. Come on, Paris. What's more important? Your bank job or shoes?"

I thought of people who cheat on their taxes and blame me when it doesn't work out for them. I thought of my boss being weird. I thought of having to turn in my loans for preapproval before submitting them. I thought of Lindsey saying that we need to live for the present. "Shoes," I said. "Give me a few minutes to come down with the stomach flu and I'll meet you there."

"Awesome. You won't believe what he's come up with."

Three days later, we sat in the PWJ offices with the rest of the team and let them in on our discovery.

"No," Greg said.

"You know how I feel," Will said.

"Oh, sweetie. I don't want you to get disappointed again," Lindsey said.

Jodi and I sat shoulder-to-shoulder on the opposite side of the picnic table from our trio of opponents.

Between us sat three pairs of women's dress shoes, designed by Orpheus, put together by the three of us. Orpheus hadn't manufactured dress shoes before, so there'd been a little trial and error. To his surprise, Jodi had been instrumental in brainstorming solutions. She'd been stumped a few times with Sfoam and had to call Will.

Will was more the Sfoam expert than she was. Will had said he wasn't able to come in to assist, but he'd offered his help over the phone. Probably trying to get in some last minute sex with She-bitch before he took off to the other coast.

Yeah, that was a comforting thought. Not.

Jodi might not have been a shoe maven, but she was a brilliant scientist with an incredible aptitude for problem-solving. Between her and Orpheus and Will's long-distance coaching, it had worked.

So maybe we'd be okay with Will on the other coast.

Maybe. I sighed and tried not to feel depressed.

We'd decided to wait until we had product before cluing in the rest of the team, and we'd worked twenty-four-seven for three days to get the product together. I hadn't been to work at the bank since Thursday. After all, strep throat will keep you down and out for quite a few days, you know?

Greg had been MIA, working on PWJ presentations.

Lindsey had been researching clown school and hanging out with a personal trainer to get herself in shape for pro wrestling tryouts. Turned out she had quite a long way to go before she was buff enough. Big surprise, huh? Just made her want to do it more.

And now we were together, and things were not going smoothly. Did I mention Will looked really cute? And he had a hickey on his neck. Not so cute.

"Manufacturing your own shoes makes no sense. We need to sell the technology." Greg set a laptop on the picnic table. "Let me walk you guys through this presentation I've put together. You'll see that PWJ has the potential to make a lot of money by selling now."

"There's potential to make even more money if we have contracts with retailers," I said.

Greg narrowed his eyes. "Yes, but . . ."

"What's the harm in waiting another week or two," Jodi asked. "Give us a chance to make this fly."

Lindsey picked up a pair of the sample shoes and studied them. "I have to admit, they're pretty sweet."

I grinned.

Greg scowled. "This isn't the direction we were planning on. Do you all have any idea how difficult it is to make a profit manufacturing shoes? We don't have the facilities, the contacts, the infrastructure. We're better off licensing the technology, and I thought we all agreed to that. It's the best financial decision." He pulled up a file on the computer and rattled off a whole bunch of evidence to support his decision.

When he finished, the table was silent.

Dreams or reality? That was the question.

He took my hand, ignoring the rest of the room. "McFee, your real dream is running shoes, not dress shoes."

"Well, yeah, but the dress shoes are pretty fun," I said at the same time Will snorted and muttered, "McFee," under his breath. "And my name's not McFee," I added.

Greg ignored both of us. "If you spend all this time trying to manufacture dress shoes, it could be several years before you have the time and resources to work on running shoes. If you license the technology, then you'll have the money flowing in sooner. It's the perfect solution." He glared at everyone else in the room. "Don't let these people take away your dream of running shoes just because they want to manufacture dress shoes. You're the leader, you lead in the direction you want."

I chewed my lower lip and thought about what Greg was saying. He was right, wasn't he? Running shoes were my dream. Dress shoes weren't. They were nothing more than a poor substitute, even though I had to admit I'd really had fun over the past few days working with Orpheus and Jodi. But fashion wasn't a passion of mine the way running was. "I agree with Greg. We'll try to license the technology."

"Paris!" Jodi threw up her hands. "What are you saying? Can't you at least try this?"

Lindsey scowled. "Greg, you're so full of bullshit. You don't care about Paris making running shoes. All you want is a fast influx of cash, and licensing Sfoam is the way to do it. You might have snowed her, but I'm not blind."

I flashed a sharp glance at Greg. "Is it about the money? Is Lindsey right?" I'd just begun to trust him again, but barely. Was I wrong? God, my head was killing me.

"What's your dream?" he asked. "Running shoes?"

"Well, yeah."

"Then do you need to look any further?"

"Look further, Paris," Lindsey said. "Definitely look further."

I studied Greg, who gave me a warm smile. Then I thought about myself. He was right. I wanted to do running shoes. "No. I don't want to do dress shoes. I mean, it's fun, but it's not what's in my soul. Running is." I stood up. "Greg, I'll research companies. Email me your presentation and I'll take a look at it." I looked at Will. "You'll get your money. You should be happy."

He met my gaze and said nothing. I couldn't tell what he was thinking. Didn't matter anymore, did it?

Lindsey picked up a pair of shoes. "Girls' night. Right now."

Greg shook his head. "I'm taking Paris out to dinner so we can talk about marketing strategy."

She pressed the spike of the heel into his chest. Hard. "You do not take precedence over me. Back off or experience death by designer shoe. Capiche?"

I glanced at Jodi, and she shrugged. What was up with Lindsey?

Will pushed back. "Christine's waiting for me. I need to go anyway."

Christine. The sound of her name made me want to vomit.

Lindsey spun away from Greg. "What? You're dating She-bitch again?"

"Yeah. Got a problem with it?"

"Of course I do. She ripped your heart out!" She threw her hands onto her hips and glared at Will and me. "So this is what happens when the two of you break up? You both go running back to your destructive exes? What's wrong with you guys? You were the happiest I'd ever seen when you were hooking up, and now you're walking away from that and going back into the torture chamber?"

Greg frowned. "I'm not a torture chamber. I think I resent that."

Jodi patted his shoulder. "Lindsey, Greg's changed. Paris sees that. You need to as well. They belong together. Totally."

Lindsey stared at Jodi as if she had a horn sprouting out of her left eye socket. "I don't understand you, Jodi. I really don't."

Will cleared his throat. "Okay, I'm out of here. See ya." He shot me a sympathetic look and then took off. I wanted to go with him, kidnap him and take the two of us off to another world.

Greg stood up. "I'll let you girls sort this out." He gave me a quick kiss. "I'll talk to you later tonight. I'll miss you."

Lindsey snorted, and Jodi elbowed her.

I kissed him back and mentally flipped off the world. "See you."

The door shut behind him, leaving us girls together, the air riddled with tension.

It wasn't the first time the three of us had conflicted, but it was the first time in five years Will hadn't stayed around to help us to clear the air.

Lindsey folded her arms across her chest.

Jodi did the same.

So I joined in on the fun.

Yeah, this was productive.

"Shoes," Jodi said.

"What about them?" Lindsey asked.

"I think Greg's wrong."

Lindsey arched an eyebrow. "You disagree with the golden boy? How can that be?"

Jodi ignored the sarcasm. "I think it's a good idea to manufacture the dress shoes. I bet we can get some sales."

Lindsey's gaze flicked to the table. "They are pretty cool."

"But I think Greg's right," I said. "I want to work on running shoes, not dress shoes."

My friends exchanged glances. Then Lindsey said. "What size did you make the shoes?"

"Paris's size. Same as yours."

"Then let's go." She swept the shoes off the table. "Into my car."

They didn't give me an opportunity to refuse, and a part of me wanted to see exactly what Lindsey was up to.

We formulated a plan en route, and by the time we arrived at the mall, I was kind of excited to see what would happen.

A test market, but without asinine testers scarfing down free pizza. We arrived at the entrance to the same exclusive store that had dissed us before.

For a moment, I felt intimidated; then I put on a pair of Orpheus's shoes and felt tough enough to take down the bitchy saleswoman and all of her predatory kind. Who knew fashion generated power? It was almost as heady as kicking someone's butt on the track.

Not quite, but almost. The nervous anticipation was the same, though. Would we be crushed or dominate?

Time to find out.

Lindsey put on another pair, and Jodi wore the third. Jodi's were a little small for her, but she claimed the Sfoam around the toes diffused the pressure enough that she could actually wear a full size smaller than usual without unbearable pain.

Lindsey strutted, I wobbled and Jodi shuffled into the store.

Under Lindsey's command, we stopped in the ladies' dress section, where Lindsey made Jodi and me buy clothes worthy of the shoes. For some reason she felt our three-days-in-a-row-in-the-lab attire didn't suffice. Can't imagine why.

It was the most money I'd spent on clothes in my life. Cumulatively. And it was only one dress.

But that feeling of power I'd had when I first put on

Orpheus's shoes? Magnified tenfold by adding the dress.

I might have to become a fashion maven after this, I thought. It was quite the adrenaline rush, to strut toward the exclusive shoe section and know I belonged, at least on the outside.

And then we strolled *into* the designer shoe section and began to flaunt. Attitude rolled off us, and we shot disdainful looks at everyone around us.

It wasn't too long before curious heads began peering around the racks at us, peeking at our feet.

I kept one hand on the racks to prevent myself from falling over and ruining the effect, and tried my best to look extremely wealthy, snobby and exclusive while I talked about money, clothes and art with Lindsey and Jodi.

It took twenty minutes for our trap to work.

A young woman in her early twenties sidled up to me as I was inspecting a pair of Manolo Blahniks. "Excuse me?"

I gave her my snottiest look. "Yes?"

"May I ask who you have on your feet?"

A thrill rushed through me, and I barely suppressed a giggle of excitement. "Orpheus M," I replied with impressive calm. I picked up a Jimmy Choo sandal and pretended to study it. Studied the two-thousand-dollar price tag, actually. And I watched her out of the corner of my eye.

This was my creation, and she was drooling. The sense of pride and accomplishment was unreal.

She continued to hover. "Um, where did you get them?"

"Specially made. You can't just buy them anywhere."

"Like, how much did they cost?"

How awesome was this? Someone wanted our shoes! I couldn't believe it. I'd always imagined people clamoring to get their hands on a pair of our running shoes. In my wildest dreams, I hadn't pictured them demanding three-inch heels, but it didn't matter. This woman was eyeing our creation with desire, and it was the most incredible feeling.

The bitchy saleswoman from before appeared at the next rack, straightening shoes and shooting occasional glances in my direction. My elation crashed. Was she going to expose me and get me escorted out the door? I edged away from her. "If you need to ask how much they are, then they're too expensive for you," I said to the customer.

The woman started to get a glassy look on her face. "Oh, no. I can afford them. How could I get a pair? Can you give me a contact?"

I sighed. "It's very exclusive. He doesn't want just anyone wearing them." Wow. I played the rich snobby bitch well. Maybe that was my future?

"That's exactly what I'm looking for. Please?"

I gave a surreptitious look around, then pulled out one of my bank business cards. I jotted PWJ's email address on the back. "Email that address. Use my name. It's on the front of the card. I don't know if they'll sell to you, but using my name might help."

"Oh, thank you." She clutched the card to her chest and spun around just as the bitchy saleswoman walked up with a box of shoes.

"I found a pair in your size," she said to the woman.

The customer glanced at me, then shook her head. "I don't want them anymore. Thanks anyway." She waved the card at me, and then bolted out of the store.

The saleswoman tucked the box under her arm and glared at me.

I whistled and did a casual scan for Lindsey and Jodi. I

could see Lindsey peeking around a shoe rack. When she caught my eye, she gave me a thumbs-up and a wink. As if one annoying saleswoman could possibly dampen my euphoria at the moment. Orpheus M designs had passed the first test. Unbelievable!

The saleswoman cleared her throat. "Orpheus M? Never heard of it."

It took me a moment to realize she was speaking to me, and she wasn't even being bitchy. She sounded curious, actually. "It's new," I said. "No retail outlet yet."

"Hmm . . ." She eyed my feet, and I tensed my legs to try to keep my ankles from wobbling. *Must stay sophisticated.*

Jodi sauntered up next to me and set her foot next to mine. "It's another Orpheus M design."

The saleswoman sniffed.

Then Lindsey popped up behind her, startling the saleswoman. She set her pair in the woman's hand. "This is also an Orpheus M design."

The saleswoman latched onto the shoes, trailing her fingers over the design and the materials. We'd gone all out on the materials, which hadn't been cheap since we weren't exactly getting bulk discounts.

I noticed the saleswoman's name tag identified her as Priscilla S. I wondered if she went by Prissy for short. It'd be fitting, don't you think?

Prissy slipped her finger inside the shoe, then frowned. "What's in here?"

"What size shoe do you wear?" I asked.

She gave me a look. "Nine."

"Those are eights. Try them on."

"I said I wear nines."

"Try them," I said.

Lindsey leaned over her shoulder. "You know you want to."

"It'll be worth it," Jodi said. "Just do it."

Prissy looked at all of us, her eyes gleaming. Then she whipped off her own shoe and slipped her foot into the Orpheus M. The look of awe on her face was priceless. It would be emblazoned on my brain forever.

"They're . . . comfortable!" She took a few experimental steps, then took off on an energetic march around the displays. "I can't believe it. What's in there?"

"Special technology unique to Orpheus M products," I said. "Disperses pressure points with the effectiveness of several inches of regular foam, even though it's less than a millimeter thick. Women can even wear a size smaller than they're used to—" apparently "—and clients love that." I was so excited I could barely talk coherently. She'd admired Orpheus's designs, and Sfoam had made her light up with glee.

Omigod! We'd done it! We'd really done it!

This was way better than winning a race! I'd worked for four years and to succeed . . . to do it . . . wow!

Prissy cruised to a stop in front of me. "We must have these shoes for our store. How do I get in contact with the designer?"

I blinked. Surely I'd misheard her in my euphoria. "What?"

Jodi's mouth dropped open.

Ever the consummate lawyer, Lindsey didn't even falter. "I'm the legal consultant for Orpheus M Designs. Lindsey Miller. Nice to meet you." She shook Prissy's hand and then nodded at me. "This is Paris Jackson,

CEO, and over there is Jodi Harpswell, one of the scientists responsible for the creation of that foam that is so marvelous." She elbowed me. "Paris? You want to take over?"

Um . . . yeah. Wow. What to say? *Thank you for making my dream come true? You couldn't have given me a greater gift?* Probably not. I settled for a smile. "Currently Orpheus M creates custom designs on an individual basis, but we're looking for a retail partner. We'd like to create an exclusive distribution with one retailer to keep the supply down and the prices high." I handed her a PWJ business card. Did she notice that my hand was shaking? "We'd be happy to set up a meeting with your buyer if it can be done soon. We're currently in negotiations for other distribution options, so time is of the essence."

Lindsey held out her hand. "I'll need those back. For security's sake, we don't allow the designs out of our control unless they are paid for."

"I completely understand." Prissy reluctantly peeled the shoes off her feet and trailed her finger fondly over the toe before handing them to Lindsey. "I'm the buyer. It's my decision. I like to be out on the floor as much as possible to keep in touch with the customer, know what they're responding to and what they're not. Orpheus M Designs is exactly what I've been looking for." She took the card. "I'll email you with an offer by tomorrow morning. If you get a competing offer, please allow me the opportunity to match it." She cast another longing look at my feet, shook hands with all of us and excused herself, hustling off to her back room.

We stared at each other for a moment, then quietly filed out of the store. We didn't say anything until we were back in the parking lot, away from probing eyes.

And then we started screaming. And crying. God, did I cry.

I screamed and cried until my throat hurt.

And then I screamed some more.

This was the best feeling I'd ever had! *Designer dress shoes, here I come!*

TWENTY-TWO

The deal was signed at two o'clock the next Friday. We had thirty days to deliver three unique designs, approximately twenty pairs of each design. We convinced them to keep the numbers down to prevent a market glut, claiming that we didn't want to give them product until they proved they could move it. In reality, twenty pairs was all we could provide until we got more efficient manufacturing facilities.

Only sixty shoes, but at a wholesale price of a thousand to two thousand bucks a pop, that was between thirty and sixty grand coming in over the next month. Lindsey was in the process of writing up a consulting contract for Orpheus. Couldn't afford to lose his services now, could we?

And that was only the beginning.

We had a hell of a lot of work to do. We needed to set up efficient manufacturing. Design facilities. Marketing. Pricing. We had to figure it all out.

It was the best week of my entire life. I didn't sleep, and I didn't need it. I didn't want to sleep and miss out on a minute of my life. PWJ had officially become a full-time job.

So what did I do?

At five after two on Friday, I walked into Thad's office, sat down, and did what I'd been dreaming of for four years.

"Afternoon, Paris. How are you doing?"

I couldn't keep the huge shit-eating grin off my face. "I'm quitting."

His easy smile vanished. "What?"

I held out my resignation. "Two weeks' notice." Two weeks and then I was my own boss! Following my dream! Yahoo!

"But why?" He frowned. "Is it because of the night in the bar? I apologized for that. It was out of line. We can resolve this and—"

I stopped him before he could embarrass both of us. "No, it's not that. My shoe company? Remember?" He nodded. "We got a retail deal. It's a full-time gig now and it's bringing in money. I'm doing it full-time!"

He looked shocked. "Really?"

"Really!" I bounced up and down in my seat. "Isn't that awesome?" Oh, forget it. I couldn't contain myself, so I jumped to my feet and did a little Snoopy dance in my Orpheus M shoes. I was getting pretty good at walking in these things. Sneakers, shmeakers. I was a fashionista now.

"So you're going to make running shoes. Congratulations. I'm really happy for you." He did look happy.

"It's not running shoes. Dress shoes. Running shoes will come later." When later? I had no idea. It wasn't as if I was going to have time to do anything with running shoes right now. And it didn't matter. The rush from designer heels was beyond anything I could ever imagine. It would keep me jazzed for quite a while. "I'm going to be my own boss!"

He stood up, walked around the desk and gave me a huge hug. "I'm really excited for you, Paris. Not many people get a chance to live their dream."

I hugged him back and was suddenly catapulted back to that night at the bar when he'd held me on the dance floor.

I felt him tense against me. Gee, you think he was having the same flashback? I guessed that little attraction would never go away. He was cute, I noticed it, but it wasn't more than that. Not anymore.

He cleared his throat and pulled back, giving a little tug on his tie. "Okay, so then, that's great." He retreated back to his side of the desk. "Before I accept this, I have to make sure you're certain. Once I accept this, we're going to start looking for your replacement and it'll be too late to change your mind."

I grinned. "I'm certain. The contract has been signed. We're in business."

He grinned back. "All right. Congratulations. And get back to work. I don't want a lame duck for the next two weeks."

"No problem." I danced my way out of his office, all the way down the hall, high-fiving every person I encountered.

This was the best day of my life! And part of what made it so good was that it was my dream, and I'd accomplished it without any outside help. I'd done it with my team. We'd fought through all the problems and driven to success.

I grinned. Okay, so maybe my mom was right that things are better if you don't take the easy way.

* * *

Six hours later, the whole PWJ gang was at Octopus 8 again, only this time it was to celebrate our future, not lament the reappearance of my ex in my life. I'd dolled up for the event like a true fashion goddess. After all, I had to do my Orpheus Ms justice, didn't I? No more running shoes for Paris!

"I can't believe this," Jodi screamed. "We're going to be rich!" She stood up and howled, swaying a little bit. It was our third bottle of champagne, after all, and she'd been right there celebrating with the rest of us. Who could blame us? We were going into business for ourselves!

Greg was leaning against the back of the booth, his arm around my shoulders. "It's not that easy. Right now we'll still be taking a loss even if we sell at two thousand dollars a pair. We don't have efficient manufacturing facilities."

I rolled my eyes. "Oh, stop being so negative. That's what we're going to work on now. Finding ways to build cheaply. All that jazz." I held up my glass of champagne. "We rock!"

He sighed and tightened his arm around my shoulders. "I guess I better get to work so you all don't go bankrupt, eh?"

"We'll all work," I said. "This isn't your business. It's ours."

"Yeah, about that. I want a new contract."

I shot a look at Lindsey, our legal consultant extraordinaire. "What kind of contract?"

"We need to revamp the management structure. With Will leaving, he shouldn't have authority over day-to-day business. I'm the business expert, and it's my money that's making this possible. My money will pay for all

273

these shoes until revenue starts to outweigh costs, which won't be for a while. I want veto power and full business responsibility."

We all fell silent and stared at him. Will's eyes narrowed and his jaw tensed. He'd been so excited for me when I'd told him, and he'd been in full support of signing the contract as long as he didn't have to put in any more money or time. A sad reminder that he was on his way out of PWJ and my life. But his excitement had been invaluable.

Unlike Greg, who'd been thoughtful and quiet. Now we knew why.

It was Lindsey who spoke. "As their legal consultant, I'll look into this matter. I'll draft up something and let you look at it." She shot me a look that said not to worry, we'd all be discussing this at length in private.

Why was Greg trying to change the rules? It didn't feel right having him as an equal partner. His only contribution had been money, none of the blood and sweat the rest of us had put in.

Besides, he hadn't even wanted us to make the shoes. He still didn't. If we gave him a vote, what would he do with it?

But he did have a point. Could we really expect to keep him boxed out since he was funding this venture? Plus he knew a lot more about business than the rest of us.

But this was our dream. The three of us, plus Lindsey. It didn't feel right to change it.

Then again, it had already changed. PWJ was about designer shoes, at least for the moment.

Greg lifted his champagne glass. "To PWJ."

We all raised our glasses, but the euphoria of the night

had lessened with Greg's comment. Why couldn't he just be excited like the rest of us? We were in business!

"In the spirit of our celebration tonight, I'd like to celebrate something else." Greg focused on me. "I came back here to make amends and move on, but in the process, I've opened the door to my past and rediscovered the friendships and love that I once had."

"Hear, hear. We're glad to have you back." Jodi raised her glass and then drained it.

"I want to raise a toast to Paris," he said.

Everyone raised their glasses, and I felt my cheeks heat up. "Oh, come on. Everyone gets credit for PWJ. It's been a team effort all along."

"Not for PWJ," Greg said. "For being willing to take a chance on me again." He glanced around the table. "Marry me, Paris. Marry me again."

Holy mother of pearl. A real proposal. My heart leapt, then crashed, then started having some sort of seizure. Marriage? Commitment? Uh . . . uh . . . panic . . . fear . . . claustrophobia . . . I took a few short breaths and tried to focus.

The table was utterly silent and still.

Then Jodi screamed and threw her arms around me and Greg.

Will looked sick, and he set his hand on my shoulder. "Are you all right?"

"No," I whispered.

Lindsey frowned. "How can you ask her to marry you after you totally shredded the vows you made to her before?"

Yeah . . . yeah . . . what she said.

"Because I love her and will honor and cherish her until the day I die."

I blinked. *Good answer.* What if he meant it? What if he was telling the truth? I still loved him, and there was something comforting about having a best friend forever. I mean, if I could get over my paranoia about trusting him or anyone like that again. "I . . . um . . ."

Will hissed softly in my ear, "Did you ever talk to Jodi about her secret?"

I stared blankly at him. "What are you talking about?" Was now the time for that? Jodi and I were good again. We were business partners. "It doesn't matter." What mattered was that Greg had proposed again, and I had to answer him. Was I going to say yes? Or no?

Greg kissed me and whispered in my ear, "Well?"

"I . . ." *I don't know. Don't know. What should I say?* How did I feel?

Will stood up then.

"Greg. A word in private."

Greg frowned. "I don't think so."

"Now."

"Fine. Because it would make Paris happy if we got along." He gave me a deliberate kiss. "To our future together, McFee."

He followed Will away from the table, and they disappeared into the crowd.

Lindsey let her breath out. "Wow. Didn't see that coming."

"Me either." I should have, I guess. I mean, he'd referenced it. But why would I really think he was going to propose? It wasn't as if I wanted him to. Denial, probably.

She studied me. "You going to marry him again?"

Jodi didn't allow me a moment to answer. "I'm so glad you guys have finally gotten together. You don't know how awful I've felt all these years." She slung her arm around me. "This is the best, isn't it, Lindsey?"

Lindsey cocked her head. "Why have *you* felt awful, Jodi? Paris is the one he left."

"Because it was my fault Greg left. Well, I thought it was for a long time." Jodi picked up the champagne bottle and drank several long swallows. "I should have told you long ago, but I was so afraid you'd hate me, but now that you guys are going to be happy and have little babies and a picket fence, it's all okay now."

I glanced at Lindsey, who shrugged. "What are you talking about?" I asked. I was too strung out to follow this discussion. Why were we talking about Jodi's issues when I had a decision to make? A life-altering decision.

Three years before, I would have jumped at the chance to have Greg in my life again. I would have been willing to risk anything to have him back.

But not anymore. I didn't want to say yes for the wrong reasons. It had to be right. Was it? I didn't know. I mean, I loved him, didn't I? So what was wrong with me? Was it leftover nerves from the betrayal in the past? I should get over that, right?

Jodi turned toward me and clutched my hands in hers. "I didn't mean to do it. Neither did he."

My heart started thudding dully. "Do what?"

"Don't be mad. You promise you won't be mad?"

I started to agree, but the words stuck ominously in my throat. "What are you talking about?" I said instead.

She took a deep, wobbling breath. "When we all got back to school in the fall of our senior year, it was really hard to see Seth's empty room, you know?"

"I know." Boy, did I know. It had sat there like an

277

empty cavern until Will had moved in and filled it with his energy and spirit.

"So one night I went in there and Greg was sitting on the floor. He was crying and stuff."

"Crying? Greg never cried about Seth." At least not to me he hadn't. Not back then. The new Greg might.

"Well, he was crying that night. He couldn't take it anymore. Felt like he'd stolen you from Seth. You know. Lots of guilt stuff. And I felt bad because I'd loved Seth too, and he was going to break up with you to be with me."

I froze as Lindsey sucked in her breath. "What? You were dating Seth while I was?" My stomach started to roil. "And you never said anything?"

She ignored my question. "Anyway, one thing led to another, and we ended up sleeping together."

I yanked my hands free from hers. "We? As in you and Greg? You had sex? In Seth's room?" Impossible. She was my friend. She wouldn't have done that. I had to have misunderstood.

"Yes." She closed her eyes. "I felt really bad, especially when I woke up the next morning and found out he'd left you during the night. I felt like it was my fault. Like I broke you two up and everything."

I pulled back from her, my heart pounding. "You . . . you . . . you slept with Greg after I was married to him? You drove him away?" Somehow the Jodi/Seth thing just didn't seem all that important right now. "You caused my husband to leave me, and you never told me?" After all those years of unanswered questions, she'd known the truth? "How could you?" My voice was no more than a hoarse, shocked whisper.

"No!" Jodi clutched at me. "See, that's the thing. Greg and I have been talking about it since he's been back, and he says it wasn't me. He would have left anyway. Sleeping with me was just a sign of everything that was wrong. Sure, it made him leave sooner because he felt so guilty and didn't feel like he could ever look you in the eye again and stuff, but it didn't change anything. He still had to leave. He still had to work out his problems."

Lindsey narrowed her eyes and her face got very tense. "Bitch."

Jodi's mouth dropped open and tears filled her eyes.

My chest was constricting. I couldn't breathe.

"Paris spent years blaming herself for Greg leaving. Years! It totally fucked her up, and you knew all along that it was your fault!" Lindsey spat out the words in disgust.

"But it wasn't my fault! And now they're back together, so it's irrelevant anyway. If it wasn't for me, they wouldn't even be back together this time. I've been working so hard to get them to reconcile and they did. I deserve credit for saving them!" Jodi was screaming now. "I felt horrible for five years. Isn't that enough?"

Lindsey leaned forward until her nose was touching Jodi's. "It will never be enough."

"But . . ."

"Get out, Jodi. Just get out."

Jodi looked at me. "Paris, you understand, don't you? I love you. That's why I had to fix it. That's why I worked on Sfoam even though I didn't care about running. For you. The last five years have been spent trying to make it up to you."

I shook my head. "I . . . you . . ." God, I couldn't even speak. The betrayal bit so deeply. My body was shaking violently, my mouth was dry, my head pounding. I'd never felt so awful in my life. So empty. So utterly alone.

Jodi hesitated, then stood up. "If you want me to leave, I'm gone."

"Go." Lindsey wouldn't even look at her.

She left.

I lifted my head and stared at Lindsey. My face felt numb and expressionless. "Did you know?"

She shook her head. "Believe me, I would have told you."

"They . . ." I didn't even know where to start. The betrayal was so enormous, so complex, so enduring.

She got up, slid next to me on the bench and hugged me. "I know, sweetie. I know."

Tears started to fill my eyes. "I don't understand how they could have done that. And let me spend all that time trying to figure out what happened. How could they not tell me?" Sobs started, and Lindsey hugged me tighter and rested her forehead against mine. "Oh, God, Linds. I'd been so close to trusting Greg again. I'm such an idiot. A fool! I have no business getting serious with anyone if I trust people like that."

"Oh, sweetie, you had no chance against him. He's an expert in manipulation, and he had a special tool to dig into your heart. It's not your fault." She stroked my hair and I let her hold me up.

I didn't have the strength to support myself. "Can we leave?"

"You bet, sweetie." She hugged me, and then we turned to get up.

Greg and Will chose that moment to reappear.

"Greg has something to tell you." Will sounded pissed. More than pissed. Furious. And smug at the same time.

Greg's right eye was swollen, and he was holding a bar napkin to his bloody nose. Will's arms were folded across his chest, but I could see that the skin on his knuckles was torn. Will, my hero. I wished he'd killed Greg while he was at it. Or at least done permanent damage to that pretty face.

"Say it," Will said. Then he saw my face, and his eyes flashed with the deepest sadness and regret. He knew I knew. But he turned to Greg. "Tell her."

I lifted my chin and willed my strength to give me enough dignity to last this moment. To survive what I knew was coming.

Greg glared at Will, then turned to me. "I made a mistake a long time ago. I slept with Jodi while you and I were married. It didn't mean anything. It wasn't why I left. But it was just another way I fucked up. It's in the past, the same as all the other shit. It means nothing now. Now we're going to get married and go into business together. I'm going to take over PWJ and make you rich. I'll make your dreams come true."

"That's it? That's your apology? You slept with my best friend, but it's all good because you're going to make me rich?" Arrogant rat bastard. It was not enough. I don't know what would have been, but that wasn't it.

A crack appeared in his confident expression. "Well, yeah. It was a long time ago. It doesn't matter. It didn't matter back then, actually. Not really. Our future is now. Money, PWJ, us getting married. I'm making your dreams come true, and that's what matters."

Lindsey let go of me, walked over to Greg and then slammed her knee into his crotch. He dropped to the ground instantly, clutching his groin and moaning. "Paris makes her own dreams come true, asshole. You aren't going to rule her life ever again."

I staggered to my feet and looked at Will. "You knew?"

"That was Jodi's secret. The one I was trying to get you to ask her about."

"And you kept it?"

He looked grim. "It wasn't my place to tell."

"Of course it was! How could you not? You let me go through all that and you didn't tell me?"

A flicker of doubt crossed his face. "What could be served by causing you more pain? You needed Jodi as your friend. Greg was already gone. He was a bastard and you knew it. I was trying to take pain away from you, not cause you more." His fists curled. "But when Greg came back . . . I couldn't keep quiet."

"But you did!"

"He told you, didn't he?" He flexed his knuckles. "Wish he hadn't given in so quickly. I was enjoying myself. Bastard deserved a hell of a lot more than what he got."

"I thought I could trust you."

"Me? It's that bloodsucking asshole you can't trust."

"I trusted you as my best friend. That you wouldn't keep secrets from me."

Confusion made his brow furrow. "I thought I was doing the right thing for you. If it wasn't . . ." He sighed. "Then I'm sorry. More sorry than you could ever know."

I stared at Will, and I didn't know what to say. I felt like he'd let me down, but in the deepest recesses of my mind, I sensed the honesty of his words and of his motives.

But I couldn't deal with it. Not now.

Greg clutched at my leg, his body still contorted on the floor. "Don't go, Paris. I love you. I'll do right by you, I swear. We'll get rich, you and I. We'll sell Sfoam for so much money you'll never have to work again. You can relax, do whatever you want. You know that's what matters."

"You're wrong, Greg. You don't even know me." What

was important was making my own dreams come true, not having Greg make me rich. "What matters to me is working hard for something I believe in and seeing my efforts pay off. Of accomplishing things by myself, or with a team of people I care about. It's not about the money, and it's not about you."

"You're wrong, babe. Give me a chance and I'll show you."

I noticed a cut under his eye that I hadn't seen before due to the swelling. I grabbed a tequila shot off the tray of a passing waitress and poured it into the wound.

His scream of pain kept me company all night long.

TWENTY-THREE

I woke up on Lindsey's couch with a dry mouth, a devastating headache and an emptiness in my soul.

Lindsey was typing at her computer, still wearing her skin treatment, her hair twisted up in curlers.

It took me about one minute to remember what had happened the night before. I groaned and pulled the pillow over my face. I wouldn't cry. Would. Not. Cry.

"Try this."

I jerked as something hit my stomach. "No." This was supposed to be the happiest time of my life, with the success of Orpheus M designs. And instead I felt as if a load of cement blocks had been dropped on my chest and left there to slowly crush the air out of my body until I died.

"Open your eyes. It's worth it."

I peeled one eye open and found a voodoo doll on my lap. It was wearing a suit and tie and a name tag that said "Greg." A plastic container of pins was attached to its ankle like a ball and chain. "Where'd you find this?"

"I had it made last week when Greg started pissing me off. Hadn't had a chance to use it yet."

I propped myself up on a pillow and opened the box of pins. I shoved one into his groin. "Think this works? You think he's collapsed on the ground grabbing his nuts right now?"

"Of course."

"Nice." I shoved another pin through his heart. "Do you think he ever loved me, or was it just about the money?"

Lindsey pushed herself back from the desk and spun around to face me. "I think he loves you in his own way. The problem is, it's not the way you deserve to be loved."

I stuck a pin through his right hand. "What is love, exactly? He wants to make me rich. Why is that wrong?"

"Because he wants to control you. He's not letting you be who you want to be. Because he wasn't honest with you."

"But that was five years ago. What if he's changed?" I didn't want to admit I'd been so wrong in trusting him again. I couldn't bear to lose my dear friend Jodi. I wanted to find a way to make that incident not important. To make it not matter. "Should I really care what happened so long ago?"

Lindsey took the doll away. "Look at me, sweetie."

I met her gaze. "What?"

"You know how I'm all about freedom and independence, right?"

"You mean your death wish? Yep, I'm aware."

"Well, Greg's trying to take that away from you. Since he's arrived, he's been setting up controls around you. Can't you feel them chafing? He's making you think you want what he wants you to want."

I frowned. "You think?"

"You were excited about the designer shoes, and then he talked you out of it."

"But I do want to make running shoes."

"Were you excited about designer shoes that night when you showed us the samples you'd made from Orpheus's designs?"

I frowned. "Well, yeah. Superexcited. Like over the moon."

"And he told you not to do it. And you agreed. If I hadn't dragged you to the mall to show off the designs, we never would have gotten the deal. He tried to stop you, and you listened."

Was that how it had happened? It was, wasn't it? Bastard.

"He wants total control of PWJ. Not an equal share of control. Total control. If he has all the control, then what? We're nothing to him. Your dreams mean zilch. He's a venture capitalist and he wants money. That's it. Money. You, my dear, are his ticket."

I held out my hand. "Give me the doll back."

She tossed it to me, and I mashed three more pins into it, one in each eye and one in his mouth. "I hope that blinds him."

"So what do you want to do?"

"About?"

"PWJ. Go forward with the designer shoes?"

I looked at her and thought about the thrill in the store when Prissy had fawned over us. The pride when Jodi, Orpheus and I had finished our samples. It might not be running shoes, but it was awesome. "I can still get my running fix through running." And the success of the Orpheus M gave me something running never had. A sense of accomplishment and ownership and pride. A team to share the joys with. I didn't want to let go. I grinned. "Let's do it."

"Right on, girlfriend." She spun back to her computer and hit "print." "I was writing up the design contract for Orpheus. He's our key figure. We need to get him under contract immediately."

"Definitely. Without him, we're screwed. With him, we're money."

We hadn't even told him about the retail deal yet. We hadn't told him during negotiations because we didn't want to give him a chance to nix them. Once the deal was signed, it would be too difficult for him to shut it down. And in the end, he'd be thrilled. He hadn't been in the lab on Friday, and we'd wanted to tell him in person. I couldn't wait to see his face.

We walked into the lab to find Orpheus working on another shoe design. Well, if you define "working" broadly. He was actually screaming epithets and throwing material swatches around while glaring at a very cool shoe.

"Good morning, Orpheus the Brilliant," I said cheerfully.

He spun around, sweat dripping down his forehead. "What did you do to Jodi?"

I tensed immediately. "It's the other way around. What she did to me."

"Us! What she did to us!" Orpheus was shouting again, his arms flailing. "She's abandoned us!"

My gut dropped as Lindsey frowned. "What are you talking about?"

Orpheus gestured at the lab bench where Jodi's research notes were usually piled. "She came in late last night and cleaned out everything. Left me a note that said she was dropping out of the business. Said it was best if she wasn't around anymore. What's going on? How am I supposed to do this without her? I don't know about Sfoam and I don't know about this fancy schmancy design shit!"

Jodi gone? As in gone forever?

Was that good? It should have been. How could I trust her again? She'd lied to me for five years and then tried to get me to reconcile with Greg to assuage her own feelings of guilt. She hadn't cared whether it was right for me. She hadn't seen that Greg hadn't changed. All she'd wanted was to take care of herself.

But damn it, she was my friend. One of my best friends. Just like that, she was out of my life? Loneliness settled across my shoulders. I should call her, I thought. Forgive her for Greg. She had tried to get us back together, hadn't she?

But what about the Seth thing? Two men. And she'd gotten both of them to cheat on me with her. What kind of friend was that? And what about Will? Had he slept with her too? I had to know how deep the betrayal went before I could decide whether to forgive her.

As Lindsey started making cooing noises to soothe Orpheus, I walked to the other end of the lab, pulled out my cell phone and dialed Will.

He answered on the first ring. "Paris. I'm so glad you called. I've felt like shit all night. Can we get together and talk?"

"Did you ever sleep with Jodi?"

"What? No. Of course not. How can you ask that?"

"How can I not?"

"Just because Greg, Seth and Jodi betrayed you doesn't

mean I deserve to be labeled as well. Not all men who share your bed are liars." He didn't sound amused.

Fine. Neither was I. "Did she ever make a move on you?"

Silence.

"Will?"

"It's not my place—"

"If you even think about saying that it's not your place to tell me, I will never speak to you again. It is your place. What the hell happened?"

He sighed. "That first night Greg showed up at your place to take you out to dinner, remember? Lindsey took off, and I was planning to stay at your place. I didn't really feel comfortable about you out with Greg after all I'd heard about him. I wanted to be there if you needed me, you know?"

My heart broke for an instant, but I steeled it right back up. "And?"

"After Lindsey left, Jodi . . . well . . . she sort of did some stuff."

I closed my eyes and felt my soul break. "What kind of stuff?"

He cleared his throat. "Well, you know, like she was touching me and sort of kissing me and you know. Stuff."

"What did you do?"

"Told her to back off. You think I'd sleep with her?"

"You're right." I took a deep breath and felt a huge load lift off my heart. Will hadn't changed. I could still trust him. "Sorry."

He grunted.

"So what happened?"

"When I told her I wasn't into it, she got pissed. Said I

had to release you because you needed to get back together with Greg, and if I was still in the picture, you wouldn't give him a chance." I could picture his shrug. "I knew then what her deal was. She was feeling guilty about everything and saw this as a chance to fix it. I stood in the way, and she was trying to get me out of the way the only way she knew. It wasn't about sex with her. It was about trying to get you back together with Greg. She was really heavily laden with guilt about the whole thing. So I blew it off. She wasn't really into me. It was just a means to an end."

I sat down on a lab bench. "She hit on you." All three of the men in my life and she'd hit on them. Only Will had said no.

"It wasn't about sex, Paris. It was about all that other shit."

"How can you defend her?"

"Because she loves you."

"This is how she shows it? What kind of warped view of love do you have?"

"She came to me years ago because she was so depressed she was considering killing herself."

My gut dropped. "Really?"

"Yes. I told her to talk to you, but she was too afraid that you'd reject her. If you had, I think it would have put her over the edge. She has no other friends except you and Lindsey. She's lived the last five years in fear of being alone, and a part of her believes she'd deserve it. Then when Greg came back, she thought she could fix everything."

I said nothing. What could I say? I felt horrible for her, but I couldn't get over the betrayal. It was a mess.

"Talk to her," he said.

"No. It would be one thing if all this had happened five years ago, but she did it again. If you weren't so moral, she would have slept with you too." Then I frowned. "And there's something going on with her and Thad, I think. Four out of four, Will. How do I forget about that?"

He said nothing.

"Damn it, Will. I don't know who to trust anymore."

"Go with your gut."

"What does that mean?" I wanted him to tell me what to do. Who to trust. Who to believe.

"Greg's been trying to control you since he arrived. He's been trying to tell you what you want and what you don't want. I'm not going to do that. Figure it out for yourself." He hesitated. "I'm heading out to California later today to look at housing. I'll be back in a week or two to pack up my stuff, and then that's it."

I bit my lower lip. He was leaving. "You're really going."

"Yep."

"And Christine?"

"Does it matter?"

"Do you love her?"

He was quiet for a moment. "In some ways."

"What does that mean?"

"I don't know. Yes, she's coming with me to look at housing."

"Oh." I slumped against the wall. "Oh."

"Are you going to accept Greg's proposal?"

I snorted. "How can you ask me that?"

Will hesitated. "I can't believe I'm saying this, but after you left the bar, he fell apart. Crying and shit. I think . . . well . . . he does love you. He truly regrets what happened in the past. I . . . he . . . well, he's . . . I think he'd be loyal to you. Treat you the way he believes his true love should be treated."

I frowned. "Why are you telling me this? You want me to get together with him?"

"It's your decision. Now that the past is on the table, well, it's not my call. I wanted you to know everything and make the right decision. I don't think he's been faking anything. He's exactly what he seems. He . . . really loves you."

I closed my eyes against the surge of confusion whooshing through me. "Damn it, Will. I don't need to hear this." It was so much simpler to consider Greg a son of a bitch who needed his testicles crushed in a vise.

"Yeah, well, sorry. I felt you should know." I heard a woman's voice in the background. "I need to go. Christine's here." He hesitated. "When I get back in town . . . dinner?"

I nodded. "Dinner."

"Right. Okay, well, then, good luck with everything. I'll call you when I return."

" 'Bye." I disconnected and let the phone drop into my lap.

As I stared at it, it rang.

Greg's cell.

I closed my eyes and let it ring.

"Paris, we have a problem."

I opened them to find Lindsey standing in front of me, her brow puckered with concern. Orpheus was nowhere to be seen. I'd totally forgotten they were there. I hadn't even been aware of my surroundings when I was talking to Will. "What's up?"

"We lost Orpheus."

"What do you mean?"

She sat down next to me and leaned her head against the wall. "He was already freaking about Jodi bailing, especially since Will has been MIA and will continue to be. When he saw the contract listing him as a designer for Orpheus M shoes . . . when he found out we'd already signed a contract . . . he sort of imploded."

I slanted a look at her. "What kind of imploded?"

"He's not a designer. Can't take that sort of responsibility. Without Jodi and Will around to help, he'll have to close down his orthopedic shoe business and then his daddy and grandpappy's legacy will be lost and what will people think if they find out he's a dress-shoe designer?" She sighed. "He tore up his consulting contract, destroyed the shoe sample he'd been working on, and left."

Wow. I'd really been in my own little world not to notice all that. "Is he coming back?"

"No, I don't think so."

"So we're screwed." I wasn't even panicking. I was too exhausted to panic. I was numb. "Totally and completely screwed. I don't even have a job anymore."

"You quit your job?"

"Yep. Friday. Thad told me it was irrevocable."

Lindsey held out her hand. "Give me your phone."

I handed it to her and watched as she dialed Greg. "Why are you calling him?" I was too tired to care. I simply didn't have the energy to deal. I supposed total numbness and exhaustion were better than an anxiety attack and passing out, though. So maybe I was becoming more adept at handling crises.

I was such a trooper. Hah.

She held up her hand to shush me. "Greg. It's Lindsey. Yes, Paris is here. No, I'm not going to let you speak to her. I wanted to know whether you were thinking of bailing from your contract for funding PWJ." She was silent. "Uh-huh. Yep." She glanced at me. "Not a chance. Okay. 'Bye."

She hung up the phone. "According to Greg, the contract becomes void when the company disbands. With Jodi and Will vacating, he's says he's no longer bound by the contract. Jodi already told him she was jumping ship, and he knows Will is gone. Unless you agree to license Sfoam and stop all manufacturing, he'll pull out." She tapped the phone on her thigh. "I think he's right about the contract. I hadn't expected PWJ to fall apart, so I didn't protect against that contingency."

I stared at her. "It's over, then." Just like that. From the top of the world to total devastation overnight. An overwhelming sense of loss and depression and panic tried to grab me, but I shoved it aside. Better not to think about things. Apparently I wasn't quite ready to grasp the enormity of the collapse. Not yet, at least.

My phone beeped a text message. I took the phone from Lindsey and opened it. It was from Greg. *Call me. I love you. We'll work it out.*

I thought of what Will had said about Greg.

"He's trying to trade your love for funding the company," Lindsey said. "Disgusting."

I frowned and dialed him.

He answered on the first ring. "Paris. Where are you? I've been waiting at your condo all night and all day. You can't do this to me."

"If I marry you, will you provide funding for PWJ indefinitely?"

"Get right to the point, why don't you?"

"Answer the question."

"PWJ is dead without Will and Jodi. They're the core of it. Sure, Orpheus is a talented designer, but he can't do it alone. I'm sorry, hon, but that dream is over. I love you, and I'd do anything for you, but I can't make it happen without them. The only thing left to do is sell the technology."

"So if I marry you, it doesn't change anything." In a way, that was the right answer. I didn't want any strings attached.

"I don't want you to think that I want to marry you because I want your business. I want to marry you because I love you. They're separate."

"But you initially gave us the money for personal reasons."

Hesitation. "Well, yes, but that was before I realized that I still loved you. Once that happened, everything changed."

I could hear the sincerity in his voice. I had my answer. "Fine. I'll talk to you later."

"Wait. When can we get together?"

"I don't know." I hung up and looked at Lindsey. "Marrying him won't get money."

"Were you planning to sacrifice yourself at the altar for the sake of PWJ?"

"No, but I needed to know." I stared glumly at the floor. "It's really over. And we're totally screwed. We signed a contract to deliver shoes and we can't. And I don't have a job as of two weeks from now. And I don't know what to do about Greg on a personal level. Will says Greg really loves me. Is that enough? And Will is leaving. And I miss Jodi. And I have this awful feeling in my gut about her and everything that happened. And did I tell you my mom married an ex-con, whom I'm supposed to meet at dinner tomorrow night?" I sighed. "Shit."

Lindsey started laughing.

"Not seeing the humor."

"That's why I'm laughing. I mean, seriously, could this be any worse?" She started to laugh harder. "God, this is a mess. We're going to get sued!"

I stared at her. "You're insane."

"I know." She wiped her eyes as my phone rang again. Greg again. "You want to get out of here?"

"And go where? Siberia, so no one can find us?"

"Maybe not Siberia, but close enough." She stood up. "Come on, Paris. It's time to see how I deal with life when it starts sucking."

I frowned, not moving from my bench. "I'm not going skydiving."

"Of course not. Didn't think you would."

"Or bungee jumping."

"Wimp."

"Or race car driving."

"It was fun."

"I think I should stay here and try to deal with this shit. Figure out what I'm going to do." My phone rang again. Greg yet again.

Lindsey put her hands on her hips. "You know what you're going to say to him?"

I let it ring. "No."

"You have any bright ideas for keeping us from getting sued for breach of contract?"

Shit. "No."

"You figured out how to get Thad to let you rescind your resignation?"

I sagged. "No."

"You figured out anything?"

"Not yet."

"Then take a break. Get some distance. Get some perspective. Trust me, it works."

"I'm supposed to go to dinner tomorrow night."

"Fuck dinner. This is your life."

I looked at Lindsey standing there with her hands on her hips and fire in her eyes. "That's why you go off doing these crazy things? Because life sucks and you don't want to deal with it?"

"Yep."

"But I thought you were so happy."

"Don't tell anyone the truth." She held out her hand. "It works. Nothing like thinking you're going to die to make you realize that your life isn't so bad the way it is. Come on, Paris. Live."

Live.

I wanted to live.

I wanted to feel that glory that Lindsey seemed to carry with her. I wanted to glow.

"You know what?"

She grinned as if she already knew what I was going to say. "What?"

"I'm in."

TWENTY-FOUR

"This is what makes you appreciate life?" I asked.

"Well, maybe not this particular moment."

We were standing side by side, ankle-deep in mud, studying our rented midsize pickup truck. It was not the poster child for off-roading at the moment.

"They aren't supposed to get stuck like this," she said. "I'm pretty sure I asked for four-wheel drive."

"The mud is up to the axles. Exactly what did you expect to happen?" I couldn't believe I'd actually agreed to accompany Lindsey on one of her trips. What had I been thinking?

"I didn't realize the mud was so deep. And it wasn't as if you tried to stop me."

"Yeah, I guess I should have done more than scream at you to stop and try to jerk the steering wheel out of your hands."

Lindsey's idea of adventure had been to rent an off-road vehicle and take to the mountains, going deep, deep, deep into the wilderness in northern Maine.

She'd thought it would be fun to drive through the small river instead of taking the bridge. Excellent idea that had turned out to be.

She grinned at me. "You have to admit, it's kind of fun having an adventure."

I slapped at a mosquito. "So fun."

She rolled her eyes. "Oh, can it. You going to call for help or what?"

"Aren't you glad I insisted on bringing my cell phone now?" Boots sitting safely on the bank, I waded through the knee-deep mud and water back to the truck and fished through my purse. I turned on my phone. *Oh, shit.* "Um, Linds?"

"Yeah?"

"No cell service."

"Really? Not surprising."

I perched inside the cab and peered at her. What exactly was up with her nonchalant tone? "So what now?" Panic tried to gnaw at my belly, but I shoved it aside. "I mean, it's been almost four hours since we've seen anyone else, and no one's going to be looking for us."

She grinned. "This is what it's all about. Makes you appreciate life."

I eyed her. "Did you get the truck stuck on purpose?"

"Well, not on purpose exactly, but you know . . ."

"Are you kidding? We're on the side of a mountain by ourselves, with a cliff on our right and mud banks on our left, enough food and water for two days of car camping, and it's getting dark. And you got us stuck on purpose?"

"You need to lighten up. I thought it would be good for you."

"Jesus, Lindsey. You're fucking crazy."

She stopped grinning. "I'm not crazy."

"You are. You're fucking insane. You have a death wish, you know that?"

"I do not! I like to take risks."

"Risks? *Risks?* Do you realize we could die out here?"

"So?"

I jumped out of the truck and tromped through the water. "So? *So?* That's all you have to say? *So?* It's one thing if you want to risk your life, but you have no right to risk mine!"

"What, are you going to live your whole life afraid of death? We're all going to die sometime, so why try to hide from it?"

"Because I don't want to die today up in some fucking mountain!"

"Well, do you think Seth wanted to die in a stupid car accident? Do you? We don't get to choose our time. Ever! So if you fear it, you'll be dead even while you're still alive!"

I was in front of her now, close enough to see the raw fear in her eyes. "Is that what all this is about? Seth dying?"

"He died, Paris! He died! He went to a stupid party and died!"

"Yeah. I was there. I know."

"He's gone! Off in heaven or maybe nowhere. Who knows what happens to our souls when we die? Poof. Gone. He was twenty years old and dead."

"I know!" I took a breath and tried to calm myself. "He died in front of me."

"That's all there is for us! We're going to be just like that. Here one day. Poof! Gone the next."

I cocked my head and studied her. Really looked into her eyes for the first time in ages. "Yeah, you say that all the time. I thought you weren't afraid to die. If you're really upset about dying, why do you always tempt death?"

"Because no matter how much I don't want to die, it's going to happen anyway." Tears trickled out of her eyes. "I'm so scared of dying, Paris. All I want to do is hide in my room under the covers and make it go away. But it's still going to find me someday, somehow. Just like it found Seth." She blinked, and her voice was nothing more than a whisper. "But if I can embrace death, if I can taunt it, if I can overcome my fear of it, then I've won. Don't you see? I've won."

"But how have you won?"

"Because I'm not afraid. Because I lived life without hiding. That makes me the winner."

"But you *are* afraid."

"But at least I'm not hiding from it."

"Maybe, but you're hiding from life."

She frowned. "How can you possibly say that? I live more than you do."

I shook my head. "All you're doing is dangerous shit that doesn't make you happy. All it does is delude you that you're powerful and you're cheating death. Well, you're not. You're still going to die and you're still not going to be ready for it no matter when it comes." I tried to blink back my own tears. "In your quest to avoid the pain of death, you've refused to let yourself really care about anything or anyone. If you don't care, then death can't hurt you, right? How is that living?"

She stared at me, tears streaming down her cheeks. "I'm so afraid. I'm afraid I'm going to die like Seth, with so much undone. I have to do it all. Don't you see? I have to do everything before I lose the chance."

"But what is it you want to do? I mean, really want to do? And don't tell me skydiving, because I don't believe you."

"I don't know," she whispered. "I don't know what I want. I'm just so afraid I won't find it until it's too late." She tugged her T-shirt free and used it to wipe her eyes. "God, Paris. I don't know what to do."

"You have to let yourself risk getting hurt." I hugged her, and she hugged me back.

"So do you," she said.

"I know." I'd been holding back for five years and it hadn't kept the pain away from me, but it had kept the joy away quite well. "When I felt that euphoria from the success of Orpheus M designs, it was the first time I'd felt happy in five years."

She sniffled. "Me too. And now it's gone and it sucks."

"So we'll find something else."

She shook her head. "No, I can't endure that much pain again. Seth's death was too hard. I won't care. I won't!"

I realized I wanted to care again. I wanted that feeling again. Was Greg the answer? Was he the risk I needed to take?

We held each other and cried for an hour.

Did we have any answers? No.

But I felt better.

I sat next to Lindsey on the bank and rested my head on her shoulder. "The truck is still stuck."

"I know," she sighed.

"The mosquitoes don't seem to be too bothered by our bug spray." I scratched my shin again. Wasn't helping.

"Cheap bug spray."

"The sun is setting." It was beautiful, but somehow I couldn't muster the energy to appreciate it.

"Yeah, I noticed."

"This sucks."

She giggled. "Sorry about that."

I looked at her. "You're laughing?"

"I can't help it. It's funny."

"It's not funny. I'm going to die up here all by myself."

"What am I, a piece of meat loaf?" She slung her arm over my shoulder. "I love you, and what better way to die than with someone you love?"

I sighed. "Yeah." Still wasn't exactly how I'd envisioned the day. I could have been at dinner with my mom and her new sex toy, and instead I was going to die on a mountain.

Dinner would have been better.

"You wish you were with Greg up here? Dying in his arms instead of mine?"

"No, actually, I don't. He'd just order us around and be annoying. I'd rather die in peace."

"What about Will?"

I slanted a look at her. "What about him?"

"You wish he was here?"

My response was immediate and instinctive. "No. I wouldn't want him to die because of me. I'd want him to live."

She lifted her brow. "That's your answer."

I looked at her. "What are you talking about?"

"The ultimate sacrifice for the one you love is if you're willing to die for them."

I frowned. "I didn't mean it like that."

"It's what you said."

"Well, I'm not ready to die."

"Me neither." She sighed and rested her chin on her knees. "Probably should have thought of that before I drove the two-wheel-drive truck through the river, huh?"

"I'm not ready to give up." I pushed to my feet, waded across the river and wandered to the edge of the cliff.

"Hey, be careful over there."

"What? Words of caution coming from you?"

"Shut up." She came to stand beside me. "It's pretty, isn't it?"

"Gorgeous." The valley stretched out before us. Trees and mountains as far as we could see. No ranger station around the next bend as far as I could tell. I frowned. "What's that?"

"What?"

I pointed. "That orange flickering light down there. You think that's a campfire?"

Lindsey frowned. "Could be. Hang on."

She sloshed over to the truck and returned with a pair of binoculars. After a moment of study, she said, "It's either a campfire or the start of a forest fire that'll cremate us."

"I'm not in the mood for death jokes right now." I took the binocs and checked it out. My heart started thudding more quickly. "I think it is a campfire. Someone's down there." I looked down the steep hillside. "It's not that far."

"We'll go first thing in the morning."

"We'll go now." I handed her the binocs and slogged back to the truck to pile water, food and my wallet into a backpack. "We'll find it only as long as we can see the flame. By morning, we won't know where it is. It's now or never."

"But what if the fire goes out?"

"It's barely sunset. We have several hours before they'll

go to sleep." I hoisted my backpack and fastened the waist and chest straps, then put my boots back on. "You might want to die, but I don't."

"But the cliff?"

I pulled a flashlight out of the truck. "Since when do you care about danger?"

She lifted her chin. "You're right. It's part of the adventure. Let's go."

Ten minutes later, we were fully loaded and standing at the top of the cliff in the fading light. "Damn, that looks steep." I wasn't exactly an experienced mountain climber.

"Yeah."

"This is your damn fault for driving through the river."

"At least you're fit. You used to run down steep trails all the time when you were training. This should be a piece of cake for you."

"True." What was my problem? Of course I could handle this. Since when had I become a citified landlubber incapable of a tromp through the woods? Pathetic. Put some designer shoes on my feet and I forgot who I was. I looked at her. "Ready?"

"Let's do it."

And with that, we were off, slip-sliding our way down the sheer rock face.

Well, okay, so maybe I was exaggerating a little. It was rock. And it was steep. Close enough.

"You know," Lindsey puffed, "it's not nearly as bad going down as it would be going up."

I maneuvered down the rocks on my butt. "We better not have to go back up. We'd never make it." I paused to pull out the binoculars. "Fire's still going. We're getting close."

"I hope they aren't a bunch of backwoods rapists."

I threw a pinecone at her. "Don't even say that."

"Well, it's true. How do we know they won't kill us?"

"I should have left you back at the truck." I stood up and tried to sort of sashay down the hill. It wasn't quite as steep here, so it wasn't too much worse than the hills I'd run during countless cross-country training runs. "Come on, Lindsey! It's leveling out."

"Wait up! I'm not as fit as you are. Or as coordinated, apparently," she muttered. "Slow down!"

"Can't." I let gravity carry me, cruising down the hill as I dodged rocks and roots. I hadn't run like this in years. I'd forgotten about the exhilaration of racing through the woods, of flying down a hill as though I were a wild animal racing after prey. "Whoohoo!"

My voice echoed through the valley as I picked up speed. This was what life was about. Racing. Running. This was who I was. This was what running was about.

And I felt Seth watching me, enjoying my happiness, encouraging me to relish the moment. And at that point, I knew he would be with me forever, regardless of whether I ever ran another step again. He would always be with all of us, and that was enough.

Even as I flew down the hill, jumping shrubbery and letting the wind smack my cheeks, I realized it was the same feeling I'd gotten from the success with Orpheus M. Exhilaration. Power. Success. Freedom. A sense of self. A feeling of completeness.

Maybe running wasn't the only thing that could make me whole. Maybe there was more to my soul after all. Maybe Orpheus M wasn't a step to getting Sfoam to work in running shoes. Maybe it was an end unto itself.

That feeling touched my soul. I leapt over a rock,

landed in a rut and flew on downward, Lindsey's shouts to hold up fading in the distance.

Adrenaline was flowing. Energy surging. Endorphins raging.

Freedom.

Life.

It was all around me.

This was me!

Can you imagine how I'd feel if I combined this exhilaration from running with the success of Orpheus M? That's what I'd have if I made Sfoam work for running shoes.

Maybe, I thought, I should keep that goal in mind after all. It would be a way to keep running in my life. The heady rush. The total and complete physical control over my world. The . . . "Crap!" My boot slipped off a rock, my hip gave out, my backpack threw off my balance and I somersaulted to the ground.

I fell with a thud that knocked my breath out of me, and then I crashed into a tree trunk. Spun past it, rolling through underbrush and rocks as gravity and my momentum dragged me. I held my arms up over my face and crushed my eyes shut as my body slammed off something hard again and then again. Something ripped my arm open and I heard myself yelp.

More crashes, thuds, pain.

And then it was finally over.

Fuck.

I couldn't move. Nothing hurt, though. I just couldn't move.

I stared at the trees above my head, barely visible in the evening light. This was like the car accident. Nothing had hurt then, either. Not at first. Should I have been scared? Probably. Should I have been in pain? I was pretty sure I should.

But I felt nothing. Except that I was cold. Yep. Cold. I was cold.

"Paris?" Rocks sprayed past my ears and Lindsey's face appeared in my view. "You okay?"

"No." I said the word, moved my lips, but nothing came out. I tried again. "No." Still nothing.

She flicked a flashlight on me. "Oh, God. You're bleeding. And your leg."

"Cold."

"What?" She squatted next to me and laid her hand on my face. "You're freezing. Shit. You're going into shock." She shrugged off her backpack and laid a sweatshirt over me, tucking it around my upper body. Did that hurt when she touched my side? I thought it did. I wasn't sure. "Hey, Paris! Don't close your eyes."

Were they closed? I tried to open them. Were they open? I wasn't sure.

"We're not that far from the campfire. I'm going to get help." She wedged a flashlight under my arm. "Keep that on. . . ." Her voice faded, then came back. "Shining . . ." Faded again. "Find you. . . come back . . ."

Gone again.

"Paris!"

I struggled to respond, to hear her. Couldn't talk. Too much effort. Needed to rest.

Her footsteps disappeared into the distance, and I was alone.

Alone with my broken body.

And trees.

The sounds of the woods. Animal sounds. Couldn't really identify them. Sort of blurry. Blending together. But it was peaceful. Nice.

Will would appreciate it. He'd like the woods. Wished he were there. I'd have to tell him about it.

Someday.

Then I got too tired to think. Needed a nap. Just a little one. For just a minute.

TWENTY-FIVE

The first thing I noticed was the pain.

The second thing I noticed was the pain.

The third thing I noticed was the pain.

I mumbled the most descriptive curse I could think of.

"Paris? Baby? Can you hear me?"

"Mom?" I dragged my eyes open. Sure enough, my mom was there. Crying. Weird. She never cried. "Why are you in the woods? Were you camping?"

She smiled. "You're not in the woods. You're in a hospital."

"I hate hospitals."

"I know, baby. I know." She held my hand to her cheek. "Welcome back."

Damn, I was tired. "Did I fuck up my hip again?"

"You use that language in front of your mother?"

I opened my eyes again. (Hadn't noticed them closing. Odd.) Turned my head to the opposite side. "Will!" He was holding my other hand, and he was crying too. What

310

was up with all these people crying? "Why aren't you in California? With She-bitch?"

He leaned forward and kissed my forehead. "Never scare me like that again."

"I'll try not to." I closed my hand around his. Didn't want him to leave. Not yet. "I have to sleep. Don't leave me."

"I won't." His hands were tight around mine. "I'm not going anywhere."

I nodded and closed my eyes again. Had to sleep.

The next time I woke up, I felt better.

Well, the pain was still there, but I could actually keep my eyes open.

My mom was sitting next to me, and a man who looked vaguely familiar was sitting beside her. They were talking quietly and holding hands. He was rubbing my mom's back, and she was gazing at him as if he were the savior of the world. Or of her world, at least. "Mom?"

They stopped talking and turned toward me. My mom dropped his hand and grabbed mine. "How are you feeling, baby?"

"Like hell." I tried to move, but pain changed my mind. "I messed up my hip, didn't I?"

"Among other things. But you're going to be all right." She pointed to my arm. "Twenty stitches."

I inspected the bandage. A vague recollection of ripping the skin open teased my mind. "How bad is my hip?"

She gave me a sad smile. "I hope you enjoyed the run down the side of the mountain."

"Because it was my last one?" Leave it to my mom to deliver the news in her creative way.

"Yes."

A lump settled in my throat and my vision became blurry. "I want to run."

Tears filled my mom's eyes. Big, tough Mom. Crying for me. Maybe she loved me after all, even though she had a new dinner partner. "I know. I'm so sorry, baby. If I could change the world for you, I would."

My throat felt thick. "I don't want surgery."

"You might not need it. With physical therapy . . . maybe . . ."

I shook my head. "I quit my job. I'm not going to have insurance. I can't pay for it." I felt a tear break through and trickle down my cheek. "This is all wrong. It's all wrong."

The man leaned forward, one hand on my mom's back, one hand on my arm. "Paris, you remember me?"

I looked at the gold band on his left hand. "You're my mom's new husband?"

He nodded. "Zach Middleton."

"Zach."

"I want you to know that you don't need to worry about money. I've already arranged to have a trust fund set up that will pay for all your medical care. Everything you need. If you need surgery, you can get the best care in the world. Don't worry about the money."

I frowned at him. "What are you talking about?"

He smiled at my mom, and that one look was so full of love that I could actually feel it in the air. "When I married your mom, she changed my world. She loves you, so I love you. I'll do anything for you. Anything for her." He looked at me again. "You might not have wanted a dad, but you've got one anyway."

"I can't accept money. I don't even know you."

"It doesn't matter if you accept it or not. It's a done deal." He squeezed my hand. "I look forward to getting to know you, so make sure you get yourself out of here quick."

I blinked hard to keep the tears from spilling free. I didn't understand how he could give me that kind of a gift. "I don't know what to say. . . ."

He shook his head. "Say nothing." He kissed my mom. "Your mom is all the reward I need."

She entwined her fingers with his and gave him the most soulful, loving look I'd ever seen. How could they love each other that much? They'd just met.

Then again, when you've been around for fifty years, you probably know what you want when it comes to a partner. They'd known it the moment they found it, and they'd had the courage to embrace it.

For the first time in my life, I was jealous.

Lindsey came in while Zach and my mom were at lunch. She sat down on the edge of my bed. "Okay, here's the deal."

"No more off-roading?"

She made a face at me. "I thought you were going to die. That was not okay with me."

"Well, thanks."

"It made me realize that I was being stupid. I can't stop death by trying to stare it down." She shrugged. "It still almost got you, and I was so scared." Her cockiness faded. "All the risks I've taken, it didn't make it any less horrible when I thought I was going to lose you. It didn't change anything. At all."

I nodded. "It wasn't my high moment either."

"And I did a lot of thinking about what we talked about. Death, Seth, living and stuff. I've decided that I need a new focus in life."

"God help us. What is it?"

"To find out what will really make me happy. Really and truly. No more being stupid. I'm going to find out what I want, and then I'm going to get it." She grinned, and I saw a gleam in her eye that I hadn't seen before. It was a good gleam.

I smiled. "You're going to be all right, Lindsey Miller."

"I know. And so are you."

My smile faded. "I don't know. I have a lot of stuff to figure out."

She cocked her head. "Will took the first flight out from California after I called him."

My heart did a little jump. "He did?"

"Yep. I've never seen him look as awful as he did when he arrived at the hospital. He was so pale and had these horrible circles under his eyes. Your mom had to lie and say he was your brother so he could be in here with you. We were all afraid he'd freak out if he couldn't get in to see you."

I met her gaze. "Really?"

"Really." She smoothed my hair. "When you were in shock, after you fell, you kept saying his name."

"He's my friend."

"He's more than a friend, and you know it. And I think he finally does too."

I didn't know what to say to that. But my heart got all weird and lumpy and I had trouble breathing.

"Think about it, sweetie. He's moving to California, and you won't get another chance."

I took a deep breath and let the air out. "You think . . . you think there's a chance?" Did I want a chance? A chance for what?

She smiled. "There's only one way to find out."

"But what about Christine?"

"What about Greg?"

I fell silent. Too many complications. It would never work.

"Jodi's been here."

I said nothing.

"Thad came by also."

"Really? To offer me my job back, maybe?"

"Yeah, not so much. But I think he likes Jodi. He was flirting with her by the coffee machine. I think she really likes him. I could see it in her face. She hasn't looked at a guy in that way for as long as I've known her."

"That would be fitting, wouldn't it?" But I was too tired to be angry. Somehow it just didn't seem that important anymore.

"He asked her out."

"And?"

"She said no. Said you came first and there was no way she was risking your friendship for him. They argued over it for an hour. He wanted to come talk to you and get you to say it was okay, and she refused. He left pissed."

I frowned. "Why'd she tell you this? To get you to change your mind?"

"She didn't tell me anything. I spied on them. She never said a word about it. Just hung around for another hour or two looking horribly depressed, and then went home." Lindsey sighed. "I think maybe, well, maybe we should forgive her. Five years ago was a long time. And she really likes Thad, but she turned him down anyway."

I thought about the recent incident with Will, but then I thought of Lindsey's pain from Seth's death. Still so raw, even though it had been five years. Jodi had been driven by her own pain, deluded into trying to salvage the situation in the only way she knew how. Plus I missed her. It would take a while to rebuild the trust, but maybe we could. I wanted to try. "Maybe I'll give her a call."

Lindsey grinned. "I think that's a good idea. When you get out, we'll have a girls' night. Like old times." A rather attractive man, a doctor judging from his white coat, poked his head in my door, raised an eyebrow at Lindsey, then disappeared. She grinned. "I gotta go."

"A doctor? Isn't that a little conservative for you? Where's the risk?"

She stood up, still smiling. "Falling in love might be all the adventure I need." She kissed my cheek. "Take care, sweetie. I'll be back later."

"Paris? You awake? I heard you were awake. Paris?"

I blinked and dragged my eyes open. "Oh. Hi."

Greg smiled, and his bonded teeth nearly blinded me. "You gave everyone quite a scare."

"So I hear." I looked at his perfect brows and his expensive suit, and I knew. Just like that, I knew what my answer was.

He set a velvet box in my hand. "I can't wait any longer. I have to know if you'll marry me again. I know I made mistakes. I won't try to deny it. But I love you, and I'll do anything for you."

I looked at the box. Ran my fingers over it. It was soft. I could say yes and have what my mom had. A man who loved me. A man who would stand by me, even if he was a little controlling and didn't always listen to what I wanted.

I wasn't afraid of marriage anymore.

I wanted it. Someday. With the right person. Like my mom had.

My fingers closed over the box. "I can't marry you."

His face fell. "Why not?"

"Because I don't love you."

"Yes, you do. I know you do. I've seen it in your face."

I put the box back in his hand. "No, Greg. I was in love with the idea of this fantasy ex-husband who'd been blossoming in my head for the last five years. When you came back, I set you in the place of the man I'd convinced myself I loved." I sighed. "But in reality, we're not right. You offer me so much, Greg, but it's not enough. I want someone who gets me."

"I get you."

I managed a smile. "I don't want to marry you again. I don't love you. Not that way." I hesitated. "I thought I did for a little while. Seeing you again made me feel safe again. Made me feel like I'd felt for those few brief weeks when we were in college. But it wasn't you. It was the feeling of belonging." I shook my head. "I'm so sorry, but it's not you I love. Not like that."

His cheek twitched. "It's Will, isn't it?"

"Maybe."

"That son of a—"

"Greg. I can't marry you. Not today. Not ever."

He sat up. "You'll regret this decision. PWJ will fail without my money."

"So it fails."

"You'll just let it fail?"

"I'm hardly going to 'let it,' but I'm not going to marry you to save it."

"I could make you happy."

"No, Greg. I have to make myself happy. That's the difference between you and me. You want to rule my world. I want to share ownership."

He frowned. "What are you talking about?"

"Nothing." The fact that he couldn't even grasp that concept told me a lot. "Never mind."

"So that's it? You won't change your mind?"

"No."

He stood up. "You'll come crawling back to me and it will be too late. You'll be so sorry. You'll wish you'd said yes."

" 'Bye."

He walked out, still espousing his greatness.

As I watched him walk out of my life for the last time, I felt relief. No regret. It was finally over and I was finally free.

God, it felt good.

I leaned back in the bed as Will rolled around the door-jamb, his shoulder pressed against the fame. "Hey," he said.

I couldn't stop myself from grinning. He looked so cute in his jeans, with sunglasses propped on top of his head. My wonderful Will. He also looked tired. Exhausted. His face was pale, the lines on his face drawn deep. "I thought you'd gone back to California."

"Not yet. Had some stuff to do first." He came in and sat down in a chair next to my bed. "How are you feeling?"

"Fine. I'm going to go for a run next week."

He gave me a half smile. "Yeah, I heard about that. How you holding up?"

I shrugged. "Well, it's not as bad as the first time they

told me I couldn't run. Been through it all before." I sighed.

"Liar. It sucks and you know it."

See? This guy got me. "Yeah, it does."

"You want to talk about it?"

"I think I'm going to be okay. I've learned that there are things besides actually running that still make me feel great."

He nodded. He knew I meant it. He knew when I was lying and when I wasn't. This is how it was supposed to be. "Like PWJ?" he asked.

"Yeah." I absently trailed my fingers over his forearm, tickling the hairs. "But I'll have to find another dream. Jodi's gone. Orpheus has bailed. Greg took the money."

"Yeah, about that." He handed me a document. "I hope you didn't mind, but I did a little work."

I picked up the document. "Orpheus's consulting agreement?"

"Flip to the last page."

I did. "It's signed? Are you kidding? How'd you do that?" My heart started beating faster.

He shrugged. "I had to make a few concessions."

"Like what?"

"Get Jodi back on board so he wouldn't have to give up his other business."

I stared at him. "How did you do that?" *Jodi's back?*

"And I talked to Thad. He said that since you won't be working there anymore, he could give you a loan. I showed him the retail contract, and that was enough for him. The loan will kick in on the first Monday after your last day at the bank." He grinned. "We don't need Greg's money."

Adrenaline was starting to surge through me. Hope

stirred in my chest. "Are you serious? You fixed everything?"

"Well, not everything. You still need to do some work on finding an efficient manufacturing option. Stuff like that. That's your side of things. I'm just the lab rat."

Tears surged in my eyes for what felt like the millionth time in the past few days, but these were the good kind. "How do I ever thank you?"

He shrugged. "I have something else for you." He reached under his chair and handed me a running shoe with no midsole except for a thin layer of Sfoam lining the footbed. "Bend it."

I flexed it between my hands. It was stiff. "What did you do?"

"I did some research. There's this start-up firm in California that specializes in injection-molded plastics. I gave them some Sfoam to work with, and they came up with that. Seems to perform well so far. Stable. Good protection. They ran a few tests at their lab. Seems like it might work okay."

I clutched the shoe to my chest. There was no stopping the tears now. Or the lump in my throat. Or the trembling of my lower lip. "You did it? You solved it?"

"It'll still require some tweaks, and you and Lindsey will have to negotiate the deal with that company. Profit sharing, probably. I told them you don't have a lot of cash now, but they're trying to break in too, so, you know, it's a good fit."

"Is that . . . is that why you really went to California?" I sniffed hard and couldn't help but smile when Will handed me a tissue. My tissue god.

"No, I really did go to check out housing for med school, but while I was out there . . ." He shrugged. "I sent them samples a few weeks ago, and they were ready for me to have a look. So I combined the trip."

"But why didn't you tell me?"

He hesitated. "You were all into Greg. I didn't want to mess things up. I didn't know if it would work. I don't know. I just did it. It's my going-away present for you."

I blinked. "But I don't want you to go."

He said nothing.

I set down the shoe and grabbed his hand. "Will, you've given me what I thought was the greatest gift any-one could give me. You've saved PWJ and you've handed me my dream of using Sfoam in a running shoe. But it's not enough."

He frowned. "But I thought that's what you wanted. . . ."

"It is. But I don't want you to go. Stay here."

"I'm going to med school. It's what I want to do."

"I know, but can't you go here?" *Please understand what I'm saying.* I didn't know if I could put myself out like that. I knew he was my friend. I knew he loved me. But did he *love* me?

He met my gaze. "Why do you want me to stay?"

"Because I . . ." The words suddenly stuck in my throat. How could I cross that line we'd so carefully erected be-tween us? If I did, would it ruin our friendship forever? Would I lose him?

"Because why?" He leaned forward slightly, his fingers loose in mine. "Why do you want me to stay?"

"Do you love Christine?"

"Answer my question first. Why do you want me to stay?" His face was serious, intense, focused. Waiting.

Waiting for what? "Um . . ."

He leaned back and let go of my hand. "I have to go.

I'm meeting Orpheus and Jodi at the lab to go over some technical details with them." He stood up. "Good-bye, Paris."

I watched him walk toward the door. Watched him hesitate. Smile back at me. Wait.

And then he walked out.

"I love you, Will." I said to the empty room. "I want you to stay because I love you."

He leaned around the door. "I heard that."

My cheeks immediately heated up. "You were eaves-dropping?"

"Yep." He walked back in and stood next to the bed. "Say it again."

I swallowed hard. It was time for me to take that risk. "When I fell in the woods, and I thought I was going to die . . . All I wanted was you. The only way dying would have been okay was if it could be in your arms. I didn't want to die without you. Without telling you that I love you."

He didn't move. Didn't respond.

"So that's it. I love you." I was so embarrassed. He hadn't said he loved me back.

"I heard you turn down Greg."

"Spending a lot of time listening at my door, are you?"

He sat down on the edge of the bed and laced his fingers through mine. "I had to wait until you made that choice on your own."

"Wait for what?"

He traced his free thumb over my lips. "To tell you that I love you."

That was the moment that my heart became whole. "Oh, Will."

He smiled. "The day I walked into your apartment at

seven in the morning and saw Greg in his boxers. That was when I realized I loved you. And by then it was too late."

I held his hand to my chest. "I didn't realize it until I saw you with Christine outside your house that night. And I knew I'd lost you before I'd even had you."

He leaned forward and gently kissed me. God, it had been so long since I'd kissed him. It was so right, so perfect. I clutched at his shirt. I didn't want to ever let go of him. Ever. "Don't ever leave me. Promise?"

"You're the one who needs that lecture. When I heard about the accident and saw you in that bed . . ." His face paled. "I knew I couldn't leave without telling you how I felt. I realized we didn't have all the time in the world."

"You're such a liar! You weren't going to tell me at all! You walked out without telling me!"

"I would have come back if you hadn't said anything." He grinned. "I wanted you to say it first."

"Why?"

"Male ego, of course."

I shoved at his chest. "You're such a jerk."

"Hey, just because I love you and I'm willing to go to Harvard Med instead of Stanford doesn't mean I'm a pushover. I have to make sure you know I'm the man in this relationship."

"You got into Harvard?" My voice was all breathy. Maybe it was because I couldn't seem to make my lungs work. They were all tight and constricted. And it was the best feeling ever.

"Acceptance came last week. Nothing like waiting till the last minute." His grin faded. "I was going to turn it down, but for some reason I didn't. I guess I was hoping something would happen to give me a reason to stay. If you'd married Greg, I would have had to leave. I couldn't stay and watch that."

I frowned. "What about Christine?"

"A pathetic attempt to convince myself I didn't care if you ended up with Greg. Didn't work."

"But what about California and her moving with you?"

Will got a sheepish look on his face. "She wanted to go, but I couldn't stand the thought of it. I let you think she was coming because, well, I guess I was trying to make you jealous."

"Are you serious?"

"Hey, I loved you. I was getting desperate." He rested his palm on my chest, over my heart. "When you get out of the hospital, I'm afraid you're going to be a little bit of a gimp. I'm thinking I should move in to take care of you. What do you think?"

I grinned. "I don't know. What if you decide to take off again?"

He lifted a brow. "Would that be a problem?"

"It might be. I'm thinking that maybe I ought to have Lindsey draft up a contract that requires a long-term commitment."

A slow smile curved his mouth. "How long-term? Ten days? That's your usual idea of long-term."

I shook my head. "I was thinking more like ninety-nine years. Or a lifetime." I suddenly got nervous. What if he wasn't thinking the same thing I was? "I mean, if you'd be cool with that."

He grinned, a huge smile that made his entire face glow. "I'll sign that contract in a heartbeat," he said, and my heart got ten pounds lighter. "Are you sure you want to commit yourself to me for that long?"

I tightened my grip on his hand and realized I didn't

feel scared or suffocated or tense. Just really excited. And happy. "Yes. Most definitely, *yes*."

It turns out I wasn't afraid of commitment anymore. I'd healed myself.

Rumble on the Bayou

JANA DeLeon

Deputy Dorie Berenger knew it was going to be a rough day when the alligator she found in the town drunk's swimming pool turned out to be stoned. Now she has some big-shot city slicker from the DEA trying to take over her turf. And Agent Richard Starke is way too handsome for his own good. Or hers.

The folks of Gator Bait, Louisiana, may know everything about each other, but they're sure not going to share it with an outsider. Richard won't be able to catch a drug smuggler without Dorie's help. But some secrets—and some desires—are buried so deep that bringing them to the surface will take a major *Rumble on the Bayou.*

GHOULS JUST WANT TO HAVE FUN

KATHLEEN BACUS

This autumn, Tressa Jayne Turner isn't enjoying the frivolity of the season. After being stalked by a psycho dunk-tank clown, all she wants is a slower pace, some candy corn and toffee apples—and a serious story she can sniff out on her own.

She's in luck! Reclusive bestselling writer Elizabeth Courtney Howard is coming to town. So, what's stopping Tressa from getting the dope—besides a blackmailing high school homecoming queen candidate, a rival reporter, and the park ranger who's kept Tressa's knickers in a knot since the fourth grade? Only the fact that the skeletons to uncover are all in a closet in a house only Norman Bates could love.